Hall
— of —
Mirrors

A Novel of Historical Fiction

Roxanne Lalande

ISBN: 978-1-7374541-0-6

Library of Congress control number: 2021913234

References to historical events, real people, or real places are used fictitiously. Some names, characters, and places are products of the author's imagination.

Front cover and book design by Stewart A. Williams.

Published by Amazon in the United States of America.

First edition 2021.

Address: www.roxannelalande.com

PRAISE FOR HALL OF MIRRORS

"The discovery of a heap of charred bones and a silver locket looms over this spirited and lush tale of political intrigue, romance and mystery set in the 17th century court of the Sun King — Louis XIV of France. In Hall of Mirrors, Elisabeth-Charlotte, the brilliant, outspoken and, sadly, ostracized second wife of the King's brother, unravels layers of deceit while investigating a secret society and the possible death by poisoning of her husband's first wife. Lalande brings the eccentric personages of the court, as well as the unforgettable Elisabeth-Charlotte, vividly to life with meticulous historical accuracy and rich prose."

— LAURIE LOEWENSTEIN,
Author of Death of a Rainmaker

"Les Français seront toujours moitié tigres et moitié singes," Voltaire once penned in a letter. ("The French will always be partly tigers and partly monkeys"...) The famous philosopher of the French Revolution might well have been describing the power-jousting surrounding the court of the Duke of Orleans from the previous century, particularly the suspicious death of Henriette d'Angleterre. There's certainly a lot of monkey business (think "court intrigue", think "serial poisoners", think hyper-jealous homosexual lovers with a penchant to punish their rivals) going on in Roxanne Lalande's Hall of Mirrors—and, as the mystery gets solved, you'll want to know how, and why, the tiger pounced.

— MARK WILL-WEBER,
Author of Mint Juleps with Teddy Roosevelt

TO MY FAMILY:

André, Eric and Jenna, William and Mary, Zoë and Beatriz

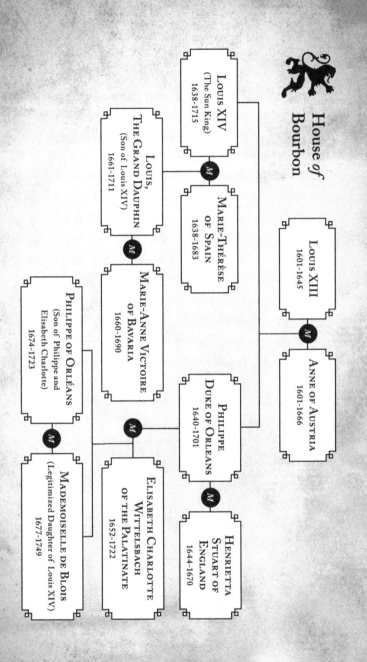

House of
Bourbon

Louis XIV
(The Sun King)
1638-1715

Marie-Thérèse
of Spain
1638-1683

Louis,
The Grand Dauphin
(Son of Louis XIV)
1661-1711

Marie-Anne Victoire
of Bavaria
1660-1690

Louis XIII
1601-1645

Anne of Austria
1601-1666

Philippe
Duke of Orleans
1640-1701

Henrietta
Stuart of
England
1644-1670

Elisabeth Charlotte
Wittelsbach
of the Palatinate
1652-1722

Philippe of Orléans
(Son of Philippe and
Elisabeth Charlotte)
1674-1723

Mademoiselle de Blois
(Legitimized Daughter of Louis XIV)
1677-1749

THE LOCKET

*D*arting through the woods, Mathilde looked back to see if Robin was still behind her, in playful pursuit. Her breath came out in short gasps, mingled with stifled giggles. The morning sun created a mottled pattern on the mossy ground, the leaves above a blurred vision. She stopped to catch her breath, but her companion was nowhere in sight. Alarmed by the unfamiliar surroundings—she had wandered away from her customary haunts—she listened intently, brushing a red lock from her forehead. A rustle here, a snap there: woodland animals at their daily tasks.

"Robin!" she called out, at first faintly, then more insistently; her panic rising. Was that a movement in the distance?

She moved forward with trepidation, now weary of this game of hide-and-seek. There, in a small clearing ahead, stood a crumbling stone edifice. The roof had caved in over the one-room dwelling, and most of the front facade was gone. As curiosity propelled her forward to investigate the premises, she suddenly felt a pull from behind and let out a loud shriek.

Robin gathered her into his arms and pressed her up against the shelter, his kisses smothering her cries of indignation. His laughing eyes and insistent caresses turned her fear to excitement, despite her distant awareness that this was wrong. The two youths had grown up together on neighboring domains near Versailles, romping through fields, wading in streams, or competing on horseback. Their favorite perch was an ancient oak tree, from which they had witnessed the slow emergence of the shining palace from the swamplands below, rising like Apollo's golden orb from the sea.

Robin was nephew and heir to the Marquis d'Effiat, whose property bordered on the royal hunting grounds; Mathilde, lady-in-waiting to Madame, the Duchess d'Orléans and sister-in-law to the king. But she knew at this moment, in a sudden flash of recognition, that they had both been living in anticipation of this awakening for some time: the inexorable result of their comradeship. A flush of desire rose to Mathilde's cheeks, and her wild locks clung to the beaded sweat on her brow as Robin probed her lips with his tongue. More tenderly this time, he pushed her ever so slowly down onto the mossy ground, pressing his weight onto her slender body, lifting her skirts, unlacing her bodice.

Suddenly, she felt ashamed of her impulse and turned her head away from Robin's tousled mane. Beneath her shoulder, she felt something hard, which she had failed to notice in the heat of the moment. She pushed Robin away and reached for the object and found it to be a silver locket. It was embossed with an emblem that appeared to represent a young man treading on a supine woman, and bore the enigmatic inscription *Qui m'aime me suive*. It was in the shape of a large cross and was fitted in the back with a small compartment, in which some tiny treasure or keepsake could be stored. *If you love me you shall follow*—the words seemed ominous, a portent of her fate: this simple act of intimacy would forever alter her relationship with Robin. Though she had always been the bolder of the two, her mate might henceforth no longer consider her his equal, his comrade in arms. Robin was already nonchalantly brushing off his trousers, impervious to her need to be cradled with tenderness. This sense of foreboding lingered as she noted the sudden detachment in his hooded eyes, a poorly concealed desire to be rid of her.

"What's that?" he asked, grabbing her wrist and forcing her to give up her find.

Robert Antoine Martin Coiffier d'Effiat, commonly known as Robin, was firstborn nephew and heir to the notorious Marquis d'Effiat, who was unmarried and had no issue—at least none he knew of—and whose scandalous life at court as one of the Duke d'Orléans's many lovers, was shielded by the king himself. *Le vice italien*, the Italian vice, as homosexuality was known in the inner aristocratic circles—undoubtedly because it was thought to have been imported from Italy a century earlier, during the reign of Henri the Second and his wife, Catherine de Médicis, was not only rampant but also all the rage. Several of the ladies at court had recently been heard complaining that womanizing had become altogether unfashionable. Robin's broad shoulders, slim hips, and angular features, his flashing eyes framed by long dark lashes, made him an object of desire for men and women alike, but he showed little disposition to follow in his uncle's footsteps. Nonetheless, there were resemblances: the haughty tone, the arrogant gaze, and, most of all, the sense of entitlement, were encoded from birth.

The discovery of the cross seemed to reawaken the child in him, so familiar to Mathilde that she suddenly felt reassured by his presence.

"Let's see what else we can uncover in this rubbish heap!" He knelt down and began combing through the grass with his bare hands. "Don't just stand there like an oaf," he said, turning toward her, then he added dismissively, "You can keep the locket if you like."

Mathilde had certainly intended to do so, with or without his permission, for it would remain a keepsake to remind her of what seemed already, in the wake of their first kiss, a momentous turning point in her young life. She clasped it in her fist, wondering where to store it, then decided to slip it onto the chain around her neck. Once again they were children, on their knees, sifting through the dried leaves and the hay, hunting for buried treasure. The old stone hearth still stood aloft and Mathilde went over to inspect the inside of the fireplace, from which wrought iron hooks were suspended in midair, bereft of their cooking pots. Robin had found a soot-covered poker and was using it to strike the blackened stones. Sure enough, he soon detected a hollow spot inside the fireplace and, upon further inspection, located an area where the mortar was chipped away. The two began to remove the blocks helter-skelter, flushed with excitement at the possibility of discovery. And discover they did! Though they didn't find what they had hoped for. In lieu of an imaginary chest, whose rusty hinges would creak as it opened to display its sparkling treasures, they unearthed a pile of charred bones from which a severed human skull gaped at them in silence. They both recoiled in quiet horror; then, as if by some unspoken accord, hurriedly began to shove the stones back into place, aware that they might have tapped into some unimaginable secret. All at once, it seemed to Mathilde that the brightly lit patches of field grass lent a discordant, garish tint to the countryside. There was a tiny shift in the air around them, subtler than a breath, secretive and alarming.

She reached out tentatively to touch his shoulder. "Do you remember that young boy who went missing during Lent last year?"

But Robin's dark gaze put a halt to her query. She quickly withdrew her hand.

"Hush! Don't speak of this to anyone. It was found on my

uncle's estate, and it could implicate him. You do understand that it will have to remain our secret."

Outside, the sun had risen to its zenith, reminding Mathilde that she was already late for her duties. Madame would be irritated, for—unlike many of the other ladies at court—she was in the habit of rising before noon. With a brief word of farewell, the girl hurried off toward the castle through meadows and swamps, treading on her gown in her haste.

"Where *have* you been?" exclaimed her exasperated mistress, as Mathilde, panting and disheveled, entered the bedchamber plunged in semidarkness. "It's nearly noon, and the king has invited me to take part in his hunting party this afternoon. You know how I count on such rare occasions to be able to speak my mind to him directly! I am surrounded by enemies who spend their time maligning me, and it is up to me and me alone to justify myself whenever I have the opportunity to speak with His Majesty. Lord knows I cannot count on Monsieur, my husband, to defend my honor! He only listens to his depraved friends: the Chevalier de Lorraine and the Marquis d'Effiat."

The voice emanating from the canopied bed was guttural and deep, punctuated by a harsh, German intonation. Mathilde moved forward to lend a hand to a rather large woman with heavy jowls and a distinctly masculine bearing.

"I have no use for fineries, but my brother-in-law the king insists that I keep up the facade at court. Thank God that you, my girl, have a flair for arranging this unruly mop and composing my ungainly appearance into a semblance of elegance."

The speaker's gentle glance belied the directness of her speech and the coarseness of her tone. Mathilde reflected on her good fortune in finding such an indulgent and generous mistress. True, the woman had her faults. One couldn't help but question her suspicions: was she indeed the victim of a

conspiracy? Or were her incessant ramblings simply manifesta-
tions of the paranoid obsession of a foreigner, whose awkward-
ness and rustic manners had made her a constant source of
ridicule and bemusement at the court of the Sun King?

Whatever the case, Mathilde had to admit that one could
hardly blame Madame for her misgivings. Her predecessor,
Henriette of England, first wife to the Duke d'Orléans, had died
twelve years earlier, in 1670, at the age of twenty-six, under
extremely suspicious circumstances. Tongues were still
wagging over the possibility of an unnatural demise. At the
time, a replacement was needed in haste, as it would not do for
the king's brother to remain a widower. Louis XIV had only to
cast his gaze across the Rhine, where the young Elisabeth
Charlotte's father governed the fertile plains and valleys of the
Palatinate from his mighty castle high above the town of
Heidelberg. Under the circumstances, and with so much land
at stake, it would be easy for his brother, Philippe, to compli-
antly overlook the uncomely features of his betrothed.
Monsieur scarcely noticed the fairer sex and, though he was
quite able to perform his marital duties, during the act his wife
knew that he preferred to imagine he was skewering a young
page. The primary obstacle to the marriage was the young
princess's faith. It would not do for the man who was second in
line to the French throne to marry a Protestant! But Karl
Ludwig had given his daughter away without any qualms of
conscience, knowing full well that such a prestigious marriage
had been beyond his wildest hopes for his unprepossessing
daughter and a great honor to the family name. The danger of
such an uneasy alliance had seemingly escaped him in his
haste. And so, at the age of nineteen, the young Liselotte, as she
was commonly known, the tomboy who had been in the habit
of roaming freely throughout Heidelberg's castle and its
grounds, was led, kicking and screaming, to the royal carriage
that would take her to her gilded cage.

Not surprisingly, Mathilde was having great difficulty tending to her mistress that morning, as her thoughts could find no anchor. The macabre discovery had chilled her to the very core and left her trembling, but the memory of the salty taste of Robin's lips was stronger yet.

"Mathilde, what the devil has gotten into you today? You know that I never wear that preposterous wig on the hunt! And where is my plumed chapeau?" Madame's breathing was somewhat hampered by her tight corset.

The young girl went to fetch Madame's hunting clothes, which the latter favored over her fancier garb. The skirt was of plain, deep brown velvet, and the waistcoat handsomely tailored in forest green with a high collar: the ensemble would have been quite becoming on a slenderer figure. The felt hat, on the other hand, was wide-brimmed and adorned with two eagle feathers, which Madame said reminded her of the homeland for which she still pined.

Mathilde drew back the heavy damask drapes and opened the windows to reveal the lavish courtyard gardens of Versailles and its fountains. Sunlight flooded the room, dancing on the mirrors, the chandeliers, and revealing the polished sheen of honey-colored wooden paneling. A fresh breeze chased away the stale, sour odor of nocturnal sweat. Madame rarely slept alone, despite her husband's neglect. In his absence she enjoyed the comfort and warmth of her seven miniature terriers, who were yapping for their late-morning meal.

"Mathilde, you can take the leftover sausage from last night's meal and serve it to the pups. They seem to love German delicacies almost as much as I do!" said the duchess, picking a bit of casing from her teeth with a whalebone pick.

Madame compensated for her isolation at court not only by lavishing attention on her pets but also by feeding her prodigious appetite. She would often request that her cooks prepare simple meals reminiscent of her German childhood, for she normally had little taste for the delicate morsels more suited to the French palate. Naturally, Mathilde had no intention of feeding the dogs. She knew her station and this was well beyond the call of duty. Madame knew it, too, but she often presumed that everyone shared her affection for those little pests.

As soon as her mistress had hoisted herself up and out the door, Mathilde summoned the chambermaid.

"Agnès! You are to feed the leftovers to the mutts, and mind that you change the bed linens today! They reek of rank, wet dog hair." She wrinkled her nose in distaste as she pushed one of the dogs off an armchair.

As a sullen Agnès went about her chores, Mathilde tended to her own grooming. When she glanced in the mirror, she was struck by the change in her reflection, staring back at her in wavy and dappled ripples caused by the uneven surface of the glass. There was nothing tangible beside the flush in her cheeks, but there was something new in her eyes: a deepened awareness that hadn't been there before, a knowing look that heightened her allure. What she had lost in innocence, she had gained in mystery. She wondered how obvious her transformation would be to the sharp-eyed, gossip-prone courtiers.

Reflecting back upon the morning's events, she relived the urgency of her passion and felt the desire to be with Robin again deep in her groin. Their terrifying discovery had lent a new dimension to their bond at the very moment it had been threatened by a change in roles. The charred bones were the strange cement of their renewed fellowship, an exclusive link only the two of them would share. She realized suddenly that she could thereby retain her privileged role as Robin's equal, because she held the key to a mystery he seemed to want to keep private. She fondled the amulet, now a pendant, dangling from her chain. *If you love me you shall follow.* Perhaps these words were more auspicious than she had thought.

Her reverie continued as she went about her daily tasks, only to be interrupted by the arrival of her best friend, Catherine de Sauvignon, who burst in without knocking. Catherine was lady-in-waiting to the grande dauphine, wife to the crown prince of France. The dauphine and Madame shared the common bond of their German heritage and had become steadfast allies at a court that viewed foreigners with suspicion. This alliance allowed the girls, who had been raised by the same governess, to maintain the intimacy of their long-standing friendship. Tall and willowy, with thick, raven-black hair, Catherine would have passed for an exquisite beauty, were it not for her unfashionably tawny complexion. Her dark eyes were alight with mischief as she carefully uncovered a parcel concealed in the folds of her ample skirt.

"You'll never believe what we found in the library!" she said, the *we* no doubt referring to her companions-in-waiting Gabrielle and Marguerite. "We were sent there by Mother Thomasine to meditate on our wanton behavior during the last banquet." Catherine set the object on top of Madame's prayer stand.

"I believe that the three of you had been drinking and were caught unchaperoned with male companions," replied Mathilde with bemusement. "It was so very unlike you. I've always considered you to be the reasonable one."

"That may be, but fate sometimes puts us in situations that are beyond our control. I'm certainly glad I don't have your wild streak! You always act first and think later."

Mathilde shrugged off the mild rebuke. She'd heard it before. "Go on with your story, then!"

"Well, we were instructed to find something edifying to read, and as I searched for devotional reading material suitable to appease Mother Thomasine, I came upon a musty volume entitled *Maxims for the Foundation of a Christian Marriage* stowed away behind several volumes of *The Lives of Saints*. It was practically sealed shut with age, and the pages were so brittle that I had to take care not to tear them. The chapters were predictably boring, filled with sound advice for the dutiful and subservient wife. The illustrations in the back, however, were quite a different matter!"

The girls huddled together as Catherine unwrapped her worm-eaten prize and pried it open to the back. There, to Mathilde's amazement, were several graphically explicit engravings, exposing sexual postures she had never dared to imagine and for which her inexperience provided no names. The girls began to giggle uncontrollably, pointing to each new discovery in turn. But it was the final engraving that made them catch their breath. It depicted a large, octagonal, ceremonial hall filled with masked bystanders, presided over by a shrouded figure seated on a throne, holding a staff. His cloak was parted to reveal an erect phallus. To his right and left, forming a semi-circle, stood eight very young, exquisitely beautiful boys, masked and naked, except for an ornately designed codpiece. Their bodies were as smooth and pale as alabaster.

So absorbed were the girls in wondrous contemplation that they barely heard the voices in the hall. They snapped the volume shut just in time to avoid disaster, as Madame bustled into the room, hat askew, flushed from her recent exertion.

"Draw me a footbath, Mathilde! I'm exhausted and beside myself with outrage and shame." She ripped her cloak off and flung it onto an ottoman.

Catherine knew better than to linger under the circumstances and was gone in the wink of an eye.

"Whatever is amiss, Madame? Did the king not acknowledge your presence at the hunt today?" Mathilde's voice was light and soothing, but it had no effect on the duchess who was steaming with anger.

"Oh, not only did he speak to me but at great length! It's the subject of the conversation that has provoked me to such indignation. According to him, I have become the laughingstock of the court because of a rumor that has spread like wildfire! That fiend d'Effiat, his cohort the Chevalier de Lorraine, and that old harpy Madame de Grancey have accused me of tolerating the advances of a certain gentleman and of returning his affection! I have never been so offended!" The volume of her voice increased with each loosened corset lace.

"I asked the king if he believed me capable of such outrageous conduct and disregard for my vows to his brother. He smugly replied: 'I am quite confident that even if you were inclined to take a lover, Madame, the opportunity would be rare indeed. I am well aware of your high moral ground and your disinclination for sexual adventures, which may simply be the direct result of your lack of suitors. However, there *has* been much ado about nothing, and that is worse and certainly more detrimental to your reputation than a successfully concealed affair.' He ended his remonstrations by quoting *Tartuffe*, that scandalous play by Molière: 'But alas tongues are wagging and that doesn't bode well.' I deemed it best to disregard the thinly veiled insult. As it came from the king himself, no retort was possible, but I was boiling inside," she said, puffing with indignation.

"When I first arrived in France, Louis was supportive and kind: a friend among strangers. Will he now abandon me, too? Bring me my pen and my inkwell, and then leave me alone to gather my thoughts!" The duchess rolled up the sleeves of her negligee and cracked her knuckles.

Mathilde knew that Madame would spend the next two or three hours writing to one of her many correspondents, as was her daily habit. This was her only consolation for her alienation in a strange land. Of course, the king's sister-in-law knew that her correspondence was strictly monitored and censured by officials before it left the palace grounds. Occasionally, she would contrive to have her letters delivered at some risk by one of her few loyal servants. The girl slipped discreetly away, looking back briefly to observe her mistress chewing reflectively on the tip of her pen before putting it to paper.

The letter she wrote that day was addressed to her aunt Sophie, the Duchess of Hanover.

No doubt, dear Aunt, you have not forgotten the strange maneuverings of the Marquis d'Effiat, the Chevalier de Lorraine, and their cabal, which I recounted to you in my last letter. My enemies have now persuaded Monsieur, my husband, to dismiss poor Madame de Théobon from my service in the same manner as he did Madame de Clérembault several years ago. They have accused her of serving as go-between for my imputed love affair with the Chevalier de Saint-Saens, but her only crime was to be too devoted to my interests. The king gives those villains free rein and seems blind to their machinations and oblivious to the fact that Lorraine has not only debauched His Majesty's son but has spread unimaginable rumors about the boy's sister as well. May God grant that Lucifer rise up from hell to carry him off to his kingdom! And so that he might not be alone and afraid, I wish him the companionship of the Marquis d'Effiat on his journey! You can well imagine what such gossip has done to my reputation and I doubt whether I will be allowed a hearing on the matter. I pray to God that you and my uncle might not give credence to such hateful rumors. I shall try to reconstruct for you the series of innocent events that may have led to such public accusations. You know how I am, very outspoken with those familiar to me. Well, the other day, during a game of cards with the queen, a dispute arose regarding the rules of the game. As usual, the table was surrounded by onlookers, and behind me stood an officer by the name of the Chevalier de Saint-Saens. As he is an avid gambler, I turned to him to ask his opinion of the matter at hand. At that very instant, Madame de Grancey approached me and inquired whether I knew the gentleman in question.

"How could I ignore his identity?" I exclaimed. "He and his comrades ride beside me at the hunt and he is often kind enough to fetch my horse for me."

"I take it, then, that he is a friend of yours," she said.

"Why do you ask?" I replied.

"Because last night he gravely offended me at the ball; he loudly claimed that I was far too old to dance. I could only assume that he was trying to please someone, a mistress, perhaps."

I informed Madame de Grancey that since I was not at the ball, I would see if I could discover the truth to the matter, but she refused my offer. Today the king informed me that Madame de Grancey had been complaining that I had used my lover Saint-Saens to insult her in public. He is well aware that these charges are fabrications designed to cause a rift between my husband and me, but he refuses to intervene on the basis that he does not want to take sides with anyone against his brother, and that Monsieur is surely aware that no one is less likely to have an affair than I. You cannot imagine how abandoned and dishonored I feel! I am sending you this letter by means of a new messenger, who seems reliable. Unfortunately, our faithful Herr Wendt, whose trustworthiness is unquestionable, has just returned from Germany, or I would have employed his services. I envy any endeavor to escape, albeit temporarily, this den of iniquity.

Your devoted niece, Liselotte

(Versailles, September 19, 1682)

While Madame was immersed in her correspondence, Mathilde had escaped to the courtyard. The weather was mild after a sudden rain shower, the sunlight was reemerging from behind a hazy curtain of fog. This gave the gardens the semblance of a veiled, mysterious, surreal apparition. The flowers formed a blurred vision of multicolored specks, the light reflecting iridescent sparks from the shrouded fountain. She blushed as she gazed at the naked statues lining the alleyway: ghostly white apparitions frozen in time. Everything today brought her reflections back to her yearning for Robin. Lost in thought, she was startled by a playful tug on her shoulder. It was Catherine, who had earlier made a quick exit from Madame's chambers.

"Do you still have the book?" she asked.

"Yes, but it's now in a secure place. Where better to hide a book than in plain sight in the library? The court has become such an austere place since the king has succumbed to the influence of that old hag he's so fond of, his mistress Madame de Maintenon. God knows what would happen to us if they caught us with that volume in our possession!"

Catherine plopped down on the bench beside her friend, seeing no need for formality under the circumstances. "What have you been up to? I was looking for you earlier today, but to no avail."

This time, Mathilde's delicate pale face turned crimson, to her great chagrin. "I was out and about . . . ," she hedged.

"Well, that begs the question *with whom*?" replied her friend, tilting her head to scrutinize her. "You seem oddly flustered for someone who barely blushed at those engravings. Don't you dare lie to me! After all, I compromised myself by showing you the book. The least you can do is to satisfy my curiosity."

Mathilde's determination to keep her secret to herself was quickly dispelled by the driving need to unburden herself of the morning's events. Her voice at first faltered, then rushed out with a sigh of relief. "Can I trust you to keep a secret?" she asked, though rather doubting that Catherine would be totally reliable.

"Certainly," her friend insisted.

Thereupon, Mathilde confessed her moment of intimacy, kindling her friend's curiosity. But the former was hard-pressed to answer Catherine's burning questions: it had all gone by so fast, and looming in the background was the horrid memory of those charred remains. Somehow, not quite understanding how it all happened, she was unable to hold back her words, once the dam had broken. The discovery had weighed so heavily on her soul that she needed to share that burden with a confidante. Pulling forth her chain, she began by revealing the silver talisman to her companion. Catherine examined it with eager curiosity, while Mathilde unveiled the rest of the morning's events. The final revelation cast a shadow over their mood, and although Mathilde felt some relief at having confided her sinister secret, she also felt a sense of dread at having unleashed a manifestation of evil straight out of Pandora's box. Catherine's previous levity was replaced by a frown of concern.

"Do you realize what this is?" she said, inspecting the cruciform locket.

"I really only took it as a memento," replied Mathilde defensively, pulling at a wayward strand of hair.

"This cross appears to be of the type that can hold, among other things, a lethal dose of poison, easily obtainable from the apothecary. This small clasped compartment here can be deftly opened and its contents emptied into the victim's goblet, while his attention is elsewhere. Depending on the dosage and the type of poison, death can result almost immediately, or overnight."

Mathilde's eyes widened as her friend pried it open to reveal a tiny lock of fine chestnut hair. She reached out to touch the strand but then thought better of it. It seemed to be a portent of sorrow.

"Whatever you do, don't mention this to anyone," said Catherine, snapping the case shut.

"I had no intention of doing so. Robin has strictly forbidden it."

"Oh? Since when do you listen to him? Watch out, Mathilde! He'll soon have you under his thumb!" Catherine's voice was scornful. She rubbed the talisman, as if it might help jar her memory. "The image and the inscription you see here are vaguely familiar, so let me make some casual inquiries. Why don't you let me borrow it, but swear not to tell anyone that it's in my keeping." Before Mathilde had a chance to object, Catherine had slipped the chain off her friend's neck and had pocketed it.

"You may keep it for a day or two, but I shall want it back!" she said.

A sudden chill in the evening breeze scattered some of the fallen leaves and reminded the girls that it was time to return to their respective duties. Dark clouds were looming in the distance, promising an abrupt change in the weather. From the windows above, a dark figure watched the two brightly clad damsels scurry through the courtyard. A hand then reached out to close the heavy damask curtains.

BLACKMAIL

*T*he duchess was startled from her slumber by a loud, peremptory rap on the door leading to her private chambers. Mathilde was nowhere in sight, as it was still well before ten, so the duchess quickly pushed aside a few of the furry creatures scuttling about in her bed and reached for her brocade dressing gown, wrapping it tightly around her large frame. Upon opening the heavy, ornately gilded door and peering out into the shadowy hallway, she discovered, much to her surprise and dismay, her husband accompanied by none other than Philippe de Lorraine-Armagnac, better known as the Chevalier de Lorraine.

"To what do I owe the honor of an unexpected visit at such an unseemly time of day?" she asked, barely masking her indignation.

Not one to be unnerved by his wife's ill humor, the Duke d'Orléans pushed his way forward, closely followed by his favorite. With a weary sign of resignation, Madame ushered the intruders into her parlor, bracing herself with foreboding for a confrontation in which she was certain to be at a disadvantage. As she positioned herself squarely into her fauteuil, she rapidly scrutinized her visitors. The two Philippes could hardly have formed a more striking contrast. Her husband's dark, feverish eyes lit up the unhealthy pallor of a pasty, powdered complexion, which no amount of rouge could conceal. Unlike his brother, Louis, he was slight in stature. A vain man, he spent an inordinate amount of time and money—certainly more than his wife—on his outward appearance, often donning woman's garb. The practice had become acceptable, if not outrightly condoned, during the regency of Catherine de Médicis, over a century prior. His companion, though thirty-nine and only three years younger than the duke, was still strikingly handsome, one might even say beautiful. Even-featured with moist brown eyes and a luminous complexion framed by soft curls, his angelic countenance belied his moral depravity. The two had met and the duke had fallen in love with the Chevalier de Lorraine at the tender age of eighteen, nearly twenty-four years earlier. They had been inseparable allies ever since. Though she loathed his sexual penchant, Madame felt that the duke was not entirely to blame for his predisposition for men, the younger the better. Fearing political rivalry between her two sons, his mother, Anne of Austria and her cohort, Cardinal Mazarin, actively strove to enfeeble Louis's younger brother by fostering his feminine side and by preventing his participation in military training or his interest in politics. It was even widely rumored that the cardinal had employed his own nephew Philippe-Julien Manzini for the young duke's sexual initiation.

Madame thought back wistfully to the early years of her marriage to the king's brother. Philippe had been kinder then; despite his conspicuous disinterest in the physical charms of his nineteen-year-old bride, he performed his marital duty, albeit perfunctorily, to ensure an heir to his title, and treated her with courtesy at court. But the chevalier despised her and did the best he could to discredit her with her husband. Years of persistent persecution and insinuations had whittled away any remaining affection between Madame and her spouse.

Contrary to the customary care he took to look his best, Monsieur appeared to have dressed with haste that morning. His wig was disheveled and slightly askew, and his shirt was partially untucked. The pale green silk of his waistcoat did nothing to improve his sickly complexion. The duchess examined him with distaste, wondering how she could have ever imagined herself happy with him. She was torn between feelings of derision, anger, and pity, knowing full well that is was the latter sentiment that would offend her husband most. She suppressed a sudden urge to laugh at this ridiculous figure and focused instead on her archenemy, who evoked in her a feeling of nameless dread. Her nose was assaulted by the smell of spent sex, reminiscent of the sickly sweetness of rotting fruit, which a dusting of lavender-scented powder could not conceal. The man's presence permeated the air with a sense of wrongness.

Monsieur declined a half-hearted invitation to sit and paced instead about the room. Meanwhile, the chevalier averted his gaze from hers, staring tensely out into space. After what seemed an interminable silence, the duke pounded his fist on the marble mantelpiece, nearly upsetting the ornately gilded clock.

"I see, Madame, that you are so unaware of what goes on at court that you can sleep soundly at a time when mischief is afoot!"

"And what sort of mischief might that be?" countered the duchess.

"My brother the king has ordered the public flogging of his own son, Louis de Bourbon! Since you were partially responsible for his upbringing, I thought this might be of some concern to you." In a conspicuous attempt to appear nonchalant, the duke took a pinch of snuff from his intricately engraved silver case, but his trembling hand betrayed him.

A rap at the door announced the arrival of Madame's tea tray. Agnès set it down quickly and disappeared with her customary sullen look.

"On what grounds? And what do you mean by his *son*? Louis is the bastard of that La Vallière whore," she replied, narrowing her eyes aggressively. Two slits of electric blue.

Despite her abrupt manner, Madame's demeanor softened visibly at the mention of the young nobleman, for she was very fond of Louis. After his mother had been replaced as the king's mistress by the ambitious Madame de Montespan, she had retired to convent life in Chaillot, leaving her children behind. The boy, who was seven at the time, had been brought in by the Duke d'Orléans. Madame, who was still grieving the loss of her first infant while expecting a second child, became very attached to the little orphan during his stay at the Château de Saint-Cloud.

"Since the king has legitimized him, he has a royal title, if not a claim to the throne. The child is only fourteen for God's sake, and his father's second favorite at that!" The duke snorted with indignation.

"I was in the king's presence yesterday during the hunt, and he said not a word to me of this affair, though he did speak of another matter that was brought to his attention by your friend here. According to Louis, disgraceful rumors have been circulating regarding my alleged amorous involvement with Saint-Saens, and the source of this gossip is all too clear to me," said Madame, standing up abruptly and stepping forward toward her husband, who backed off defensively.

"As a matter of fact, I, too, have heard such reports, Madame, and we shall need to address the incriminations shortly, for a husband's honor is at stake in such matters. However, there is a far more pressing matter at hand, and one in which I most urgently beseech your help," said the duke, attempting unsuccessfully to temper the irritation in his voice.

The duchess cocked a quizzical eyebrow. She could not help but be astonished at such an intercession, particularly in view of the fact that it was pronounced with such acrimony. Her husband, who was used to giving orders and being obeyed unconditionally, was visibly annoyed and unaccustomed to the posture of supplicant. He looked like he had just swallowed a spoonful of lye.

"Well, if indeed you need my help, it might behoove you to use a gentler tone of voice. You can catch more flies with honey than with vinegar, as the saying goes." She went over to the side table where her morning tea was getting cold and poured herself a cup, not bothering to offer any to her visitors. The duke disregarded the obvious slight.

"I won't beat around the bush on this matter. It is imperative for you to intercede with the king on the chevalier's behalf," said the duke haltingly, the words nearly sticking in his throat.

Madame was adding a liberal dose of sugar to the brew when she stopped in mid-action. She swiveled to face the duke, spraying sugar on the carpet. Her face was frozen in disbelief, as she stared at her husband in dumbfounded silence, waiting for some further clarification. How could he possibly prevail upon her to promote the interests of her sworn nemesis?

Sensing this, the duke continued rashly, "The chevalier has been unjustly charged with molesting Louis's bastard, an accusation he most vigorously denies! He runs the risk of exile from court, or worse yet!"

The chevalier simply nodded and smiled contritely at his benefactor.

"So I gather that this is the reason for the boy's punishment. It would certainly be far more fitting to have the chevalier flogged in his place!" At these words, the chevalier visibly had to hold himself in check. His face was flushed with anger.

Madame began to stir her tea with deliberate slowness. She yearned to ring the service bell—it was just within arm's reach, for someone, anyone, to break the unbearable tension. She reflected that the accusation seemed perfectly plausible and that the chevalier's exile could only benefit her peace of mind. Nonetheless, she also had to recognize the danger of provoking a man as powerful as the Chevalier de Lorraine, whose influence extended into the darker reaches of the Sun King's domain. Her predecessor, Henriette of England, the duke's first wife, had dared to request the banishment of the chevalier and his friend, the Marquis d'Effiat. It was rumored that the king had granted this favor to his sister-in-law, in return for favors of her own, for she was a comely woman with a vivacious wit, and all too often neglected by her husband. The duke, however, managed eventually to obtain the chevalier's pardon and return from Rome by pleading incessantly with his brother. By this time, the king had tired of Henriette and had turned his attentions to Louise de La Vallière, her lady-in-waiting. Ironically, the king and Henriette had used Louise as a pretext for His Majesty's frequent visits to his sister-in-law's private chambers, for even *he* had scruples about bedding his own brother's wife.

The king had understood the political expediency of Philippe de Lorraine and Antoine d'Effiat's return to court. Though he personally condemned homosexuality, he was willing to overlook it in the case of his brother. The chevalier's presence would keep his occasionally meddlesome sibling well occupied, out of the way, and, more important, gratefully indebted to him for his magnanimous pardon. But the king had ignored, or had purposefully overlooked, the danger such a pardon would represent for Henriette. Her unprecedented request for the chevalier's banishment was widely known. She died in her twenty-sixth year writhing in agony. Only a handful of devoted friends were stalwart enough to endure the stench of her vomit. The official autopsy revealed an acute peritonitis due to a perforated ulcer, but many at court thought otherwise.

Madame had often wondered if her father had known of these rumors when he came to her room that day, on her nineteenth birthday, to casually announce her betrothal and imminent departure for France. Her mother had long been sent away by then, as the woman's fits of jealously disturbed the peace of mind of Karl Ludwig's new mistress.

"I fail to see how I, of all people, could be of help," she began hesitantly, measuring her words.

"Nor do I believe the chevalier's claim to innocence," she continued, more assertively now.

At these words, the chevalier, who had been standing to the side, glowering in frozen silence, like a serpent coiled for the attack, suddenly sprang to life. "I am sure that you will find it in your best interest to cooperate, once you have heard our terms."

"And in what way would that be to my advantage?" The duchess set down her cup and folded her arms defiantly, standing her ground.

"It is not what you have to gain but what you have to lose that should concern you, Elizabeth Charlotte," he hissed, lurching forward with untoward familiarity.

"How can you stand by, Monsieur, and allow your wife to be threatened in such an insolent manner?" The duchess, struggling to maintain her dignity and to subdue the violence of her reaction, turned to confront her husband, whom she outweighed by a stone or two. She pulled her morning gown more tightly around her bosom. Splotches of scarlet had spread over her normally ruddy face, giving it a frighteningly intense glow. The duke stepped back to shield his lover.

"Let us keep our calm, for this is a matter of mutual interest," he prevaricated. "First of all, I believe that having you stand in defense of the chevalier would have all the more impact in view of the fact that the animosity between the two of you is common knowledge. What we want—would like—from you is to testify on the moral depravity of young Louis. Who knows him better than you, who practically raised him? The chevalier maintains that it was the lad who sought to seduce *him*, rather than the opposite. And I, for one, believe him. Secondly, whatever one might say of you in jest, your reputation for integrity and often brutal honesty is undeniable. It would give *weight* to our testimony."

The sarcasm was not lost on the duchess, who sniffed with distaste. "Well, that may be, but isn't it ironic that the chevalier himself, along with his cronies, has jeopardized his own chances in this matter by actively undermining my reputation for moral decency? Furthermore, why should I risk tarnishing my one advantage at court through outright perjury, since the boy's fate has already been determined and your friend here is undoubtedly implicated?"

"Here is why, you German cow!" the chevalier bellowed, his handsome features suddenly distorted. "The king intends to appoint my intimate friend, the Marquis d'Effiat, governor to your son Philippe, heir to the Duke d'Orléans. Should you decline to help me now, I shall see to his education personally, if you catch my drift." Lorraine could not suppress a malevolent chortle.

This is what the devil must look like, the Duchess thought, *at once irresistibly attractive and intensely repellent.* She fought back a violent urge to spit in the chevalier's face. Instead, she spoke in carefully measured words and in an ominously soft tone of voice.

"All too well, I am afraid, buy why would the king allow such an abhorrent thing? Especially in view of the punishment he has reserved for his own son Louis!"

"Bastard or not, Louis de Bourbon is still his son, whereas your offspring is already tainted by heredity in the king's view."

"If it weren't for my husband, none of your kind would be

allowed at court. And it would be a good riddance." At this pronouncement, Madame gritted her teeth and opened the door to her chambers, unceremoniously gesturing the two visitors to leave. A look of unadulterated hatred grazed her face as they went past. As the door closed, she leaned back on it, in an attempt to regain composure. Gasping for her breath, she groped her way to her writing table, took up her pen, ripped a sheet of paper from the pile, and, still trembling, began to scratch her way through yet another lengthy letter.

She scarcely noticed the arrival of her lady-in-waiting, who prepared the washbasin and selected a dress of blue satin, embroidered with gold thread, and a blond wig for Madame to wear for her appearance at court that evening. Outside, the wind was howling. A loose shutter beat against the facade of the palace. Mathilde opened the windows to secure it, but the wind blew sheets of rain into the chamber, so she hastily closed them again. Although by now it was almost midday, ominous rolling clouds darkened the sky and made it necessary for the maid Agnès to light the chandeliers.

Madame's prose was as blunt and direct as she was: her letters reflected her despondent longing for home and her exasperation with the hypocrisy of life at court, but they also revealed an indomitable, sardonic, and often bawdy sense of humor. Her aunt Sophie of Hanover, with whom she had lived for several formative years during her youth, was her staunch supporter and ally in times of trouble, and her most frequent correspondent. Nonetheless, she felt that in her imminently perilous situation she required more immediate help.

"Mathilde," she said, "please request an audience with Madame la Dauphine. The sooner the better!"

Maria Anna Victoria of Bavaria, otherwise known as the grande dauphine or the Dauphine Victoire, had arrived in France two years earlier to marry Louis XIV's oldest legitimate son and heir to the throne. Although she was a woman of great personal charm, culture, and intelligence, she suffered from ill health and spent most of her time in her private chambers, unable to fulfill her social duties, much to the chagrin of her father-in-law, who felt that she had let him down. With the exception of the dull-witted and docile Queen Marie-Thérèse, it was Victoire who held the rank of foremost woman in the social hierarchy at court. She suffered from her marriage to the affable, but childlike grand dauphin, of whom it was said that the apathy of his mind was second only to that of his senses. Most of all, however, she suffered from ostracism due to her unsightly appearance. Her face was almost revolting to look at: a weak chin combined with a strong overbite and buck teeth contrasted with distended, pouched cheeks, in which she appeared to be conserving nuts. Two beady slits above a crooked nose completed the rodent-like impression. It was hardly surprising, then, that the two compatriots, each one a misfit in her own right, sought and found comfort in each other's company.

Mathilde went out in search of Catherine, the dauphine's lady-in-waiting, whom she found by one of the great-room windows, bent over an embroidery frame, deep in thought. Her friend's dark lustrous hair was swept up into a chignon, and the sheen of a pearl earring drew the gaze to her swanlike neck. She was dressed in black velvet with a touch of white lace at the wrists, a shadowy figure set across the dark-lit sky.

"My mistress seems to be in urgent need of a private audience with the dauphine," Mathilde announced, interrupting her friend's reverie.

"She's in Chantilly visiting the Prince de Condé and won't be back until tomorrow or the next day. I'll give her the message as soon as she returns. What's the matter this time? Another case of indigestion? What can they possibly have to chatter about in that barbaric language of theirs?" she said irritably.

"What's gotten into you, Catherine? You know how they're treated. Is there any wonder they should wish to commiserate? Besides, their chats leave us ample time to roam the grounds. I thought I might take you to the site of our discovery, if you have the stomach for it."

"The weather outside isn't fit for a dog!" Catherine protested, with a slight shudder.

"Exactly! We won't risk running into some busybody. I'll return as soon as I have reported back to Madame. As for you, go fetch our cloaks!"

A short while later, two hooded figures, huddling together, dashed into the rain and through the woods bordering the grounds of Versailles. The rich, heady scent of damp moss and decaying pine needles permeated the air, while glistening leaves covered the ground with speckled patterns of gold and russet that stood out against the dark green hue of the trees. The girls' boots sank into the spongy loam and their capes occasionally snagged on the dense underbrush. As they advanced into the darkness, their courage began to falter. Mathilde had been sure she could find her way back to the collapsed structure by following familiar landmarks, but in the gloom it was difficult to distinguish one clearing from the next. She was nonetheless determined to conceal her rising sense of panic from her friend. Her heart nearly stopped when suddenly she perceived a brief glimmer of light through the branches ahead. Catherine had observed it, too.

"What do you make of that? I wonder who could be out in the woods in such weather," she whispered, crouching behind a stand of river birches.

"Well, *we* are here, are we not?" replied Mathilde ill-humoredly.

Unable to decide whether to advance or retreat, and unsure of their exact location, the girls stood wavering when the light appeared again, more distinctly this time and accompanied by a distant, high-pitched whistle. Suddenly, a huge mastiff crashed through the undergrowth, yellow eyes aglow. Mathilde let out a sharp cry and attempted to climb the nearest tree, but she became embroiled in her long skirts and petticoats and fell to the ground. Catherine had gathered a long branch and was brandishing it feebly toward the dog. This only served to enrage the hound. Growling deeply, he bared his teeth and braced for the attack, his smooth gray flanks heaving with fury. Catherine stumbled to the ground, and the two girls huddled together in an attempt to shield themselves from harm.

"Well! What have we here? Two damsels in distress?" a mocking tone announced. "Come here, Goliath! These girls couldn't harm a fly if they wanted to." The dog leaped forward toward his master, wagging his tail.

"Would you like to bet on that?" Mathilde declared defiantly, brushing the wet leaves from her gown.

"Chrétien Desforges at your service," the youth replied cheerfully, as he bowed in mock deference. "Whom do I have the honor of rescuing on this dark and stormy day?"

"I would scarcely call that a rescue," said Catherine, having recovered her wits. "I would advise you to keep that beast at bay if you don't want him to come to harm." Despite her words of defiance she was inching away from the hound.

"I see that you're overwhelmed with gratitude! But you weren't looking so proud a moment ago," shot back the young man.

"How dare you speak to us with such insolence? We could have you flogged for much less!" Mathilde's hackles were up.

"You would have to catch me first, and I know these woods like the back of my hand. They're the king's hunting grounds, and I am one of the groundskeepers. I was checking for poachers. They come in all shapes and sizes, you know. Perhaps I should check what you are carrying there, beneath your cloaks!"

He held his lantern high and appraised the girls from head to toe. His broad grin revealed a healthy set of teeth, a rare enough feature among the courtiers at Versailles, let alone the common folk. Catherine could not take her eyes off him. Broad-shouldered and tall, Chrétien's unruly mop of golden curls suggested Norman origins and crowned a striking, raw-boned face with soft brown eyes. Mathilde, who was known for the quickness of her wit, was at a loss for words, aware that her own impetuous foolishness had led them into a potentially dangerous situation. For here was a stranger, and a commoner no less. His open demeanor and cheerful countenance, however, inspired confidence. She reasoned that whatever the case, they had no option but to trust him. He was familiar with the terrain and could guide them back to the castle gardens. Just as she was about to swallow her pride and ask for guidance, a violent downpour erupted.

"I know an abandoned shack near here, on d'Effiat's estate," he shouted. "We can take refuge there until the storm subsides. If it please your ladyships . . ." Another mock bow and a sweep of the arm.

Chrétien led them directly to the crumbling ruins that housed the hidden remains. They had not been so far off the mark, after all. As they gathered close together in the lantern light under what remained of the thatched roof, Mathilde and Catherine were visibly edgy, as they averted their eyes from the directness of the young man's bold scrutiny. Despite his mockery, Chrétien seemed unable to take his eyes off Catherine. Her glistening hair was matted down by the rain, and a few strands clung to her forehead and cheek. He reached out to gently sweep them away, but appeared to think better of it and withdrew his arm. As she shivered in the radiance of the lantern light, her wet skin gave off an iridescent, honey-colored glow and a faint but undeniably musky scent. The spell was suddenly rent by the sound of Mathilde's voice.

"The rain has died down, and I believe that your presence is no longer required," she said haughtily, regaining her composure. She thought it best to remind Chrétien of his lowly station.

"Are you sure to be able to find your way back?" he inquired, visibly concerned all of a sudden for the girls' safety.

"Don't worry! We won't leave your service unrewarded. Tomorrow at noon, Catherine will wait for you at Versailles by the fountain of Apollo with a small token of our appreciation. Now leave us!" Mathilde abruptly turned away. Catherine remained standing there, looking forlorn, arms dangling at her side.

"Hurry up now, and good day to you!"

◆

Chrétien made a show of turning on his heels and whistling for his hound as he stomped off into the forest. He felt deeply humiliated by the condescending dismissal and the assumption that he would expect compensation for his help, but he made an effort to suppress his irritation. At twenty-three years of age, he had certainly had his share of country girls and tavern wenches, willing to lift their skirts and spread their thighs for a few coins or a beer or two. But it seemed to him now that Catherine had an otherworldly aura different from that of any woman he had ever known. The promise of a meeting with her was more than enough reward for him. Once he was well out of earshot, he tied up Goliath and silently retraced his steps to the place where he had left the girls.

He was quite astonished to find them still at the site, removing bricks from behind the hearth. They labored together awkwardly, for they had no tools but their bare hands. Nonetheless, it was apparent that they knew what they were looking for and that the bricks had been loosened previously.

Chrétien hoisted himself nimbly into a nearby tree. Propelled by curiosity, he leaned forward to hear their conversation, nearly losing his balance in the process.

"It's not here!" cried Mathilde, straightening up. She wiped her forehead with the back of her hand, leaving a trace of soot behind. "Someone must have come here recently to remove the evidence!"

"And could that someone be Robin d'Effiat, perchance?" asked Catherine. She seemed exasperated as she peered once more into the hearth.

"If Robin had some motive to remove the skull, why would he have offered me the locket?" replied Mathilde. "It makes no sense!"

Catherine removed a kerchief from her sleeve and wiped the smudge off Mathilde's face. "That was before you found the remains. A possible connection between the cross and the skull had not yet been established. Has it occurred to you that if it was someone else, you and Robin may have been followed and may even be in danger? Someone may be aware of your discovery. Someone who doesn't want further inquiries. If you don't watch out, you may be the next person to be 'removed.'"

"I think you are suffering from an overactive imagination, girl," said Mathilde offhandedly.

Nonetheless, Chrétien observed an abrupt change in the girls' demeanor as they hurriedly wedged the bricks back into place before starting back through the woods, their rising panic causing them to break into a run. He climbed down from the tree and followed them silently, determined to make his way back to the ruins to investigate the site for himself once the girls had safely reached the palace grounds.

At the palace gate, he saw them hesitate before parting ways. Catherine seemed to breathe with difficulty as she asked, "Don't you think we should speak to our ladies of this matter? The fact that the remains have been moved points to the possibility that they're recent. Madame and the grande dauphine are bound to have more resources at their disposal for a discreet investigation than we do, and should they decide that the matter be dropped for the sake of caution, then so be it. Unfortunately, you, Mathilde, are going to find it difficult to extricate yourself from this muddle. You'll have to find out if Robin was the one who disposed of the evidence."

"I know, I know," said Mathilde distractedly, twisting her finger around in her hair. "It's time to seek the protection of the two most prominent women at court, if not the most powerful, but if Robin finds out, there'll be hell to pay."

THE PORTRAIT

*R*obin was sitting at a desk of inlaid rosewood in the library of his uncle's country estate, watching the massive storm clouds heave their heavy bulk across the afternoon sky and wondering fretfully whether he had been a fool to give up the locket, which might be a key piece of evidence in the likely event of foul play on the grounds of his family manor. It had seemed like a generous impulse on the spur of the moment, but in retrospect he felt that he had been too impetuous. Mathilde had always been a chatterbox, and the recent turn of events lent greater uncertainly to their alliance. As a childhood friend, she had been his trusted comrade, but what type of conduct might he expect from her if they crossed the line and became lovers? Would she be prone to histrionics or fits of jealous rage? He was at a loss to explain his unease, but there it was, nonetheless, gnawing away at his gut. *If you love me, you shall follow . . .* the inscription echoed somewhere in the dark recesses of his memory, and the image seemed vaguely familiar as well. Where had he heard or seen them before? The words enclosed an enigma. They were decidedly ambiguous, for they could be interpreted equally as: *I command those who*

love me to submit to me. Did they form an order, an appeal, or an invocation?

Had Robin's relationship with his uncle been closer, he might have summoned up the courage to ask him if he had ever heard the phrase, but Antoine d'Effiat's only concern for his nephew's welfare was linked to his own self-interest. He had recently contracted an extremely advantageous marriage agreement between Robin and the widowed countess Madeleine de Noailles, fifteen years his nephew's senior, an arrangement of which Mathilde was thankfully unaware. Of course Robin, who was heir to an immense fortune, could not envision the possibility of a marriage founded on love, let alone to a woman of impoverished, albeit noble lineage. He stood up listlessly and went over to the bookshelves, where he scanned row upon row of leather-bound volumes. They were not arranged in any particular order, and Robin, who had never shown much inclination for study or introspection, was not keen on examining their contents. He wandered over to the window seat and pulled the miniature portrait of his newly appointed fiancée out of the satchel hanging from his belt. He rumpled his nose at the thought of marrying a thirty-four-year-old woman, but his uncle had argued that her status as a widow had left her the freedom to fully dispose of her own huge fortune without the inopportune intervention of a family patriarch. And she had set her sights on Robin from the first moment she saw him. People at court claimed that having been married at the tender age of fifteen to a wealthy sexagenarian, she felt it was now time to claim pleasure as her rightful due. Her husband had been impotent, but not without a taste for sexual perversion, and she had been made to suffer for her rise in status.

As his gaze lingered over the portrait, taking in every detail of the pale, thin, elongated face, the delicate bejeweled hand clasping a prayer book, and the wide collar of Belgian lace adorning an alarmingly frail white neck, something jarred his memory and brought a similar image to the surface. Then it all came back to him. Somewhere, a few years ago, in the seemingly endless gallery of family portraits, he had seen a similar pose, a figure holding a book inscribed with the same enigmatic logo as the locket in the ruins. But he was at a loss to establish the connection or the reason this image had suddenly flashed in his mind. Robin wondered why one particular painting among so many others had seduced him as a youngster. Perhaps because of the vaguely androgynous beauty of the subject. He now distinctly remembered having asked his governor, half in jest, whether the venerable subject was a man or a woman. His question was met with awkward silence. A short while later, the portrait had disappeared, replaced by that of yet another valiant ancestor astride a magnificent steed.

Following this revelation, Robin spent the better part of the afternoon searching every room in the castle for the painting, but his quest proved unsuccessful. He then decided it was time to make inquiries about the whereabouts of the portrait and what better place to start than with his former governor, Gaston de Liancourt, who was currently residing in the west wing of his uncle's estate. Once a formidable swordsman, Liancourt had suffered the effects of debilitating arthritis and was only a shadow of his former self.

At the annex, Robin was invited to take a seat in the antechamber, where he spent his time fidgeting until finally three physicians in long robes, with equally long faces befitting their station, exited from his former master's chambers. As he approached the bedside, he was struck by the frailty and ashen complexion of the man who had once governed him with an iron hand.

"What brings you here, my boy?" Liancourt asked in a faint voice.

Robin knelt down beside him and bowed his head. "How fares your lordship?" he asked in a low, deferential voice.

"Come, come, my boy. You don't give a toss about my welfare. I've been shackled to this bed for nigh on a year, and not once have you come to visit."

Liancourt knew him all too well. Any attempt to proclaim disinterested concern would only make matters worse.

Robin looked him squarely in the eye and said, "I've come to ask you about a bit of family history."

"Ah! That's more like it, Robin. I taught you to avoid the fawning manners of the common courtier. Now get to the point!" There was a malicious twinkle in the man's eye that reminded Robin of many a thrashing.

"If you wish, sire. I am hoping to locate the portrait of one of my forebears that was suddenly removed from the gallery a few years back. The ancestor in question was a handsome young man with auburn hair and strikingly feminine features. I seem to recall that he was carrying a book, but I have no recollection of his identity."

"Well, that is a long and shameful story. Neither your dear departed mother nor your uncle would favor the telling of it. And I am too weak to tell it at present or to bear the brunt of the marquis's anger. As for your mother, I'll have to account to her on the other side. But why the sudden interest in unearthing dark family secrets? Let the dead dogs lie." The man's voice kept trailing off.

"It is not a matter of idle curiosity, sire, but I am looking for clues in what appears to be foul play. I have no intention of revealing any of this to my uncle, as it's not in my interest to incur his wrath, either."

"I can't see how an ancestor's portrait could provide any clues, but should you really want to know the truth behind the Marquis de Cinq-Mars's sordid past, for that is his name, you only have to consult the *Historiettes* by Tallemant des Réaux. They've not been published, as they've been censored by His Majesty the king, but the manuscript is circulating clandestinely at court. It would seem that everyone but you, one of the chief concerned, is aware of the squalid details. He was beheaded some forty odd years ago by Louis XIII for the crime of lèse-majesté. There, I've said enough." The old man coughed up some phlegm and laid back against his pillow. The short conversation had apparently sapped much of his strength.

"One more question, I beg of you! Can you tell me where to find the painting?"

"I haven't a clue. The portrait was removed when you became too inquisitive and I believe that, aside from your uncle, the house steward is the only one to know of its whereabouts." With that, the old man nodded off, leaving the young man to his vexation.

Back in the main hall of the estate, Robin decided that the next step in his search for the painting was to inquire among the domestic help. They were the ones who kept the estate running efficiently from within the bowels of the castle. He hurried down the back staircase, where he was met by the surprised glances of the scullery maids, cooks, butchers, stablemen, and guardsmen stationed in the lower depths of the building. Robin rarely ventured into the domestic quarters, having little interest in the administration of the household. He passed by the kitchens, which occupied a good third of the lower level. The head chef was shouting at the saucier who had, by the smell of it, burned the roux. There were dried herbs hanging from the rafters, baskets overflowing with fresh onions, carrots, beets, and apples, pails of foaming milk, large wheels of cheese, and hefty cakes of churned butter. The rich scent of baking bread loaves mingled with the pungent aroma of smoked meats. Robin stood watching as the butcher raised his mighty cleaver over the carcass of a freshly slaughtered boar, when his attention was suddenly diverted by the strident voice of Jacques Molinier, the castle steward, who was arguing with the local fishmonger over the price of the daily catch. The dispute came to an abrupt halt as Robin approached and was met with obsequious bows.

"May I have a word in private?" he asked Molinier.

The steward was tall and gaunt, with stooped shoulders and a permanent scowl etched on his stubbled face. He eyed Robin suspiciously.

"But of course, sire," replied the steward, discreetly but firmly ushering Robin into the courtyard. Molinier's function was to oversee every aspect of the running of the estate, from the buildings and grounds to the domestic staff and the household finances. Robin noticed that his hands were muscular and gnarled from years of toil.

"Can you tell me where we store the canvases that are no longer on display?" Robin carefully avoided making any direct reference to the exact tableau.

"We sold several of them recently," replied Molinier cautiously, "but we keep the most valuable portraits of family ancestors in an enclave next to the wine cellar."

"Who has access to the storage site?"

"Your uncle and I, sire. No one else."

"I would like to gain access to the premises, if that's at all possible, and without my uncle's knowledge."

The steward's eyes glazed over; he was clearly evaluating the odds of angering the uncle in order to please the nephew.

"No one need be informed of this, and I'll make it well worth your while," added Robin. As sole male heir to the fifty-one-year old Marquis d'Effiat and his vast fortune, many already regarded Robin as their future employer.

Molinier hesitated and looked wary. Finally, he whispered, "I shall 'misplace' the key before midnight tonight. It will have fallen into an empty urn by the kitchen entrance. Please be sure to replace it before dawn. I am sure that you realize the risk I am taking for you." Such flagrant disregard for the marquis's orders could mean immediate dismissal or worse.

"Rest assured that the key will be there . . . along with a louis d'or," replied Robin.

◆

While Robin was waiting for the stroke of midnight, pacing through the hallways and racking his brain to make sense of it all, Chrétien made his way back to Goliath, who greeted him with great leaps and bounds.

"Down, boy, down!" he commanded while unleashing the hound. "It's time to put your talents to the test." Upon returning to the site of the ruins, he took out his hunting knife and wedged it in between the loosened bricks of the dilapidated hearth, removing them with ease. He scooped up a handful of ashes and held them out for Goliath, who eagerly plunged his wet nose into the gray powdery substance. The dog looked up at his master in anticipation of the signal.

"Go!" Chrétien shouted, and Goliath shot off through the forest like a bullet, his tail bobbing up and down, stopping periodically to track the scent. As Chrétien caught up with him, the dog had his paws propped up against a stone wall surrounding an abandoned well and was straining his massive neck over the edge.

"Good boy!" he said as he petted his heaving flanks. Peering over the side, Chrétien was unable to distinguish anything in the murky depths. He found a sturdy branch nearby, tied his lantern to it by means of a length of rope he carried in his satchel, and lowered it slowly down into the dark. There, leering up from the pit, was what appeared to be a pile of bones, ashes, and several human skulls. He recoiled in horror and tripped over a jagged stump, falling on his backside.

After having dusted off his trousers and regained some of his composure, the young man was struck by the oddity of the situation. Was there a connection between what the girls had been searching for in the ruins and the findings in the well? If so, what was their level of involvement? And if, as Chrétien surmised from what he had overheard, someone had recently moved the remains with the knowledge that they had been discovered, then was there a possibility that the girls were in danger? He wondered whether he should warn Catherine, but in so doing, he would also have to admit that he had been spying on them. In the mud surrounding the well he caught sight of multiple sets of footprints, but the soft soil had been trampled to such an extent that it was difficult to distinguish one set from the other. Goliath, however, had no problem picking up the direction of the most recent visitor and started off again, this time toward a spot where someone had ostensibly mounted a horse, for there were deep-set hoof prints leading away from the marquis's estate in the direction of Versailles.

Chrétien decided that he had already dallied too long, for he had chores to attend to back at the kennels. Despite an attempt to slip onto the premises unnoticed, the barking hounds alerted his father to his presence.

"Don't think that you are too old for a beating!" his father warned as he whacked his son on the back of the head with the handle of a riding crop. "The terriers need to be fed and let out for a run so that they'll be in condition for tomorrow's royal hunt. The king is most anxious to impress a visiting emissary with the splendor of Versailles and its grounds. Nothing can be left to chance, and should anything go wrong, there will be a heavy price to pay!"

Despite this admonition, Chrétien went about his chores distractedly. His thoughts were absorbed with the afternoon's events and more specifically with the mesmerizing beauty of Catherine. It was late when he finally finished, and he knew that his seven siblings would have left him very little to eat, so he headed down to the local tavern and ordered a draught of beer, some sausage with mustard, and a hunk of dark bread. The innkeeper of L'Auberge du Cerf Blanc was a dour-faced man with heavy jowls and a bad disposition: the regulars knew better than to cross him the wrong way. The only one who could both govern and humor him was his wife, Guillemette, whose ample hips swayed from side to side as she hustled to and fro with frothy mugs of beer and cider. Guillemette's face was covered with freckles, and when she smiled, which was often, her missing front tooth lent her a foolish expression. Nonetheless, she was both a shrewd businesswoman and the local gossip.

"Greetings, Chrétien! It's been a while since you've graced us with your presence. Juliette and Sylvie have been pining for you, and each one believes herself to be your favorite. I keep telling those silly creatures that your heart isn't so easily stolen, but they hold on to their fantasy."

The two serving wenches were in fact the reason Chrétien avoided the place. Their rivalry was so obvious and the attentions they lavished upon him so overbearing, that he often did not have the stomach for a meal at the inn. He was, however, too courteous to show his annoyance and so continued to suffer their behavior during his rare visits.

Guillemette lowered her backside onto the wooden bench beside him with a sigh of relief. She always enjoyed taking a moment to inform her patrons of the local goings-on. Without any prompting, she began to recite a litany of scandals: the coal merchant's wife had caught her husband in the act with Louison, the half-wit; Monsieur Jeannot had accused the butcher of altering the weights for his scale and a fight broke out in the marketplace; Martin, the village drunk, had been found dead in the gutter . . .

"Has anyone else disappeared of late?" Chrétien asked, trying not to sound too eager for information.

"Well, I can only think of the blacksmith's daughter, who

ran off with a gypsy. She'll have a hard time earning a living off fortune-telling, that one! Oh, yes, and then there's that Yves Roussin. According to his neighbor, he went out to gather firewood the other day and never came back." She turned toward the kitchen to call out "Jules! Bring Chrétien here another drink! This one's on the house."

Her husband grunted in disapproval, but poured the beer nonetheless. The mention of Chrétien's name brought the two servant girls scrambling into the front room to fawn over their favorite patron. Sylvie was the quicker of the two, managing to wedge herself between the innkeeper's wife and Chrétien. Meanwhile Juliette bent over him, placing herself at an angle that allowed for maximum exposure of her opulent bosom.

"Scat!" said Guillemette. "You've no business here. Get on with your chores! Can't you see that you're making a nuisance of yourselves?" To Chrétien's relief, the girls obeyed by retreating ever so slowly back into the kitchen.

"If Yves was hurt or killed as the result of an accident, his body would probably have been discovered by one of the groundskeepers," said Chrétien, attempting to get the conversation back on track.

"Well, all the townspeople sighed good riddance when he disappeared, I can tell you that!" added Guillemette. "There was something quite queer about him, lurking about the young boys and such. He didn't fit in, never married, kept to himself. Some caught sight of him creeping off to God knows where in the middle of the night, only to return at daybreak. It's not natural, I tell you!"

Seeing that it was getting very late, Chrétien threw a coin on the table and stood to leave, trying to be as inconspicuous as possible so as not to attract the girls' renewed attention. As he was approaching the tavern gate, he heard a stifled giggle from behind him and when he turned around, Juliette clutched him by the neck and kissed him full on the mouth. He struggled to disengage himself, and once he had, the wench darted back to the inn. Everything was over in a flash.

◆

The bells tolled midnight as Robin reached down into the urn to retrieve the key to the storage room. His shadowy silhouette slid down the wall of the stairwell and into the basement. As he passed furtively through the wine cellar the moldy scent of musty bottles and fermentation assaulted his nostrils. The only light source was the faint reflection on the wine bottles of a moonbeam that had slipped through the window grating. He felt his way to the door of the storeroom and inserted the key. Once inside the windowless space, he locked the door again and thought it safe to light his lantern. The room was filled with crates full of fabric and outmoded clothing, furniture in various states of disrepair, and worn-out riding gear, but Robin went straight to the paintings. There were several lined up against the wall, but the one he was searching for was hanging in full view of the entrance. He studied it for some time. The subject portrayed had wild waves of auburn hair, delicate features, a regal bearing, and a disdainful expression in his eyes. He wore a short-waisted doublet with full slashed sleeves and an unstarched ruffled lace collar, which Robin recognized as the fashion worn during the reign of the king's predecessor Louis XIII. The inscription on the heavy gilded frame read *Henri Coiffier de Ruzé, Marquis de Cinq-Mars et d'Effiat* (1640). Robin's memory of the portrait had not been entirely accurate, for the book was the Bible, however he was startled to discover that the marquis wore a large cross identical to the one that was now in Mathilde's possession, bearing the same design and inscription. As he pondered the meaning of this discovery, he was startled by the sound of muffled voices and approaching footsteps. He snuffed out the light and hid behind a wooden crate. The portrait suddenly began to shift, revealing the rotating panel of a secret passageway. Several hooded figures appeared and exited through the storeroom door, locking it behind them. Robin distinctly heard the voice of his uncle and trembled at the thought of his narrow escape. It took him a while to regain control over his jagged breath and pounding heartbeat. Once he was sure that the premises were vacant, he made a quick exit. He was about to return the key, when he thought better of it. Robin stole into the kitchen, cut off a portion of lard, and made a quick impression of the key before dropping it back into the urn. Back in his room, he stared out at the moonlit gardens, glistening with moisture in the aftermath of the storm. Attempting to recall what little he knew of his family history, he regretted not having paid more attention to his governor's long-winded lessons in genealogy. Without bothering to undress or to turn down the bedcovers, he tumbled heavily onto his mattress and drifted off into a fitful slumber haunted by pale phantoms.

◆

The next day, Chrétien arrived at the fountain well in advance of the appointed time. Every time he caught sight of a feminine form in the distance, his heart would pound against his chest. Catherine was late, and he cursed himself for having fallen prey to her feminine charms. Perhaps she was already promised in marriage to some pampered nobleman. He imagined her at court, surrounded by admirers, and his face flushed with jealousy. Although he found this feeling preposterous, he couldn't overcome it. How could he, a mere peasant in her eyes, presume to spark her interest? Catherine was unattainable, yet he longed to see her again, despite his sense of foreboding that no good could come of it. He had never concerned himself much with matters of love, for he had an easy, effortless appeal to women of his own class.

When Catherine finally appeared, she was unmistakable. The wind had picked up and was whipping her long ebony hair wildly about her face. Her black cape was billowing around her slender body, and he crossed himself superstitiously, for he thought he beheld an enchantress, a shimmering mirage appearing miraculously out of thin air. He found nothing to say and was sure that she would find his discomfiture laughable. But to his surprise, she too was tongue-tied and ill at ease. After an awkward silence, Catherine held out a satchel containing a few coins and turned to walk away, when Chrétien finally ventured to speak.

"Milady, I did not come for my reward but for a chance to speak to you of an matter of interest." Again, he resisted the urge to touch her, swallowing hard instead.

"And what might that be?" she replied, drawing closer despite her haughty tone.

"Meaning no disrespect, milady, I watched over you and your friend yesterday by the abandoned cottage to make sure you were safe. I couldn't help but hear part of your conversation."

"How dare you eavesdrop? What we were doing at the site was none of your business." The flare of anger in her eyes exposed a fierceness that the young man found both tantalizing and amusing.

"Ah, but I made it my business, didn't I?" replied Chrétien, recovering some of his cockiness. He had no intention of being bested or bullied by a damsel, beautiful or not. "I think that you should hear me out, because your interests and your very safety might be at stake. If it comforts you, I can swear to secrecy on this matter."

Seemingly torn between disdain and attraction, Catherine

eyed Chrétien with wariness. He drew closer yet, at the risk of making her retreat. But she stood her ground.

"Goliath and I returned to the ruins and he tracked the remains I assume you were looking for to an abandoned well. What we found at the bottom was more than I had reckoned for."

"Take me there!" she demanded impulsively, but then winced as she bit her tongue.

"Perhaps this is not the best time," Chrétien replied, looking beyond her toward the palace. "It seems like the well is a mass burial site, and should its discovery become known, the people involved would not take kindly to further interference. Besides which, based on fresh footprints, it's likely that the person of interest resides at Versailles, if not in permanence, at least occasionally. Since it appears that foul play's involved, the possibility that a murderer lives in your midst is to be taken quite seriously."

Catherine shuddered involuntarily. "I still fail to see how all of this adds up." For the first time since they'd met, she lifted her gaze to look him squarely in the eyes. Chrétien felt his knees go weak.

After a moment of silent consideration she added quietly, "Perhaps we can meet again on Saturday, providing Mathilde is willing to place her trust in you a second time. She won't be happy to hear of your spying on us."

"She's already made her dislike of me painfully clear," said Chrétien.

"Be that as it may, she will want to satisfy her curiosity. The matter is of personal interest to her. On Saturday, the king is offering a musical fete and fireworks for the Turkish ambassador. Our absence would scarcely be noticed if we make haste and return before the grand finale."

"How can I resist?" said Chrétien cheerfully, attempting to hide his disappointment at the prospect of a third party but knowing nonetheless that it would be inappropriate and fool-hardy for the two of them to venture out alone after dark. He agreed to meet again in order to arrange the nocturnal visit and turned to leave. Glancing back over his shoulder, he was surprised to see that Catherine's gaze was still lingering on his shoulders. Then she blushed and turned away.

◆

When Robin awoke that same morning, he had already decided on his course of action. He called for the stable boy and asked him to saddle up his horse at once. The discovery of the night before provided a definite link between the locket and a distant family member, so he thought it prudent to reclaim the pendant without delay. The young man was well aware that his uncle's scandalous lifestyle had brought unwanted attention to his family and had tainted his own reputation. Another scandal might cause his social disgrace and Robin, though young, was intent on protecting his family's name and fortune.

When he entered the stables, Robin was met by the eager snort of his black Arabian steed, who began to pace excitedly in his stall.

"Calm down, Sarrasin!" he commanded, offering the horse a handful of oats before hopping into the stirrup and swinging his leg with agility over the horse's ebony flanks.

Antoine d'Effiat's country estate was only a short ride from the palace of Versailles, but Robin was ostensibly trying to cut the time in half. Sarrasin had the proud bearing of a thorough-bred and scarcely needed the spur to accelerate into a full gallop. Robin had planned his arrival well before noon, to ensure that Madame, the duchess, would still be in bed. Upon dismounting, he summoned the nearest page and asked him to send for Mathilde. It didn't take long for her to join him in the royal stables. He led her by the hand to a quiet place behind a haymow where no one could see or hear them. Her face flushed with pleasure as she embraced Robin, but she backed away immediately when he shrugged off her embrace. If the disappointment was reflected in her crestfallen manner, it barely registered with Robin, as he came straight to the point.

"Mathilde, I want you to give me back the locket!"

"And why should I?" she asked, a trace of spite in her voice. "You gave it to me as a keepsake, and I fully intend to keep it!" She crossed her arms unflinchingly.

Robin understood Mathilde's body language well enough to know that he had to take a different approach or he would get nowhere with the headstrong girl. He reached out for her and stroked her red curly mane, gliding his hand down the nape of her neck and onto her back.

Coming very close now, with his lips brushing her earlobe, he whispered, "I will replace that ordinary silver cross with a finer one, made of gold and precious stones." He saw that his cajolery had taken effect.

The girl stepped back for a moment to eye him suspiciously, but in the end she broke into a smile.

"Why do you want it so badly? It must surely be of little consequence to you," she teased.

Robin was beginning to lose patience with Mathilde. He wanted to explain as little as possible, and she was making it difficult for him to conceal his motives. "I believe that I may have discovered some information as to its origin, and I wish to investigate the meaning of the motto, is all," he replied guardedly.

"So it *was* you who removed the remains from their hiding place!" she cried, with a breath of relief.

Robin recoiled in disbelief: "What are you talking about? Have you gone mad?"

Madeleine suddenly seemed to realize that she had said too much and that it was too late to take it back. She attempted, rather lamely, to explain her reason for returning to the site, but skirted the issue of Catherine's presence.

"Care killed the cat, you know. I certainly did not remove the remains, nor have I been back to the site since the other day. Your meddling has revealed a turn of events that bodes no good and should convince you to return the cross to me for safekeeping. It's in your best interest, so turn it over!" Robin demanded, towering over the wisp of a girl.

Biting her lip, Mathilde reluctantly replied, "It's no longer in my possession."

Robin, who had managed to contain his temper until that moment, exploded with rage: "You stupid fool! I should have known better than to trust you! No woman can keep a secret, least of all you! I demand to know who has the locket and how much of our story you've let slip. It is not merely your safety that you've jeopardized but mine, too!"

Forgetting her solemn promise, she muttered, "I gave it to Catherine, who seemed to know something about it, and she's set out to investigate the matter. I trust her implicitly to return it in due course," protested Mathilde with tears in her eyes.

"Well, there's another meddlesome wench for you," replied Robin, his anger waning at the sign of Mathilde's distress.

Her tears softened her beauty in a way of which she was wholly unaware, and his own discomfiture caught him off guard. Robin had mostly known her as a willful tomboy whose burgeoning womanliness was veiled by her hard edge.

"There, there," he whispered, gathering her into his arms. "We'll simply have to get it back from Catherine before she begins to nose around."

Still trembling, Mathilde laid her head against his chest. Robin caressed the soft down on her neck until he had to surrender to desire. Pressing her against the door of the stall, he lifted her up onto himself. This time she embraced him eagerly as he undid the laces of his trousers and took her, moving back and forth, slowly and gently at first, then harder and faster until he had to place his hand over her mouth to stifle her moans. A while later, smoothing their hair and adjusting their garments, they furtively left the stables, glancing around to make sure they passed unnoticed. They parted ways without a word of farewell.

The moment Mathilde had left, Robin's anger returned. He blamed himself for having trusted her, and even more so for having forgiven her so easily. She had assured him that she would get the cross back from Catherine within the hour and would hand it over to him at their next meeting. Upon leaving the castle grounds, Robin caught sight of a broad-shouldered young man with curly blond hair taking leave of Catherine by the fountain and slipping out the castle gate. As he rode back home, Robin suddenly decided to change his course.

Keeping at a safe distance behind her, he tied up his horse and skimmed the palace walls as Catherine, oblivious to his presence and lost in thought, crossed through the garden passage and entered the north wing, where she stealthily opened the door to the library. Robin stooped forward to look through the keyhole and was able to observe that the young woman had reached for a volume from one of the shelves. A shaft of light illuminated her neckline and shoulders. As her back was to him, he was unable to determine what she was doing, but she quickly tucked the book back on the shelf after having slid something into the folds of her gown. To avoid discovery, Robin swiftly entered the adjacent chapel, as Catherine flounced past. Hoping to find the pendant, Robin returned to the library to examine the volume Catherine had removed. The title was bewildering: *Maxims for the Foundation of a Christian Marriage*. But as he opened it, several images fell to the ground. The etchings were highly interesting.

THE LOST BOYS

*C*atherine rapped discreetly at the door of her mistress's chamber. She heard a muffled *"herein"* and could not help wondering why the grande dauphine, who spoke adequate French, still clung to her harsh-sounding native tongue. The dauphine's red-rimmed eyes gave evidence of weeping, though she turned away toward her mirror as if to avoid her lady-in-waiting's gaze. Catherine was extremely fond of her mistress, and she felt a pang of sadness at the thought of her lonely plight. She brought out the washbasin and a pitcher of warm water she had heated in the hearth. The Dauphine Victoire looked up at her through puffy eyes, submitting passively to the morning ritual. Catherine noticed that her nails had been bitten down to the quick.

"The Duchess d'Orléans has requested the pleasure of your company, Madame."

"I am feeling rather indisposed at the moment, my dear. Could we not put off this visit a day or two?"

"Without wishing to alarm you, Madame, I should point out that the matter appears to be rather urgent. Mathilde didn't tell me the nature of the concern, but she indicated that her mistress was extremely distraught."

"Very well, then!" said the dauphine with a sign of resignation. "She is my dearest and most trusted friend. When I came to court from Bavaria she was the first to befriend me. I cannot deny her in her time of need."

Catherine chose a simple frock of white silk and a strand of pearls. The back of the skirt was gathered into sweeping folds by a series of pink bows, but the front was plain. Her mistress had a distinct preference for understated garments, having no desire to draw attention to her physical appearance. At court gatherings and festivities she stood in the shadows, self-effacing and unnoticed, yet thanks to her invisibility she had become a shrewd observer of her entourage. As she laced up the dauphine's stomacher, Catherine impulsively decided to reveal the events of the past few days. She was aware that the moment was awkward. Victoire seemed preoccupied with her own worries, not to mention those of Madame, but Catherine knew that her friend's and maybe her own well-being were at stake. As she recounted her recent adventures, Catherine observed that the dauphine's expression, at first detached, became increasingly alarmed.

"This discovery of Mathilde's is a foreboding of worse to come, and I would advise the two of you to abandon your amateurish sleuthing before you come to harm. As your mistress, I feel a keen sense of responsibility for your plight, so I shall take up the matter with Madame during our visit today to seek her opinion on the matter. You mentioned that you're in possession of a cross that was found at the sight. You *must* hand it over to me for safekeeping."

"Thank you, Madame!" replied Catherine with a sigh of relief but also a twinge of guilt, handing over the object.

The dauphine rolled the locket in her fingers, examining its shape and opening the compartment to discover the lock of hair. When she read the inscription, a glimmer of recognition passed over her face. She did not, however, comment on the words. Instead she replied, "Save your thanks, my dear, for there is something more we need to discuss. Your story corroborates certain allegations regarding your reckless behavior that I have tried to deny in your defense. Yesterday the king, who was with that intrusive old prude, Madame de Maintenon, called me aside. I find it hard to believe, but that shrew has managed to sink her hooks into His Majesty and gain such influence with him! When she was simply Madame Scarron, the governess of his brats, she did not put on such airs, but since she has become the king's favorite with a noble title, she has single-handedly dampened the mood at court. She believes herself to be the upholder and enforcer of moral standards, and her accusations of misconduct are unfailingly upheld by the king. Now it would seem that she has plans to create a finishing school at Saint-Cyr for young girls from the minor nobility, where she proposes to instruct them in the conduct of virtuous and thrifty Christian wives."

Catherine could barely suppress a sardonic smile at the thought of Maintenon's unfortunate young pupils. She went over to the giant mirrored armoire, from which a carved eagle looked down on her as she searched for a pair of pink satin slippers. The grande dauphine distractedly extended her foot as she continued.

"So as I was saying, yesterday that old hag was positively gloating as the king publicly rebuked me for my permissiveness in allowing my ladies-in-waiting to have suitors. I suppose that he now believes himself to be a paragon of virtue for no longer sleeping with young maidens. Maintenon added that most of the young people at court today spend their days drinking themselves into a stupor, using profane language, and wallowing in depravity, but that the worst behavior came from my own entourage. She must have spies everywhere, for she even mentioned the fact that Madame and I had dismissed such misconduct without sanctions on more than one occasion. We Germans have a saying: *Wo der Teufel nicht hin kann, da schickt er ein altes Weib.* Where the devil cannot go, he sends an old woman! You, my dear, were one of the principal parties named. I believe that you were punished for your recent indiscretion by Mother Thomasine, were you not?"

Catherine's face flushed with anger and embarrassment at the memory of the incident. She, who had been so careful to shield her immaculate reputation from gossip-hungry, dissolute courtiers, had been publicly admonished for a moment of weakness, a minor peccadillo. It occurred to her that the dauphine's exchange was a plausible reason for her present state of distress. The slightest censure from the king could bring about public disgrace, which her mistress, already the target of ostracism, could ill afford.

"Madame! I can assure you that although I have indeed been punished for that single unfortunate episode, my behavior has generally been beyond reproach!"

Catherine reflected with indignation that although she had acted foolishly in cavorting with a group of her peers, she was far less to blame than it appeared, and that singling her out had been unfair, for she was far from being the worst offender. Unlike many of her friends, she drew the line at a modest flirtation with members of the opposite sex.

Despite her desire to vindicate her reputation, Catherine refused to provide further clarification, knowing that she had one secret she could not share with her mistress. One of the young "men" who had been involved in the scandalous affair and with whom she had been compromised was the audacious Julie d'Aubigny, an exceptional swordswoman with a penchant for cross-dressing. So effective was the latter's transformation into a swaggering buccaneer that many an impressionable maiden had fallen prey to her charms. Julie was, in fact, a distant relative of Catherine's impoverished noble family.

Her thoughts drifted back to the day they first met. Upon learning of Catherine's appointment as lady-in-waiting to the grande dauphine, Julie's mother had written to Catherine, prevailing upon her to help her daughter gain admittance to the court of Versailles. Under pressure from her mother, Catherine had reluctantly consented to use some of her sway, and her appeal was granted. But on the appointed day of Julie's arrival, when Catherine went out to greet her carriage, she found, not the third cousin she barely remembered from fleeting childhood encounters, but a slender, prepubescent boy of about fifteen years of age with the face of a cherub, who introduced himself as the Chevalier de Maupin. He explained that his stepsister, Julie, had been obliged to delay her trip, and that she had sent him in her stead. The chevalier's appearance caused quite a stir at court, where every new arrival served as a pretext for gossip, speculation, and scandal-mongering. Gabrielle and Marguerite in particular, two sisters with a penchant for trouble and a reputation for wantonness, were all aflutter and keenly interested in meeting the handsome, if somewhat effeminate newcomer. So insistent were they, that Catherine finally conceded, albeit reluctantly, to arrange an assignation. But the situation quickly got out of hand, as Maupin, unabashedly flouting the sisters, made a brazen play for Catherine instead. Having had a bit much to drink, she let down her guard just long enough to be enticed into some physical explorations that were sufficiently probing to lead to the discovery of the chevalier's true identity. As Catherine was recovering from her initial shock and readjusting her garments, Mother Thomasine flew in like a bat out of hell, alerted by one of the guards that something suspicious was going on in the north wing of the palace. Maupin was mildly reprimanded for his misbehavior, but the girls' conduct caused a public scandal.

Julie must have been well aware that passing herself off as a man had more than one advantage. Catherine's thoughts were interrupted by a further admonition from her mistress.

"My dear, in your case, you have to be twice as vigilant as others in order to avoid disrepute. Maintenon has you under close surveillance."

Catherine anchored her fists on her hips, but the dauphine ignored her silent protest as she went on.

"The king's mistress is acutely aware that whatever looks she had are rapidly fading, and she is extremely jealous of the young beauties at court, and of you in particular. This may surprise you, as you seem to be unaware of your effect on men. You may recall that the king recently made an offhand comment about your many charms for all to hear, and Maintenon, who was standing by, turned green with envy. Moreover, your close relationship with me and the duchess puts you at risk, because the old witch heartily despises us both and has more than once joined forces with the Chevalier de Lorraine and the Marquis d'Effiat in their attempts to discredit us. Despite her self-righteous sermonizing about Christian self-denial, Maintenon is ever the politician and has taken the side of the duke's entourage in the presence of the king, simply to spite Madame. Then, when she is out of His Majesty's earshot, she decries and vilifies them for their debauchery."

This tirade was interrupted by a soft knock on the door, followed by the swift entrance of Mathilde. She curtsied as she said, "My mistress has sent me to inquire when she might expect the pleasure of your visit. She is in considerable haste to speak to you of an urgent matter, and has been awaiting your return from Chantilly with great anticipation."

"I was just about to leave," replied the dauphine. "No need for either of you to accompany me. I have two sturdy legs, and despite my poor health I am not as helpless as many of these Frenchwomen at court appear to be! By the way, Mathilde, I have told Catherine—and the same goes for you—to stop meddling in that gruesome affair and to leave matters to me and the Duchess d'Orléans. We have the means to conduct a discreet investigation into the matter, should we choose to do so." And turning on her heels, she promptly left the room.

Mathilde balked at the dauphine's revelation. "Catherine!" she cried out. "How could you have talked to Victoire without my consent?"

"I thought that we had agreed to confide in our mistresses, and the sooner the better, as matters already seem to have gotten out of hand. Are you having second thoughts?"

Mathilde's face was etched with misery. "I swore to Robin that I'd return the locket to him and that I'd keep our discovery a secret. He was very cross with me for having turned it over to you and for returning to where we found it. Now it would seem that I've inadvertently perjured myself, because this incident has taken on a life of its own." She looked down at her feet in dismay.

An involuntary shudder, prompted by an intense feeling of apprehension, coursed through Catherine's body. "That's quite true, and I should add that our mistresses and Robin are not the only ones to share our knowledge. That young groundskeeper we met in the forest also knows a bit too much. He followed us back to Versailles and then, with the help of his mutt, did some scouting of his own. He discovered the missing bones and skull at the bottom of an abandoned well that apparently has served as a mass gravesite for other victims."

"What? That ruffian? It's deeply unsettling to think of him watching us from a distance like some animal on the prowl."

Exasperated, Catherine countered, "As for Robin, I'm of the opinion that *he* is the one to be kept in check. Why should he be so intent on getting back the pendant? His motivations are suspicious, and he seems to know something we don't. But you, my dear, are so enthralled with him of late that you lose your sound judgment in his presence."

"Be that as it may," said Mathilde, visibly miffed by her friend's criticism, "I did promise to return the cross, and return it I shall."

"The Dauphine Victoire ordered me to hand it over to her. I had no choice in the matter, so there's no use crying over spilled milk. I know that everyone is urging us to give up our search, but somehow that just makes me want to do exactly the opposite."

"Despite the possible risks involved?"

"I'd like to pursue with discretion. Chrétien has offered to lead us back to the abandoned well where he discovered foot-prints leading back to Versailles." Catherine failed to mention that her primary motivation was to see the groundskeeper again, for she was only barely conscious of this herself.

"*Chrétien*, is it? I see you're on familiar terms with that peas-ant. If I didn't deem it impossible for someone of your social rank to find interest in a rogue like that, I'd find your present demeanor highly suspect. That's not to say that I'm not equally curious, and after all, it was my own brash behavior that's led you into this. So I will go, but you can rest assured that I'll be watching the two of you like a hawk."

"He is beneath contempt!" cried out Catherine, but her laughter rang slightly hollow, signaling her sense of malaise at the unsettling truth of her friend's words and her own bad faith.

◆

"*Ja, meine Liebe, was ist denn so dringend?* Whatever is the matter?" The two compatriots greeted each other in a warm embrace. They formed a striking contrast: the effects of melan-cholia had somehow manifested themselves in opposite ways in the two women. Madame found solace in food, whereas the dauphine's depression had suppressed her appetite. As a result she had become rake-thin in the two years since her arrival at court, a fact that did nothing to improve her looks. On the other hand, Madame's double chin could not disguise the fact that she would have been considered a handsome, if not a beautiful woman, were it not for her girth. That double chin was now wobbling with emotion as she choked out her grievances.

"Never would I have imagined that my husband could have such disregard for our son's education and his moral character! The Chevalier de Lorraine has Monsieur wrapped around his little finger, and the two are about to propose the Marquis d'Ef- fiat as little Philippe's governor."

"How could the king possibly allow such a thing? He who is revolted by the mere mention of buggery," objected the dauphine.

"Knowing how I would oppose their deviant ways, they have offered a trade of sorts. Should I intercede with the king on Lorraine's behalf in order to defend him against the charge of debauching Louis de Bourbon, they will withdraw their choice of governor. But whom can I trust? Surely not them! I see this as an intentional ploy. Once I have defended the Chevalier and his lot, any protests against d'Effiat as governor will fall on deaf ears: I will have lost my credibility, my only asset at court."

A thin line creased the dauphine's forehead as she reflected upon the situation. "You are perfectly right. Since you've asked for my counsel, I'll give it to you. From what I've been able to observe, you're known for your brutal honesty in a court where language is used to conceal rather than reveal its true meaning. Despite your status as outsider, you are feared and respected for your straight talk. I would even go so far as to claim that it is the true source of your credit with the king. Lose that reputa- tion for honesty and you lose whatever power you may have.

That's your enemies' ultimate goal! Despite the imminent threat to your son, your only choice is to do the opposite of their bidding. You must find a way to publicly discredit the chevalier de Lorraine and his cohort the Marquis d'Effiat!" Victoire pulled a handkerchief from her sleeve and handed it to her friend to wipe the sweat from her brow.

The duchess mopped her face and readjusted her wig, regaining her steely disposition. "My husband's first wife, Henriette, was able to achieve that by simply sleeping with the king, but even should I wish to persuade him to rid us of Lorraine by means of my feminine wiles, I have no bait with which to ensnare him. Besides, Henriette's victory was short-lived. She was soon replaced by her own lady-in-waiting, Louise de La Vallière, and shortly before Henriette's death the king gave in to Monsieur's unrelenting pleas and called the chevalier back to court from his exile in Rome."

The dauphine could not repress the hint of a smile, as she went on to say, "What we lack in beauty, we make up for in wit, for lacking beauty we have had to resort to other means of empowerment. I believe that fortune may be favoring us at this very moment, so let us not let this opportunity go to waste." Saying this, she removed the cross from her satchel and handed it over to her friend. "Before I tell you where this was found, I want to ask you if you recognize it."

The duchess eyed it cautiously, as if it were from the devil himself. "I know this all too well! My husband was only able to perform his marital duties when he wore this around his neck, in an effort, presumably, to ward off the lure of feminine evil. You cannot imagine how disconcerting it was to watch it dangle back and forth while he was huffing and plowing away!"

Victoire blushed deeply and lowered her gaze to her folded hands. She had still not grown accustomed to her friend's blunt speech. "I had no idea, my dear."

The duchess smiled compassionately as she added, "I doubt

whether the nighttime visits from that dull-witted husband of yours are any less excruciating."

"Can we perhaps get back to the point?" said the dauphine rather more sharply than was her custom. "I've seen the very same emblem on a signet ring worn by none other than Philippe de Lorraine. I asked him about its meaning, and he had the audacity to reply that it was a trinket he wore in honor of the late Marquis de Cinq-Mars!"

"You mean that it's a tribute to Antoine d'Effiat's infamous ancestor? The impudence of that fiend never ceases to astound me!"

The two women both knew the story well. At the age of eighteen, d'Effiat's uncle, Henri Coiffier de Ruzé, Marquis de Cinq-Mars, was a strapping young man possessed with grace and exquisite beauty, an advantageous attribute that many of his male relatives and descendants seemed to share. The ambitious Cardinal Richelieu knew that the Sun King's father, Louis XIII, was partial to the charms of budding young boys. He persuaded Cinq-Mars to maneuver his way into Louis's bed, which he did with great alacrity and ease. This enabled Richelieu to tighten his grip on the reins of power by using the king's young lover as an intermediary. But Cinq-Mars paid for his short-lived favor with his life, for the arrangement didn't last long. Drunk with power, Cinq-Mars falsely assumed that his influence over Louis had made him untouchable. Little did he know Louis XIII. The king's first love was always himself and compassion and sensitivity were not traits that ran in the Bourbon family line. Tired of acting as go-between, Henri attempted to supplant the cardinal in order to govern the king directly, but Richelieu's hold on the monarch was well anchored, and when the cardinal got wind of this treason, he sought the young man's execution. Louis granted it without blinking an eye. As rumor had it, the king didn't even attend the beheading, but is said to have uttered the following words about his former lover at the designated hour of his death: "I would give anything to see the expression on his face at this very moment!"

"But in what way does this ridiculous pendant help further my case against the chevalier?" said the duchess.

"The motto on the locket, which, if we are to believe Lorraine, was commissioned by Cinq-Mars, confirms the late marquis's conviction that the present king's father was so infatuated with him as to satisfy his every whim. It may interest you to know, however, that this locket was found suspiciously near a remote site where charred human remains were discovered by none other than your own lady-in-waiting." The dauphine waited for her revelation to have its desired effect.

The duchess's eyes widened slowly as the dots connected one by one. "But why didn't Mathilde inform me of this directly? Why was I not the first to know?" Her voice was steeped in disappointment.

"I believe that the reason may lie in the fact that Robin d'Effiat was involved as well. She knows how you loathe his uncle and may have felt that you would regard their friendship as a betrayal, even though it dates back to their childhood." Again, Victoire offered her friend the kerchief, now caked with powder and rouge.

"I can't say much for her taste in men, but she would not be the first maiden to have fallen for a handsome scoundrel. I don't believe that she would purposefully deceive me by divulging confidential matters to d'Effiat via his nephew, however I will have to be more circumspect in the future, for she could very well do so unwittingly," answered the duchess, gnawing on her lip.

"I believe that neither girl would have come forward, were it not for a strange series of events that has led them to be concerned for their safety. Someone involved in this macabre affair may know of their discovery, and they've appealed to us for protection. Aside from the fact that I have a great deal of affection for Catherine and Mathilde, I also suspect a possible connection to others in your husband's inner circle. If that's so, we must keep the cross in our possession at all costs, and make inquiries as to its significance. It may be nothing, or it may be a key factor in discrediting your enemies."

"Don't forget that it wasn't found with the remains but nearby, so this may be wild speculation on your part. Nonetheless, I am desperate for some proof that will banish my sworn enemies from court for good. The locket is an unambiguous link between them, and this association is no secret as they apparently have the audacity to occasionally wear the emblem in public. The difficulty will lie in determining the nature of the link."

"You'll recall that the chevalier was suspected of involvement in the murder of a young waffle vendor two years back. The child was no older than thirteen, but since he was a commoner, the entire affair was hushed up. When one of d'Effiat's pages went missing last spring, there were rumors that he might have met with the same fate, but the powerful have ways of covering their traces. I believe we should begin by calling upon the silversmith who crafted the identical lockets. He shouldn't be too hard to find."

The two women's deliberations were interrupted by the announcement that dinner was about to be served. As part of the king's closest entourage, they were required to attend most public functions. This was a full-time task, for Louis's life was governed by public rituals, protocol, and ceremonies. He had crafted his own myth, that of the Sun God, Apollo, toward whom all gazes converged, mesmerized by his spectacular radiance. In so doing, he had become an actor who could never leave the stage or remove the mask of his own making. Every bowel movement became a matter of state. And of course, he commandeered the courtiers' attention. To deny it to him would have been a serious offense.

The two women rose with reluctance. "Time to put on our masks," said the dauphine with a sigh.

◆

Chrétien, meanwhile, had arrived at similar conclusions based on local gossip and decided to make a few inquiries of his own. It was market day in the hamlet, an excellent opportunity to hear the latest drivel. First, however, he had to find a way to dodge his father's watchful eye, for Chrétien had overheard him complaining to his wife that his eldest son had been distracted and remiss in his duties over the past few days.

No surprise, thought Chrétien, whose mind kept wandering back to Catherine. He was quite besotted with the wench, much to his own dismay, and wanted nothing better than to make himself useful to her.

It was a brilliant day and the market place offered a dizzying riot of colors, sounds, and odors. Competing voices, high and low, called out to advertise their wares, while chickens clucked, pigs grunted, and flies buzzed around the meat stall. The young man's nostrils were assaulted by the smell of over-ripe fruits and cheeses baking in the sun. Passing by the fish-monger, he lingered a while, taking in the pungent tang of the sea, for which he longed but had never seen. Finally, he found the old man, nearly blind and dressed in rags, whom he had come to see. Pierre Simon had once been a farmer. He had married late in life, and his wife had died in childbirth with their second son, who did not survive infancy. He mourned his wife and vowed never to remarry, but to raise his firstborn son, Gilbert, on his own. With only one son to ensure his livelihood in old age, Pierre became a very protective and devoted parent. One fateful day, however, when Gilbert was thirteen years of age, he disappeared, never to be heard from again. There were suspicions of foul play, but the matter was soon put to rest, for lack of evidence. Pierre never recovered from this second stroke of fate. He was shattered, a broken man, who aged ten years in a single night. He stopped working and soon lost his land and everything he owned. People said he had lost his mind as well, yet Chrétien knew that was not the case. During the core of winter, the Desforges family would often provide shelter for the homeless man, who survived on alms for the poor. Over the years, Chrétien had befriended Pierre, who saw in him the man his son might have become. The man's eyes lit up for a moment as the two embraced.

"Chrétien! It seems you've grown some stubble since last we met!"

Reluctant to open old wounds, Chrétien approached the matter with circumspection. "How are you faring, old friend? You've been avoiding us of late."

"There's no place for the likes of me in a happy home. The black cloud floating above me is my only fit companion."

"Now, now, Pierre! You know full well that's not so. You look like you've had little to line your belly these days. Let me take you down to Guillemette's tavern for a pint and some bread," said Chrétien warmly.

"I manage to beg enough for scraps of food. It's the appetite that lacking, son. But you're a sight for sore eyes! I'll take you up on that, if only for the company."

Once seated across from each other at the rough-hewn table, the old man went on. "You've grown to be such a strapping young man. No dearth of ladies, I suppose."

Chrétien found himself unable to meet the man's gaze. "Enough with the niceties, Pierre. There's been a finding that may have something to do with your son's disappearance twelve years ago, but there's no way to be sure."

The old man's weather-beaten face remained expressionless as he listened to the story of Chrétien's encounter and subsequent discovery. The young man added that he had inquired about recent disappearances with the innkeeper and found that the only one to fit the puzzle so far was that of Yves Roussin.

At the mention of that name, Pierre's stony countenance crumbled. He clenched his gnarled, leathery hands in despair as he said, "I remember him. Before Gilbert's disappearance he was often seen loitering in the vicinity of our house, and I even caught him speaking to the child on several occasions. I thought nothing of it at the time, but after Gilbert vanished I couldn't help but find the man's behavior suspicious."

"I remember quite well that you harbored suspicions at the time regarding Roussin's connection to the disappearance, though no one paid you heed. But now that he himself seems to have vanished into thin air, your supposition seems more plausible. Still, I only have a vague remembrance of the man, as he lived a solitary life on the outskirts of town. Can you describe him for me?"

A bitter, throaty laugh, followed by the comment: "He was more of a ghost than a man. Pale, ill-kempt, colorless hair, bad teeth, of medium build. His only distinguishing characteristic was a stutter, which he tried as best he could to keep under control. He was invisible in a crowd, and no one seems to remember his occupation or whether he had any friends. I don't believe that he had any family in the county. He made his home in a dilapidated old shack near d'Effiat's estate and was rarely seen in town. If he's disappeared, good riddance! But he can't have gone far for lack of money."

"Is there anyone who might have known him well? If he's still alive, he'd have to make contact with someone, if only to get food." Chrétien tried to temper the eagerness in his voice by taking another swig of beer.

"Well, if he's the one whose remains were found, he's

scarcely in need of food. I assume that you believe his disappearance is the result of treachery."

"At this point, there's no way of knowing."

"The only person I can think of who might know of his whereabouts is Margot Ledoux, but I doubt whether she'd be willing to talk. I believe Roussin lived off her income as a whore for a while."

With a word of thanks and a few coins for a meal, Chrétien bade the old man farewell, eager to pursue this new line of inquiry. Glancing back at Pierre one last time, he noticed that the old man's sunken face was moist with tears.

THE ENGAGEMENT

*M*adame was awakened, as she was every morning, by a strong whiff of dog breath and a rough, wet lick of the tongue. Struggling to free herself from a tangle of bedcovers, sheets, and her twisted nightdress, she hauled her ungainly mass onto arthritic feet. In the wake of the upheaval, several bewildered pups tumbled out of bed. She then made her way stiffly and unsteadily to her dressing table, where a pitcher of warm, lavender-scented water awaited. Her eyes were two small pouches under swollen lids, peering out over pleated, ruddy cheeks that had been creased by a heavy slumber. She stared at herself in the mirror, then abruptly turned away, reflecting bitterly on the number of flattering portraits of her that adorned the palace walls. No court artist would have dared to portray her thus, in all her natural glory! She had often wondered whether beauty would have brought her greater happiness, but she suspected that it would have only worsened her plight. As it was, she was greatly relieved that men left her alone to do as she liked.

Until recently, she had settled into a state of gentle lethargy, mildly indifferent to the turbulence of life at court. But the unsettling events of the past week had thrown her back into the fray. She was determined not to give in to her husband's bidding to exonerate the chevalier, despite mounting pressure from all fronts. It was only a matter of time before the Marquis d'Effiat would be appointed as little Philippe's governor. Madame felt her bile rise at the thought of her impressionable eight-year-old son. She took the threat quite seriously, due to the ominous precedent with Louis de Bourbon. How dare those monsters use him to bait her? What had she ever done to them, save sleep in her husband's bed on rare occasions?

With less attention than usual, she hastily threw on the garments that had been laid out for her by Mathilde and summoned the palace silversmith.

While waiting, she wrote yet another lengthy letter to vent her rage and frustration to her brother Karl, prince elector of the Palatinate. Her hand flew across the page, leaving a blur of sharply pointed scratches and dots, ripping the paper here and there. So absorbed was she in her task, that she scarcely heard the knock on the door, followed by Mathilde's announcement: "Julien de Grosménil, silversmith to the king, Madame."

Startled, Duchess Elisabeth Charlotte jumped to her feet, upsetting the ink bottle and spilling the contents onto her morning gown. Flustered, she looked her visitor up and down with contempt as she attempted to blot out the damage. The man seemed quite unsettled by her summons, as he stood before her, slack-jawed and disheveled, nervously picking at the hem of his waistcoat.

"What pleases your ladyship?" he inquired with a slight tremor in his voice.

"Is this cross of your making?" she said, getting straight to the point and displaying the silver locket in her palm. The directness of the question clearly caught him off guard. His shifty eyes narrowed as he examined the sizable object, hunched over, stalling for time.

"No, Madame, it is not," he replied haltingly.

"Out with it, then!" she commanded. "Who commissioned it, and who fashioned it? I am sure that you've seen it before."

"I . . . I . . . do not recall," he stammered, cowering under her imposing physical presence.

"I, for one, believe you do! For even I, who care little for such finery, have an idea, which you, as royal silversmith should be able to confirm. Can you identify this locket as one that once may have belonged to Cinq-Mars?" She jabbed him in the shoulder with her index finger, defying the rules of etiquette.

Julien de Grosménil was jolted back. He could no longer feign ignorance, not only out of professional pride but out of fear and expedience as well, for lying to Monsieur's wife would be tantamount to treason, and he had mouths to feed. "I trust you are right," he finally admitted. "Although I do believe that it's not the only one of its kind. It seems to me that my father, who served under the previous reign, forged it originally for the former king's lover and according to his specifications, but after Cinq-Mars met with his doom, the cross was passed on to his nephew, Antoine d'Effiat. I believe that the marquis then commissioned a number of copies bearing the same emblem."

"I can see that you have miraculously recovered your memory," the duchess said wryly. "I want a list of all those who are in possession of a replica of this cross!" When she was angry her German accent became more pronounced.

"With all due respect, Madame, only my father would know for sure, but he has long since departed to a better place." He offered her a half-frozen smile.

Madame was visibly riled, but she continued, undeterred. "Better place, indeed! There must be financial ledgers recording your father's business dealings. I'll make it well worth your while if you can locate a transaction record listing the buyers. Now go!" she commanded, with a dismissive wave of the hand.

Grosménil bowed deeply, inching backward toward the door, then, with a sigh of relief, he hurriedly turned his skinny backside and left. Madame returned to her writing desk to seal her letter, then called impatiently for Mathilde, brandishing the letter at her imperiously.

"Be sure to send this out as soon as possible with one of my German servants and take care not to draw attention onto yourself as you do!" she said. "But first, bring me a change of clothing! I seem to have ruined my favorite morning gown with my usual clumsiness."

After rummaging through the massive oak armoire to find the appropriate attire for her mistress, Mathilde curtsied and left, disturbed by the conversation she had just overheard, for she had been eavesdropping behind the door. She now understood Robin's haste in attempting to recover the cross, as well as the potential difficulty in retrieving it from her mistress, for Madame would no doubt want to keep it as evidence, depending on the results of her inquiries. Of course, the fact that multiple copies existed gave her hope, be it ever so slight, that Robin's family might not be implicated in any wrongdoing. She was unsure how much, if any, of this information she should share with him. One way or another, she was compromised. She felt the urgent need to consult with the more level-headed Catherine on the matter.

As Mathilde dashed through the galleries, in search of Madame's faithful manservant Hermann Wendt, she crossed a group of her peers, whose huddle of wide-skirted organdy gowns resembled a gauzy bouquet of pastel-petaled roses. The girls were all aflutter at the prospect of divulging the latest blather. As she slowed her pace to greet her friends, Marie-Hélène called out, "Well, if it isn't Mathilde! If anyone has heard the latest rumor, it's surely you!" She made no attempt to suppress the malicious grin that had etched its way across her face.

"I haven't the slightest idea what you are talking about. I have better things to do with my time than to spread idle tittle-tattle," Mathilde replied haughtily.

"Better things? Such as cavorting with Robin d'Effiat, I suppose!" Marie-Hélène was widely known to be infatuated with Robin, a fact that had recently soured her friendship with Mathilde. Robin dismissed her blatant adulation with contemptuous mockery, often mimicking her cow-eyed stare behind her back.

"Better even than that," Mathilde shot back.

"Well, then, perhaps it won't disturb you to hear of Robin's engagement to Madeleine de Noailles! It was announced unofficially only this morning," she pronounced triumphantly.

Mathilde's heart began pounding so hard against her chest that a deafening sound reverberated in her ears, but outwardly she kept her composure. "Robin and I are good friends, nothing more. Of course I knew of it!" she lied, desperately attempting to save face. "I was sworn to secrecy by Robin himself, because of his understandable embarrassment and distaste for a woman nearly twice his age. Your malice is written all over your face, Marie-Hélène. Shame on you!"

Mathilde turned on her heels and left abruptly, using her errand as an excuse to be alone. She felt as if all the wind had been knocked out of her. What false hopes she had entertained in secret! It had always been clear to her that her destiny was not to be married above her station, but as long as the thought remained an abstraction, she had no trouble relegating it to an indeterminate and hazy future. Confronted as she was now by an impending reality, she felt unprepared and betrayed. Robin had to have been aware of his uncle's choice for some time now, but he was far too self-centered to be bothered by the thorny task of softening the blow. She hadn't mattered enough to him for him to use his persuasive charm, which he deployed to easily whenever it suited him. The more she thought of it, the angrier she became. When she reached Wendt's living quarters in the servants' wing of the palace, she issued a few curt orders and handed over her mistress's letter to him unceremoniously.

She determined to seek out Catherine at once. By now, her hot temper had gotten the better of her, and she was no more able to reverse her unbridled impetuousness than to tame a herd of wild horses. She knew that in her current state she needed someone's counsel, lest she do something brash that she might later regret. Marie-Hélène's revelation had had at least one positive effect: she no longer felt any compunction or obligation to help Robin protect his family name.

Let them all be damned! she thought.

She found Catherine in the gallery, returning from the Grande Dauphine Victoire's private apartment. Her friend was walking slowly, glancing out the windows absentmindedly as she went along.

"Well met!" she called out, startling Catherine out of her reverie. "I must talk to you straightaway. Have you heard that Robin is to be married to Madeleine de Noailles? The engagement was just announced." Her voice wavered.

"Calm down, dearest!" replied Catherine. "Are you sure of what you heard? How could Robin consent to such a mismatch with that goose! But leave it to Antoine d'Effiat to disregard his nephew's inclinations in favor of material gain, as if the family weren't rich enough!"

Catherine gathered her friend in her arms and cradled her soothingly, murmuring softly into her ear. Mathilde burst into tears as her anger gave way to waves of sorrow. Catherine had rarely seen her friend cry, for Mathilde was as fierce and proud as Catherine was gentle. Not wanting to draw attention, the two friends ventured into a remote wing of the palace, intended for the servants of visiting dignitaries. The heavy paneling in the small quarters generated a stifling, claustrophobic atmosphere, but had the advantage of rendering the room virtually impenetrable to the would-be eavesdropper.

Once Mathilde had regained her composure, she bristled again with indignation. "I shall find some way to get even, and I have the means to do it," she said. "Despite Robin's outward bravado, he cowers before his uncle. He is a weakling who always follows the line of least resistance. I should know, for I have had many an opportunity to witness his spinelessness. If only I hadn't been born a woman!" She bit her lip in frustration.

"Hell hath no fury, as the saying goes! It's quite true that you were always the bolder of the two, but the chink in your armor, my dear, lies in your physical attraction to him. As long as you fail to overcome that limitation shared by so many women, you will never be able to see him for the person he really is. You must not allow him to govern you, for there is no worse tyrant than a weak one." The look in Catherine's eyes was compassionate, yet elusive, as if she were under the spell of a distant vision.

"It's true that I have no regrets for not having returned the cross. Why should I fear Robin's wrath? I have nothing to lose, and I have far more reason than he to be incensed, and if anyone should fear a row, it is he! He showed no regard for my feelings, though he has had me once. I have certainly been made to play the fool! I thought that our childhood bond would mean enough at least to prevent him from treating me like some common wench." Mathilde's hands had twisted and turned her handkerchief into a knotted mess, as she sat hunched over, arms clenched to her sides.

"Mathilde, you knew all along that this would be your fate. How blinded you've been by your feelings! The Marquis d'Effiat would never consent for his heir to marry beneath his rank.

What's more, any woman who marries into that misbegotten family is in for a life of grief and sorrow."

"You're right, as always, Catherine. But that doesn't make the truth easier to swallow. Ever serene, and ever governed by common sense! But I might protest that you've never loved."

The words brought a blush to Catherine's face, but in her state of distress, Mathilde barely noticed her friend's discomfiture.

"That does remind me, though, that I have some information regarding the cross, which I happened to overhear while waiting on Madame this morning," said Mathilde.

"No doubt you couldn't help but linger by the door, in your effort to be of service to your mistress," replied Catherine sardonically, grinning like a well-fed cat.

Mathilde looked out the window evasively. The stalwart columns supporting the terrace cast oblique shadows across the diamond-patterned tiles. The rigorous symmetry of the view was broken in the distance by the twisted forms and the lacy mist of the ornamental fountain of Apollo.

"I won't make excuses for my eavesdropping, because I truly doubt whether Madame intends to share her findings with us. But here's what I've learned: the locket was fashioned by the royal silversmith and can be traced back to Cinq-Mars, an ancestor of Robin's. It would appear, however, that a number of replicas were commissioned by the marquis. Who received those copies remains a mystery. Perhaps this explains Robin's insistence on my returning it to him." Mathilde's voice was unusually shrill, despite her efforts to remain calm.

"That may be. But Robin presumably has no idea as to the origin of the cross. He's not the most observant fellow, and he didn't seem to recognize the emblem or the inscription. If he had, he would have insisted on keeping it himself. Could it be that he's since then discovered the connection to his family, or worse, that he's reluctant to leave you a keepsake that might compromise in some way his engagement?"

This second possibility had not as yet occurred to Mathilde, but now that it had been suggested it supplanted her earlier suspicions and became firmly anchored as the prime motive. "Of course! Why hadn't I thought of that? I intend to confront him and to get to the bottom of this matter as soon as I can, but I'm willing to bet that he'll avoid me now that his engagement has been announced."

"If I know anything about men, though it's true that I know very little, he'll try to dodge any form of confrontation. Even then, he'll probably lie through his teeth, protesting his innocence," said Catherine. "I just hope you won't fall prey to his charms. He's got a silver tongue, as you well know." She couldn't help smiling at her private joke.

"You're right. It will be difficult to corner him, but I'll have an opportunity next week at the masked ball, which the king has commissioned to please Madame de Maintenon, though she has little use for such frivolities. Robin will hardly be able to avoid me there, especially if I'm wearing a costume."

"I doubt there is a costume in existence that will mask your fury. You might as well choose one that calls attention to it instead. I've heard it said that the best masks conceal and reveal at the same time."

"Like a well-designed bodice neckline?" said Mathilde, forgetting her wrath for a moment.

Catherine didn't react to the quip. When she spoke, it was with concern. "You want the truth at all costs, but the truth won't benefit you in this matter. Can't you put it all to rest?" She reached out to her friend, who turned away distractedly, preparing to leave.

"Not in my present state of mind," replied Mathilde, looking back over her shoulder. "I must know if Robin has any feelings for me. I must put him to the test."

"In that case, I'll try to help as long as you're willing to follow my advice. First, you must abandon your plan to confront Robin directly, because it will only result in widening the breach between you. Temper your reaction and act as if you were indifferent to the news, despite your unruly disposition. This can only fire Robin's curiosity and wound his male pride. Secondly, let's consider employing the services of my cousin, Julie d'Aubigny. She's indebted to me on more than one account. I can enlist her to spy on Robin. I have a hunch that she would enjoy the adventure."

At these words, Mathilde turned about abruptly. "Tell me more about this eccentric cousin of yours. You've told me about her double identity, but can she be trusted with men? Isn't it possible that she might succumb to Robin's charms?"

Catherine repressed an indulgent smile. "Not everyone sees Robin with your eyes, my dear."

Reluctantly, Mathilde agreed. "I can see certain advantages to your stratagem, however, I'm disappointed to have to forestall venting my rage. Let's start by enlisting Julie's help and arranging for the two to meet at the ball. I hope that she's an excellent improviser."

"The best!" said Catherine. "Come now, it's time for us to plan our disguises!"

◆

During this time, Robin was pacing fretfully back and forth in the library of his uncle's estate, while the latter sat back languidly in his fauteuil of blue satin brocade, appraising his heir's lithe body from head to toe, as if for the first time. It was rare for him to turn his attention to his descendants, but the marriage contract was a momentous event, a real coup for the family fortune. Unaccustomed to such scrutiny, Robin was nervously biting his lower lip, wondering how best to register his dissent.

Clearing his throat, his uncle spoke in a forceful voice, firm in the knowledge of his authority. "I know that she's older than you, but consider the fact that Henri the Second was mad about Diane de Poitiers his whole life long. And she was a full twenty years his senior. She had also been his father's mistress until she was put in charge of the son's sexual initiation, I might add."

"I am in no need of an initiation," replied Robin, "and you may recall that Diane was a great beauty, whereas Madeleine de Noailles is all skin and bones, with a dreary disposition."

"*La beauté ne se mange pas en salade, mon fils,*" sighed the marquis. "Beauty is not a material commodity. It is something to be savored on the side, but it, too, can become tiresome as a staple. Your marriage won't prevent you from tasting the delightful delicacies served as side dishes at court."

Robin scrutinized his uncle's handsome face, which had recently begun to show the ravages of a lifetime of debauchery. A spray of tiny creases fanned out around his eyes, and his skin had become sallow and weathered. Nonetheless, the man was still a force to be reckoned with. Robin had to concede that his uncle had a point, but he was deeply embarrassed by the derision he would have to face from his mates. Not being used to the company of homely women, he wondered how he would be able to fulfill his martial duties, both public and private. Robin was also justifiably nervous about a possible encounter with Mathilde. He cursed himself for not having broached the matter sooner, but the premature public announcement came as a surprise, even to him.

"The king's masquerade ball next week will be an opportunity for everyone to pay homage to you and your betrothed. Be sure to keep up appearances by making a display of good countenance. You may go now, for I have much to attend to today."

Robin came forward to kiss his uncle's hand, and in so doing was astonished to see that the ring on his right hand bore the same design and inscription as the locket Mathilde had found near the ruins. He wondered whether it had escaped his notice before. "*Qui m'aime, me suive.* What an interesting logo!" he said. "What does it mean?"

"Just an old proverb," replied his uncle cagily, narrowing his eyes. "It's the motto of one of our more notorious ancestors."

"Is that the only one of its kind?" asked Robin, immediately concerned that he might have overstepped an invisible boundary.

His uncle squared his shoulders and replied tersely, "Why do you ask?"

"I seem to recall having seen the inscription before," Robin hedged.

"I may have had a few made for my most trusted friends, in honor of our bond. The inscription serves as a reminder of the obligations of friendship."

Robin would have liked to pursue the matter and inquire about the meaning of the image on the cross, but his uncle's voice allowed for no further questioning. It would perhaps be more prudent not to inform his uncle that he had made the connection. Feeling ill at ease, he let himself out of the room, followed by the suspicious gaze of the marquis's dark eyes. He sensed with renewed urgency the need to recover the cross, but was loathe to confront Mathilde so soon after his engagement had been made public. He wondered whether he should allow her time to digest the information, or if that would simply make matters worse. He considered approaching Catherine, but he was well aware of her aversion to him. Damned if he could understand women! Suddenly it dawned on him that he might have some leverage over her. Leverage that could be used to his advantage.

◆

Chrétien was eager to glean any information that might lead him back into Catherine's presence and earn her gratitude. He set off the next day in search of Yves Roussin, wondering where the trail might lead. When he reached the outskirts of the hamlet of Versailles, he found the man's gloomy dwelling, teetering on the edge of a marsh. Scattered here and there were run-down structures, like a sparse cluster of rotting teeth. It was still early morn, and a fine mist rose off the surface of the wetland, shrouding the shelter with a filmy pallor that announced a damp day to come. The door stood slightly ajar, like a gaping mouth, from which emanated a terrible waft of decay. The stench was amplified by the humidity of the interior. Chrétien entered cautiously, finding his way in the shadows, stirring up a few rats along the way, until his eyes became adjusted to the dark. On the table stood a dusty, half-emptied bottle of wine and putrefied food particles resembling a greasy oil slick. In the corner he caught sight of a coarse straw mat covered with a grimy blanket, and peering out from that blanket, two feverish eyes, wide with fear. A clawlike hand drew the blanket protectively higher as Chrétien approached.

"I haven't come to harm you," he said to the skeletal figure he assumed to be that of a woman, once his eyes had grown accustomed to the dark.

A raspy voice answered back, "Get yerself out o' here! What d'ye or yer likes want from me in this godforsaken place?"

"I'm looking for Yves Roussin. I've heard that he's gone missing."

"That he is. He ain't brought me rations for nigh on a week. What business d'ye have with 'im?" came the suspicious reply.

"My name is Chrétien Desforges, and I prefer not to discuss my reasons, but I can assure you that they're honorable." The young man was fighting back the urge to plug his nose.

The woman's head fell back like a deadweight against the wall. "Water! Fetch me some water!" she gasped.

Chrétien ran out to the well and filled his flask to the brim. The woman grabbed the recipient with surprising strength born from desperation, and drank in long gulps, until she began to choke and cough.

"More honorable than Yves, no doubt!" she said, once she had regained her voice. Spittle was running down her chin as she spoke. "Ye don't look like the type o' fancy man he's usually with!"

"So I gather you must know the man fairly well, and that he's given you permission to squat on his property?"

"He owes me that much, and a lot more, if he's still alive, that is." Her tone was truculent, despite the frailty of her condition.

As Chrétien grew more accustomed to the dimness, he became aware of the woman's revolting appearance and could not suppress an involuntary convulsion and an urgent desire to flee. A closer look at her face revealed deep crevices, scaly lumps of dark pigmentation and open sores, signs of the advanced stages of syphilis. Her glassy, distant stare was glazed over with an iridescent, yellow-white coating. Margot Ledoux, the village prostitute, was a ghastly shadow of her former self. Her fingers were hideously misshapen into twisted claws. Chrétien suddenly understood the reason for the smell of decay.

"How long have you had the pox?" he asked, kneeling beside her with as much compassion as he could muster.

"Long enough to know me time has come. I prefer to die alone, and with a last shred o' dignity, rather than in the agony and horror of an insane asylum!" She suddenly grabbed his hand and clung to it. Chrétien felt as though a banshee had him in her clutches and would drag him down to hell with her. He shuddered as he remembered how once as a child he had witnessed with horror a madwoman being hoarded off to an asylum, shrieking and wailing in her misery.

Attempting to steady his nerves, he spoke: "I swear to keep silent and not to reveal your whereabouts, for a dying wish is sacred, but first we must talk. What do you know of Yves's connection to the disappearance of young Gilbert Simon?"

Margot looked him up and down scornfully. "It's a bit late for all ye concerned to be askin' 'bout such matters. Little good it'll do to reveal the ugly truth, as justice'll never be served for the likes of that young lad."

"It certainly won't if no one breaks the silence. What have you got to lose?" insisted Chrétien.

Margot let out a long rasping breath, then she croaked, "That bastard Yves weren't satisfied with the meager income he got 'imself from me whorin'. He were connected to a number of brothels to serve the fancy men. There were boys 'n' girls a plenty involved. But he were also a scout fer some people of the highest rank. He supplied 'em with beautiful boyos. And I remember that the young 'uns couldn't be more than fourteen. Older than that and they's less likely to knuckle under. Yves didn't share much more, but Gilbert's looks and age would've fit the bill."

Chrétien shuddered at the thought of Gilbert's possible fate, and said, "Do you know who these people were and if they were capable of violence?"

"The Chevalier de Lorraine were the ringleader, for sure, and he's known to boast of his exploits, if you catch my drift, bending those poor young 'uns to his will. I know he were given to violent fits of rage, and even Yves, who's hard to the core, lived in fear of 'im. That beast were once accused of murder or manslaughter, I ain't sure which. That must've been a couple years back."

"Anyone else you can think of?"

"The chevalier's chummy with the Duke d'Orléans, but everyone here knows that."

The woman was visibly fatigued by the inquest, and Chrétien realized that she had reached her limit. He offered her a hunk of bread, which she gummed down as fast as she could, and he promised to return with more. As he left, she was mumbling incoherently, and he was forced to reflect on the boundless forms of human misery.

THE COUNCIL OF RATS

*H*ermann Wendt was not what some might call a handsome man, but he commanded attention. Liselotte found herself musing that he was perhaps the only man at court to whom she felt more than remotely drawn. Those ludicrous accusations that she might be enticed by some French fop like Saint-Saens! She felt renewed indignation at the slight to her impeccable reputation. Wendt had been serving at the French court since 1670, when Liselotte's aunt Sophie of Hanover had recommended him to the king as a man of unimpeachable integrity. Unlike many other domestic servants, he had managed through his diplomacy and tact to survive numerous cabals and keep his position for over a decade, despite the disadvantage of being both German and Protestant. Twice a year he returned to Hanover to visit his wife and children, who had stayed behind. When Liselotte came to court to marry Philippe d'Orléans, it was deemed fitting that he be assigned to her as her personal messenger, and so it came to be that the two established a bond of trust and familiarity despite their difference in rank. He was privy to many of her confidential matters and was often charged with the role of secret messenger when discretion was required. Rugged and broad-shouldered, with a chiseled face and a high forehead crowned with dark blond hair that was streaked with strands of gray, he was her anchor in the treacherous maelstrom of life at court. More than once, she had felt a tug of desire in his presence, but she had too much self-respect to follow her instincts. She imagined that his arms would feel like home to her.

The duchess had been kneeling in her bedchamber at her velvet prie-dieu, but found herself distracted from her daily prayers by the massive gilt image of the sun emblazoned on its central panel, reminding her of the king's sovereignty and his claim to divine authority. Ever since her forced conversion to Catholicism, she had become increasingly cynical in the knowledge that at Versailles it was the king, not God, whose commandments were absolute. Knees creaking, she rose to greet her countryman Wendt, who stood before her now, bowing slightly, and tending her a sealed envelope from Julien de Grosménil. She promptly ripped open the seal, cutting herself on the edge of the paper in her haste. A droplet of blood smudged the sheet, but she barely noticed.

"Needless to say, this list of commissioned works is highly confidential, my dear Wendt." The servant signaled his acquiescence with a short clip of the heels.

"Let's see what we have here: Antoine Coiffier de Ruzé, Marquis d'Effiat. And my dear husband Philippe I de Bourbon, Duke d'Orléans . . . so much I already knew! Ah! As I suspected, Philippe, Chevalier de Lorraine-Armagnac!"

"And furthermore Jean-Baptiste Lully, the court composer; Louis de Bourbon, Count de Vermandois, the king's legitimized son by Louise de La Vallière," added Wendt.

"The poor boy's about to receive a flogging for his involvement with the chevalier. He's only fourteen, by God! Sadly, the king has also determined to send him into exile in Normandy and to marry him off as soon as possible to avoid further scandal," said the duchess, choking back the tears and wiping her eyes with her sleeve.

"The Prince de Condé, his *son* the Duke d'Enghien, *and* his nephew the Prince de Conti are also on the list," added Wendt, peering over her shoulder. Their arms brushed, and Wendt stepped back quickly. Too quickly, thought Madame.

"There are a few surprises, though. Françoise-Athénaïs de Rochechouart, Marquise de Montespan. How the devil did she get on the list? And then there's Martin de Vasselot, Squire de Brouilly. I thought his reputation for devotion was beyond reproach. He seems to spend every waking moment genuflecting in the chapel. The last two on the list, Guy Armand de Gramont, Count de Guiche, and Gaston de Porentruy, Baron de Guéret are known to be intimate friends and political allies. But what is the connection?"

"I would have said a penchant for young boys, were it not for Madame de Montespan, the king's former mistress, who doesn't seem to fit the picture. For one thing she is quite obviously the only woman on the list," said Wendt.

The duchess nodded and walked over to the fireplace. She looked up at her reflection in the mirror above the mantel and saw that the firelight had softened her homely features with its amber glow. Wendt was still standing at a respectful distance, his features inscrutable.

"Perhaps," she added, "but this wouldn't be the first time she was associated with a ring of disreputable individuals. Remember the *Affair of the Poisons*! Were it not for the king's intercession, she and her chambermaid, Claude des Œillets, would have assuredly been put to the question along with the rest of that sorry lot! There's no doubt that she had dealings with Catherine La Voisin, who was burned at the stake as a witch two years ago for her involvement in a series of commissioned poisonings. Her daughter Marguerite's confession implicated Montespan, albeit under duress of torture."

"Who could forget? What a terrible ordeal! The rumors spread like wildfire! Poisonings and black masses with the butchering of infants. But are they to be believed? The marquise had countless enemies at court, mostly women, who were eager to connect her to the poisonings and take her place in the royal bed. It was said that when Montespan found the king's interest to be waning, she employed aphrodisiacs to stiffen his resolve, so to speak." Madame could not suppress a smirk. Was Wendt actually blushing at her words? "That was when she first employed the services of La Voisin, who provided blister beetle powder to add to the king's food in small doses. In large quantities, though, the substance can cause miscarriages in women, and even death."

The two looked at each other knowingly. Everyone was familiar with the story. The events were relatively recent. Despite the marquise's best-laid plans, no amount of aphrodisiacs could divert the king's attention from a new trophy, Madame's very own maid of honor, Marie-Angélique Scorailles, Duchess de Fontanges. Montespan and Maintenon, who were rivaling for the king's affection, were both incensed by this young interloper, whose dewy-eyed beauty had the middle-aged king at her beck and call.

"May Marie-Angélique rest in peace!" The duchess did her best to look and sound bereaved, but failed to muster the emotion. She'd never been much of an actress, so she dropped the pretense altogether when Wendt raised a disbelieving eyebrow.

"You know very well that she was imposed on me as a companion by my brother-in-law. I never had any use for that insufferable little bitch, who was dumber than a bag of hammers. Her mere presence made my skin crawl. But she helped the man feel young again, and he showered her with gifts. All those foolish ladies at court imitated her headdress and ridiculous hairstyle . . . à la Fontanges. Montespan was green with envy!" Madame offered Wendt a candied cherry, which he declined. She stuffed one in her mouth, as she was feeling rather peckish.

"It's hard to blame her for her parents' ambitions. She was sent to court to increase the family fortune, but it all ended tragically last year when she died shortly after giving birth to a stillborn child by Louis." Wendt didn't seem to share her acrimony toward the late maid of honor.

"Montespan isn't above suspicion in the matter, as she was heard making death threats to Fontanges and to the king himself during a violent row. In a fit of demented desperation, she went so far as to release two bears in Marie-Angélique's private quarters. They ripped and clawed everything to shreds, including some priceless tapestries. The woman is mad, I tell you! I reckon she could have had something to do with the stillbirth, and perhaps even Marie-Angélique's death." The duchess absentmindedly took another cherry from the box.

"One of La Voisin's associates, Françoise Filastre, admitted to having served as go-between, providing poisons and aphrodisiacs to Montespan, however she later recanted her statement. So once again, the king's former mistress came out unscathed," replied Wendt.

"The rich and the powerful have long arms, as they say. Before you leave, what do you make of the emblem on this cross?" said the duchess, pulling open a drawer to reveal the object. "The iconography seems to represent St. Michael defeating the devil, as painted by Raphael, however in this case Lucifer is embodied by a woman. What would any self-respecting woman want with such a medallion? And what do you make of the inscription?"

Wendt brushed the engraving with his thumb. "*Qui m'aime me suive* . . . May he who loves me follow. Follow what? My example? Submit to me, perhaps? Whatever one's interpretation there is an apparent allusion to the connection between

Satan, sex, and power, which isn't surprising considering the originator."

The clock struck five and Madame exclaimed, "My goodness, I completely lost track of the time! I have to prepare for yet another one of Louis's divertissements. The whole palace is bustling with activity as the king prepares to receive the Turkish ambassador. In the meantime, use your advantage as court messenger to scour for information on a possible connection between Montespan, the chevalier, and the other people on that list. That's of primary importance to me, not idle tongue-wagging about a whore who has fallen out of favor with the king. Now where's that girl? Mathilde!"

As Wendt opened the door to leave, Mathilde nearly fell through the opening. Madame went about her routine distractedly, appearing not to notice. She was too preoccupied to let Mathilde's clumsy attempt at eavesdropping get her riled up. In fact, she found the girl's curiosity faintly amusing, and she was still feeling the euphoric effect of Wendt's presence. But it was a feast day and duty called: time to don her best apparel. As Mathilde scurried back and forth with assorted garments, she tossed repeated glances at the list, left open on the writing bureau, trying to commit the names to memory, noting the smear of blood. She helped Madame squeeze into her gold brocade dress, over which she slipped a transparent three-tiered black gown adorned with gold satin bows. The subtle glimmer of gold beneath the outer garment was stunning, but the duchess sighed with discomfort at the constraining corset, from which it seemed like her breasts were about to burst like corks from fermented wine bottles.

While Mathilde was skillfully brushing and arranging her mistress's thick, unruly locks, and adorning them with a string of pearls, Madame asked, "What do you intend to wear to the reception for the Turkish dignitaries, my dear?"

"If it please your ladyship, I am feeling indisposed and

would prefer to stay in my private quarters this afternoon."
Mathilde made a lame attempt at a raspy cough but realized
that it was unconvincing.

"You don't look unwell to me, but please yourself! These
affairs are such a bore, and if I could, I would gladly stay home
with my darlings," said the duchess, eyeing her pups with affection. "I've heard, though, that the ambassador has brought with
him such a magnificent train and such extravagant gifts, that it's
put the French court to shame. I am eager to see the king's reaction and his attempt to save face. That alone should be worth
suffering through the whole ordeal," the duchess added gleefully. "The gifts have been put on display outside the newly
appointed Hall of Mirrors, and I cannot wait to see them. For
now, I think I'll join the other ladies for a game of tarot, while
we wait for the men to return from the hunt. Meanwhile, be
sure to rest, for I shall need you in attendance later this
evening."

Once Madame had left, Mathilde rushed to the door, nearly
upsetting a lavishly adorned *guéridon*, which teetered on the
brink of crashing to the floor before settling back into place.
Gathering up her skirts, she ran through the adjoining gallery,
where Catherine was waiting, nervously gnawing at her thumb.
Aside from a few servants, the private quarters were empty and
the girls had no trouble slipping out unnoticed.

The first cold snap of the season the night before had
abruptly changed the landscape. It was a brisk afternoon, and
the air was razor-sharp to the scent. A dense, cottony blanket of
fog hovered just above the ground, and the dark of the forest
was like a hallucination in the mist. Here and there a sparse
array of luminescent leaves on the branches and the path twin-
kled through the lighter patches of fog, like specks of gold. The
girls hesitated at the edge of the chase, mindful of the eeriness
of the setting. Catherine felt the grass clutching at her ankles,
pulling her back.

They were late and wondered if perhaps Chrétien had tired of waiting, when they heard a shrill whistle, followed by his sudden emergence from the mist. He was standing there, fierce and proud as a knight, blazing white between the shadowy trees.

"Good afternoon to you, my ladies! My time is at your command," said Chrétien with a curt bow. He then turned and walked into the forest, leading the way. The young man's tread was soundless, but the girls wrestled with their frocks, stumbling occasionally on the uneven terrain. From somewhere deep inside the forest came an ominous muted hum, a vibration almost too low to hear, like the sound of a bow grazing a distant cello. Chrétien stopped to listen, then walked on in silence. When they arrived at the well, Mathilde and Catherine approached its rim with trepidation, but the darkness of its depths concealed its secret. As before, Chrétien lowered his lantern by means of a length of rope he had attached to the pulley. The girls peered over the edge, and though they had been forewarned, they recoiled at the sight of the chalk-white skulls gaping up at them from the dark pit.

"Now that you have seen the evidence, let's not tempt fate by staying any longer than necessary," suggested Chrétien, checking their reactions. "Whoever removed the bones from their previous location must not suspect that this mass burial site has been discovered. I suggest we return to the park to discuss some further findings that may be of interest to you. That is, if your nerves haven't been shaken by the ghastly scene that you just witnessed."

With her hackles up, Mathilde boldly stood her ground, then strutted toward him defiantly, "We're not as fragile as you might think! I know just the place for a private conversation once we're back in the formal gardens."

When the three youths reached the eastern park gate, known as the Grille du Mail, they headed down the Allée de l'Automne until they reached the Bosquet du Labyrinthe. Once there, they turned into one of its many transversal paths leading into a dense, intricate maze of privet hedges. Although it was embellished with thirty-nine ornamental fountains, each representing a fable by Aesop, there was little else to distinguish one alleyway from the next in the fog, so the girls soon got off course. Enjoying this prolongation of their encounter and not wishing to provoke them any further, Chrétien followed them, offering no suggestions as to their whereabouts, though he was an expert scout. At long last, they stumbled upon the heart of the labyrinth, where stone benches arranged in a circle provided a place to converse in private. The faint murmur of gurgling water from a nearby fountain droned on as a distant accompaniment to their revelations.

Chrétien spoke first, in the knowledge that he had to prove his usefulness or he might be dismissed from the inquest. He told the girls about the recent vanishing of Yves Roussin and the latter's possible connection to the disappearance of prepubescent boys. Boys who might have been recruited, or forced into sexual bondage by members of the higher echelons of the aristocracy. He spoke of allegations of wrongdoing on the part of the Chevalier de Lorraine and the latter's imputed involvement in the death of a young vendor two years earlier.

When he was done, he knew he had won their trust when Mathilde, who had hitherto been hostile to his presence, let down her guard and her shoulders.

She chimed in: "Just before we left the palace, I overhead Madame discussing a list of people who commissioned replicas of the cross I found at the original site, on the ground by the old ruins." She blushed, as she recalled the pendant digging into her shoulder under Robin's weight. She reasoned that no one, not even Catherine, could read her mind and, after regaining her composure, revealed the names she could recall from the list. "The chevalier was among them, and so was d'Effiat. There is also the incriminating fact that the run-down shanty you searched was on the marquis's estate, from where the remains were later removed. These can't be mere coincidences. But like my mistress, I have to question the connection between Madame de Montespan and the others on that list. Have you anything to add to this, Catherine?"

"I brought this along on a hunch," she said, pulling forth the etching from a fold in her skirt. "This may, or may not have anything to do with our investigation, but it obviously depicts the subornation of young boys. In view of what the two of you have brought to light, it may appear highly relevant." This time it was Catherine's turn to blush.

Chrétien's arm grazed Catherine's shoulder as he reached for the paper. The gesture, though innocent, caused a stirring in her that she had never felt before. She looked away, hoping he hadn't noticed.

"Where did you find this?" he asked in amazement.

"In the palace library, in an old volume entitled *Maxims for the Foundation of a Christian Marriage*," she answered.

Chrétien could not suppress a wry grin at the incongruous find.

"Are you so eager to be married, then, milady?" he said, with an impudent wink. "I think the print will be of more use to you than the maxims when it comes to the realities of marriage."

"What business is that of yours? You won't be the one to tutor me in such matters, as far as I know," came the prompt reply. She reached out and well-nigh ripped it back out of his grip, nearly tearing the image in the process.

In the distance, the sound of a horn announced the return from the hunt. Alarmed at the lateness of the hour, Mathilde stood up to depart.

"I must return to the palace before my absence is noticed. Madame has insisted that I cater to her this evening. Catherine, can you stay a while longer to determine what to do next? Chrétien's freedom to roam the estate may be of use to us after all." With that, she gathered up her skirts and ran off.

Catherine suddenly felt awkward, alone in Chrétien's presence. As they made their way back to the entrance of the maze, they discussed the girls' scheme to employ the charms and brazenness of Julie d'Aubigny to investigate d'Effiat's involvement in the affair. Chrétien promised to follow the lead on Yves Roussin, whereas Mathilde would be assigned to make inquiries into the charges against the chevalier and his connection to Montespan. The conversation faltered when they came upon one of the many fountains in the grove, which they stopped to admire. The basin was a hexagonal structure bordered by seashells. On each of the six points of the hexagon stood a rat on hind legs, from whose mouth spewed water. In the center of the fountain, the leader of the pack dominated the scene. The jet of water that surged from its snout soared higher than the rest, gurgling and splashing as it fell on the shells beneath. The myriad fountains of Versailles used more water than the entire city of Paris, and most of the smaller water features in the minor groves were only operated on special occasions. It was obvious that today the king had every desire to impress the Turkish dignitaries. The fountain was surrounded by an elaborate copper dome-shaped grid resembling a giant cage. *The Fable of the Council of the Rats* was inscribed on a bronze plaque, which the two read in silence. It was the tale of a fearsome cat on the prowl, a feline devil who terrorized the unfortunate rats, who were starving to death. One day the cat went a-courting and while he was caterwauling with his mate, the rats deliberated and came up with a defense strategy: to attach a bell to the cat's neck so that they could hear his approach. Unfortunately not one of the rats had enough courage to risk its life to secure the bell, and so they all perished under siege.

Catherine read the moral of the tale out loud. "'When advice is all that's needed, the court abounds in counselors, but when it's time for action, everyone has vanished.'" The story seemed pertinent somehow. She smiled as she said almost under her breath, "I hope that I can count on *you* at least to be a man of action."

She felt the pull of Chrétien's body heat as he stood behind her. The hair on the back of her neck tingled with the shudder of anticipation. She turned to look up at Chrétien, as a sudden breeze whisked a strand of hair across her face. He reached for the back of her neck, splaying his fingers through her thick dark locks, and tilted her face toward him. A sudden surge of excitement left her no choice but to follow her desire, as she yielded to his insistent embrace. It was Chrétien who broke the trance, knowing better than to trust the moment or to take advantage of the situation.

Coming back to her senses, Catherine said distractedly, "I can't do this," knowing full well that the spell had been cast and that her conduct had already demonstrated the contrary. They parted ways silently at the end of the path, though Chrétien's hand reached out to touch her cheek one last time, and Catherine, departing with great reluctance, suddenly grasped the pain of yearning, loss, and regret.

◆

Meanwhile, Robin was distractedly patting his courser, waiting for the king to go in for the kill. Despite the fog, the hunt had been a success, and Louis delighted in showing off his skill as a huntsman. A magnificent twelve-tined hart was at bay, rearing and bucking in panic, cornered by the wailing hounds: a ghostly apparition in the mist. The Turkish ambassador, however, seemed less than thrilled and paid little attention to the bloody display of the slaughter. During the unmaking and the *curée*, he made no attempt to conceal his boredom, preferring instead to converse with one of his attendants. His blatant disrespect was causing quite a stir.

After it was over, Robin patted his vest pocket to make sure that his copy of the cellar key hadn't fallen out during the chase. In his haste to join the hunt he had not yet had time to consider a secure hiding place. He threw a few bloody scraps of flesh from the dismembered carcass to his hunting dog, who tackled his reward and wolfed it down, flashing shard-like fangs. Robin knew that his uncle would not want to miss the lavish fete planned for the foreign emissary that evening, but his own presence would not be mandatory. The dinner party would provide an ideal occasion to explore his uncle's cellar at will. Or so he hoped. He had been burning with curiosity since his recent discovery of the secret entrance.

As he broke away from the hunting party to make his way home to the estate, he came across Catherine, who was heading toward the palace. Halting abruptly, he blocked her path.

"Well, if it isn't the little busybody Catherine!" he said. "I hear you have something of mine, and I want it back! Mathilde has no doubt informed you of this." He placed both hands on her shoulders, keeping her at arm's distance and eying her darkly.

"Get your hands off me!" she said, irritated, shrugging him off. "The cross doesn't belong to you. Claiming ownership will only implicate you in what may prove to be more than simple misconduct. If I were you, I wouldn't meddle in this sordid affair. Besides, it's my understanding that Mathilde was the one to find the locket, and you yourself allowed her to keep it."

"What do you know that I don't?" Robin was visibly shaken.

"I doubt very much that you would want to compromise your family name any more than it already is. Why, in heaven's name, should I tell you anything?" replied Catherine, turning to leave.

"Look here, I have a lead of my own and I'm willing to trade information for the return of the cross." He decided to change tactics and graced her with a full-blown smile. He could be disarming when he wanted to and he knew it. But his charm had little effect on Catherine, it seemed.

"To avoid being compromised yourself. I saw you in the library today. By all appearances you removed a sheet of paper from a book. What was my surprise when I opened the volume after you left, only to discover a series of pornographic illustrations. That kind of reading material can get a young wench like you in serious trouble," he said with false concern in his voice.

"If you intend to blackmail me on that account, it's hardly worth the effort. Madame de Maintenon has already cast doubt on my reputation before the king, so the damage is done. What's more, I handed the pendant over to my mistress, the grande dauphine, at her request. If you really want to know what I was taking from the library, no need to spy on me. Here it is!" replied Catherine insolently. With that, she removed the etching from the folds of her gown.

Robin stared in amazement at the disturbing image. To his dismay, he turned beet red. "What's this got to do with anything?" he asked.

"Nothing, necessarily. But unlike the other etchings, this one clearly shows some mysterious ritual involving beautiful young boys. We're simply wondering if the chevalier might be the central figure here, given his sexual interests."

Robin examined the etching more closely now, attempting to take in every detail. "The number fifty-three must have some meaning. Can you see it here on the staff and on the back of the throne?"

Catherine shook her head. "It means nothing to me, and it could be that this image has absolutely no bearing whatsoever on our inquiry."

"I believe it's time for us to join forces rather than to work at cross purposes with each other. We have more to gain than to lose in the process. I have to attempt to undo the damage that the two of you have caused by sharing our information with the dauphine, and presumably the duchess," said Robin, folding the document and attempting to pocket it.

"Give it back! It's thanks to Madame's inquiries that certain things have some to light. Without her influence, we would have made very little progress at all. What's your interest aside from putting a lid on the matter?" She looked at him skeptically.

"You may be aware that I have very little affection or esteem for my uncle, but I *am* his heir, and you know that he and the German are sworn enemies. She may attempt to destroy him, and that can only harm my own interests," said Robin.

"Exactly! Which is why I have to question your motives in assisting us."

Robin put his arms around Catherine's shoulder. Again, she squirmed and wriggled out of his unwanted embrace. "Call it a preemptive strike. I need to weigh all of my options in the matter."

"Madame may hate the marquis, but she isn't vindictive by nature. We all know that her real target is the Chevalier de Lorraine, and even there she only wants to thwart his conspiracies against her. She picks her battles wisely and knows that she can't win on all fronts. Before I can share any information with you, Robin, I must first ask for Mathilde's consent. At the moment, she's not particularly well disposed toward you. You could have had the decency to share the news of your engagement with her before the public announcement."

Robin shrugged his shoulders. He never liked being found in the wrong, and he always reacted to criticism by counterattack.

"I never lied to Mathilde, nor did I promise her anything I couldn't deliver," he said haughtily. "What's more, I only gave her what she wanted. Do you think I want to marry that dull-witted Madeleine de Noailles? It's no pleasure for me to know that my friends ridicule me behind my back."

"Nonetheless, you must be willing to treat Mathilde as an equal if you want her cooperation. Enough said for now, but I'll let you know if we intend to barter information next week, during the masquerade. Adieu."

On his way back to the estate, Robin mused whether he was wise to join forces with the girls. But he needed to have access to whatever information they possessed, and he knew he could employ all his charm, which was considerable, to make amends to Mathilde. He wasn't in love with her, he thought, far from it, but their longstanding friendship was one of the few things on which he could depend. He cursed himself for having taken their relationship to a heightened level of intimacy merely for the sake of a moment's lust.

Robin hopped off his horse and handed the reins to the stable master. He entered the premises through the servants' quarters in the back and crept downstairs. It was late afternoon, and since the marquis and his current lover, the actor Dancourt, would not be home till the wee hours, the house was quiet. Some of the servants were no doubt enjoying a rare moment of respite in the master's absence. As Robin passed by one of the chambers, he thought he heard the muffled moans of fornication: the mice were at play, he thought. So much the better.

The new key slid easily into the lock and turned without a squeak. Robin had taken care to oil the hinges the day before, so the heavy door opened soundlessly as well. Once inside, he secured the door again to guard against intruders. At that point he knew that only those two people who had right of entry could surprise him: the head steward Molinier, who had risked lending him the key in the first place, and his uncle, who was away at Versailles. A trace of filtered gray light had found its way into the cheerless space, settling on the dusty bottles of vintage wine. Dusk would be falling soon, so he had no time to waste. He preferred not to use the lantern until he was sure he was in a windowless space. The air was chill and damp. Robin shuddered as he approached the tableau of his ancestor and scrutinized it for further revelations, he was suddenly struck by an association that had escaped him earlier, while examining Catherine's etching. The number fifty-three, or rather the numbers five and three, were an obvious—and not too subtle— allusion to the fifth of March, *Cinq-Mars*! The print was indeed connected to his lineage, as was the cross. But so far, the only person implicated was his notorious forebear, who had been executed by royal command forty years earlier, in 1642. It was time to delve further into this affair and to face whatever secret loomed in the shadows. After fumbling around behind the portrait, Robin finally located a mechanical lever that unlatched the panel to the underground. As the portrait pivoted, his ancestor's face appeared to be leering at him indecently.

TURKISH DELIGHT

*O*ne can learn a lot about court politics by studying the seating chart at official dinners, thought the duchess. The king, handsome and resplendent in a gold-embroidered red velvet waistcoat, presided over the main table, reserved for visiting dignitaries and members of the royal family and their favorites. Tables close by included princes of the blood, dukes, counts, and marquis. As was customary, the rectangular tables had been set up on trestles, to be disassembled after the event. Each one had at its center an elaborate floral arrangement of hybrid roses and variegated parrot tulips, the latest rage from Holland. The bouquets were large enough to hinder prolonged cross-table arguments, thus reducing the noise level considerably. Members of the minor nobility, such as Mathilde and Catherine, were at the periphery of the grand reception hall. It was a well-ordered world in which everyone knew his or her place. Liselotte observed with some satisfaction that the Chevalier de Lorraine and the Marquis d'Effiat had not been placed at the same table as her husband but at a remote table with the Marquise de Montespan, whose demotion from *maîtresse-en-titre* was plain for all to see.

Queen Marie-Thérèse shuffled in on tiny feet. She appeared to be hovering above the floor like a little humming-bird in her ample pastel gossamer skirts. Dutifully, she took up her position to the right of the king, who patted her hand distractedly as she smiled at him, displaying a mouthful of decaying, blackened teeth. To his left throned Madame de Maintenon, who wore a plain high-necked gown of black satin. The contrast between the diminutive childlike queen and the stately, self-possessed widow could not have been more strik-ing. Montespan, on the other hand, desperate for attention, was babbling away incessantly to the jaded Chevalier de Lorraine and casting sideways glances at the king's table. Her loud prattle was occasionally punctuated by a strident cackle. She looked ridiculous in the turban and kaftan she had donned to honor the foreign envoy.

The dauphine nudged her dinner companion, who was ladling a spoonful of soup into her mouth. "Not only is Montespan seated far away from the king, but she's been forced to sit next to her former *entremetteuse,* Claude des Œillets. The two women despise each other. Everyone at the table is obvi-ously shunning that sullen bag of bones, perhaps in deference to Montespan, or perhaps because she is a commoner by birth."

In her prime, the marquise had had a predilection for homely companions, not apt to stir the king's carnal appetite. And yet, even *Claude* had had her day. At times Louis had sought solace with her during the night, when Montespan was away from court. It was rumored that she had even entertained ambitions to become the royal favorite, but when she gave birth to a daughter by the king, he refused to acknowledge the girl as his own. Louis farmed her out to a certain Philippe de Maison-blanche to raise as his own child. This had left des Œillets full of loathing toward Louis and the woman who at the time was his new favorite, Marie-Angélique Scorailles de Fontanges.

Madame added, "One reason the marquise hates her

former companion and go-between is that she seems to have mysteriously amassed a fortune. Despite her lowly origins as the daughter of actors, she now owns several important residences in Paris and has more money at her disposal than Montespan and myself combined."

The dauphine leaned forward. "Don't forget that Claude was in charge of procuring aphrodisiacs for Montespan from La Voisin, and that she shared some rather compromising information on her mistress at the time of the Affair of the Poisons. Whoever placed the two women at the same table had trouble in mind. It must have been Maintenon, as the king prefers to sweep such matters under the rug."

The Turkish ambassador, Suleiman Aga, and his translator were seated across from the king, at the opposite end of the table. This made it necessary for them to converse rather loudly in order to hear each other over the general brouhaha of the assembly. Very few things were left to chance in daily rituals at Versailles, and one could only surmise that this, too, had been intentional. The public exchange was halting and awkward, putting the ambassador at a distinct disadvantage.

Compensation for the ostentatious display of Turkish opulence, perhaps, mused the duchess.

Indeed, Louis had been showered and humbled with extravagant gifts, including bags of shiny gold doubloons, velvet satchels filled with pearls and precious stones, bolts of lustrous silk, vibrant oriental rugs and wall hangings, multi-hued mosaic tiles, and intricately carved arabesque panels. The courtiers had stopped to gape at the riches on display outside the Hall of Mirrors but were equally fascinated by some of the trendier items that were all the rage: coffee, tobacco, and opium. The splendid reception hall was nearing completion and scheduled for a ribbon-cutting ceremony in the spring, but the king had not been able to resist making use of it on this occasion to impress his guests.

During the exchange of gifts, the ambassador had invited Louis to sample the quality of the opium powder, which His Majesty had declined peevishly, explaining that the royal druggist had advised him against taking it through the mouth but rather to insert it into the anal cavity, so as to avoid stomach upset. Monsieur and his entourage had found this information quite amusing and couldn't stifle a collective snicker, until they met with the king's icy stare.

Despite Louis's apparent discomfiture, he had an ambitious political agenda, to be discussed in a more private setting, which went well beyond the social niceties of entertaining the representative of Mehmed IV, sultan of the Ottoman Empire, and his general, the grand vizier Kara Mustafa. The Turks had expansionist ambitions and were eager to wage war in Eastern Europe, a war that would weaken France's political rival, the Holy Roman Empire. Although Louis had initially supported the Austrian emperor, Leopold I, in the latter's attempt to keep the Turks at bay, he later understood the value of favoring the Ottoman initiative. Of course, the fact that his wife Marie-Thérèse of Spain was herself a Habsburg, prevented Louis from openly entering into an official alliance with the sultan, but the ambassador's visit was prompted by the promise of an agreement of French neutrality and a pact of nonaggression with the Ottoman Empire.

Liselotte's stomach was growling in anticipation of the sumptuous meal she saw displayed on the banquet buffet. She had not yet grown accustomed to French manners, which prohibited noisy belching, public farting, or licking one's fingers. The king refused to use a fork and commanded his guests to do the same, so it was fortunate that napkins and bowls of rose-scented water were provided and frequently changed. Iridescent oysters gleamed in the light of the chandeliers, a large two-handled porringer offered pureed chestnut soup with truffles, and a royal ballotine of pheasant wiggled in its gelatin mold. The maître d'hôtel, sword at his side, ruled over an army of waiters, one of whom rushed to Madame's side to fill her goblet the minute she emptied it. The aromas of an assortment of main courses, which included wild duck in brandied cherry sauce, rabbit stew chasseur, and truffle-scented turkey, mingled and wafted across the room enticingly. She was famished, but the formalities had not yet begun.

When the king rose commandingly and raised his glass, a hush descended on the assembly. Only the ambassador realized a bit late that a moment of silence had begun. Louis toasted his honored guest, thanking him rather tersely for his generous offerings and alluding obliquely to a new era of cooperation between nations. Not to be outdone, Suleiman Aga impressed the courtiers, albeit through his interpreter, with an eloquent oration brimming with fawning adulation. His dark eyebrows and beard, and his guttural speech lent him a gravity of countenance that seemed out of place amid the playful banter of the clean-shaven, wig-bedecked French elite. As soon as the homilies had ended, the entire waitstaff sprang to life, hustling here and there, offering libations on gold and silver platters. The steady drone of conversations, the occasional bursts of laughter, the clinking of crystal against crystal, and the scraping of chairs on the parquet resumed, as the noise level escalated again to its previous volume. Madame rolled her eyes at the grande dauphine, who answered with a wicked grin.

The grande dauphine had scarcely touched her *vol-au-vent* before the first-course dishes were whisked away. Madame, on the other hand, had filled up on the *jambon persillé*, a specialty of Burgundy that reminded her of the hearty fare she had enjoyed as a child. Suppressing a small belch behind her napkin, she waited for the evening's first entertainment interlude to begin. A head of wild black curls emerged from the wings and bowed before the assembly. It was Gianbattisto Lulli, or Jean-Baptiste Lully, as he preferred to be called in his adoptive land, composer to the king. He brandished his violin with a flourish and stretched out his arm to invite the court musicians to take their seats on a circular platform stage that had been erected for the occasion. Once they had tuned their stringed instruments and settled into silence, the master tapped his bow on the music stand and a young woman appeared, curtsying deeply to general applause. A brief moment of speculative chatter was again silenced by a tap of the bow. From the back of the room, Catherine gasped. It was none other than her chameleon cousin, Julie d'Aubigny. Lully had obviously taken her under his wing, and when the music began, Catherine understood why. Julie had the voice of an angel. It lifted up into the air, swooped and soared, then descended again like a soothing caress down the backbone of the night. The aria was from the opera *Atys*, with Julie singing the libretto of Cybèle, a goddess who has fallen in love with a mere mortal. It was Louis's favorite opera and a command performance. Some saw it as a homage to his mistress Madame de Maintenon, who was a commoner herself.

Ce mortel dans mon Cœur est au-dessus des lois.

Trop d'égalité rend l'amour sans appas.

In my heart, this mortal is above the law. Too much likeness lessens love's appeal. The lyrics spoke directly to her! Catherine realized that since her first encounter with Chrétien, she was smitten. Everything in her life was taking on fresh meaning and new dimensions. The difference in rank, which had at first seemed an insuperable barrier, was starting to crumble. After all, she reasoned, even the king seemed to disregard matters of class when it suited him. The tradition of marrying for title or wealth was so entrenched in her family that it seemed preordained that Catherine should remain a spinster. Generation by generation, her forebears had let a fortune slip through their fingers. Compulsive gambling, outrageous spending, and poor property management had been the primary culprits. Even her unconventional beauty could not make up for the lack of a dowry. What had initially seemed a disadvantage to her, she now saw as a blessing in disguise. Among her possible suitors, none struck her fancy, and since she had met Chrétien, she knew that none ever would. One kiss had sufficed to spoil her for life. She was startled out of her reverie by a question from the Baron de Rougemont, whose drivel she had been enduring for the past half hour. Attempting to disguise her distaste, she answered politely, then turned to her other neighbor, who was not much better. Discordant hues of red met her eyes: copper hair, crimson cheeks, vermilion waistcoat. She became unfocused, escaping once again into her imagination, where Chrétien eagerly awaited her under a swollen autumn moon.

Mathilde had been staring at her from another table, trying to get her attention. When the musical interlude ended, she quickly stood up and went over to her friend.

"You seem addled," she said in a hushed voice, leaning over her friend. "I have been signaling you for some time now. It seems that your cousin Julie has been raising some eyebrows, as people are starting to speculate on her recent appearance at court and her strong resemblance to the Chevalier de Maupin, who's conveniently been called away these past few days. I wonder how long it will be before her secret is discovered."

"It may not matter at this juncture. She has somehow managed to establish close ties with Lully. Didn't you say that his name was on the silversmith's list?" Catherine poked half-heartedly at her ballotine.

"Yes, in fact we may have more use for the singer than the swordsman. Lully's first soprano Marie Aubry has gotten so fat that she can hardly walk onstage and is speaking of retiring to save face, because the writing's on the wall. It looks like Julie may be a prime candidate to replace her. We'll have to speak to her before the masquerade."

"On a related matter, I have to tell you that I ran into Robin this afternoon, on my way back from the grove. Have you seen him here this evening?"

The Baron de Rougemont attempted to draw his chair closer to Catherine's, but Mathilde unceremoniously wedged herself between them, blocking out any possible communication. The Baron sighed and turned to the young lady to his left.

Mathilde was trying to maintain her composure by appearing indifferent to the news, but her facade was thin and ready to crack. "He is not here and I couldn't care less," she replied, looking around unhappily. "What did he have to say for himself?"

"I told him exactly how you felt, and he'll no doubt try to make amends at the first opportunity. Beware of his charm! He has an ulterior motive." People at the table were starting to take notice and listen in to what was being said.

Mathilde lowered her voice even more, to the point where Catherine could barely hear her. "What could that be? Does he still want to get his hands on that cross?"

"It's more than that. He wants an exchange of information. He's apparently made a discovery of his own but is only willing to share it with us if we do the same. I doubt whether he'd be so communicative were he not aware that we've made some progress in our inquiries, which places him at a disadvantage. I told him that no exchange would take place without your consent. "

Mathilde considered this a while, wondering at the fragile balance of power between her and Robin. At this moment he was the one who had something to gain from her and she could lord it over him if she so desired.

"Tell him that my decision to share what I know rests on calling his bluff. I want to hear what he has to offer first. If it's valuable to us, it will no doubt be compromising to him. That would put us all in a position of mutual dependency, which would secure our position and give us bargaining power. Those are my terms. Take them or leave them!" With that, she brusquely returned to her seat. Rougemont promptly turned back around to beleaguer Catherine.

It was time to serve dessert, which was presented in silver bowls overflowing with fragrant oranges, mangoes, kumquats, melons, and passion fruit. Muscat grapes were draped over an ice sculpture of Apollo. In the center stood a pièce montée, a mountain of caramel-glazed profiteroles artfully surrounded by a moat of custard cream with floating meringue islands. Madame was anxious to seize the first opportunity to speak to the king about the choice of d'Effiat as governor to her son, and she was watching his table like a hawk. At one point, she was surprised to see Hermann Wendt pass a document with the official seal of state to Louis, who glanced at it briefly and dismissed the messenger with a quick nod. Then, having wiped his mouth, the king clapped his hands to signal that it was time for the dancing to begin.

Once again, Lully took up his position to conduct the martial beat of *Le Triomphe de l'amour*. Tables had been moved to create a dance floor, around which torches were lit. The king, as usual, took center stage, beckoning his wife with an exquisitely elegant flick of the wrist. At forty-four he could still cut a fine figure in his red silk stockings and platform heels. As other couples took to the dance floor, the duchess awaited her turn to be asked to dance by the king. She would be fourth in line after the queen, the grande dauphine, and Maintenon.

It was hard enough to concentrate on the intricate inter-weaving steps of the gavotte without having to attempt to plead her case to the king. It was he who opened the conversation.

"My brother, the duke, informs me you have something to tell me."

"That is so, but I am afraid that it's not what he expects me to say. He's implored me to beseech Your Highness to spare the Chevalier de Lorraine, who's accused of involvement in the debauching of your son. As you can imagine, I cannot bear to endorse that man's loathsome behavior, let alone try to exonerate him."

"I myself can't imagine what my brother sees in that lout. He's always causing some kind of trouble and boasting of his depravation. As you know, your predecessor, the duke's departed wife, asked me to exile him from court." The king raised his arm, and Madame, who hadn't been paying attention to the signal to twirl, almost lost her balance.

No need to mortify the king, she thought.

"But why let him return, only to cause more turmoil?" The duchess was out of breath, her chest heaving. Louis, on the other hand, seemed slightly amused at her discomfiture.

"Because he keeps my brother happy, Madame. Something I wish you were better able to do. When it comes to ruling the land, too many cooks spoil the broth, as they say. I don't want Philippe meddling in politics."

"You are a great leader, sire, and your rule is absolute, so why do you always cater to him?"

The king was indeed an excellent dancer. He could glide across the polished floor as if he were skating on ice, and his tongue was just as smooth as his dance movements.

"Because like most men, I try to avoid arguing with women at all costs," he replied with a smirk.

As the dance ended, Liselotte quickly clutched her brother-in-law's hands: "Your Majesty, I implore you: if ever I have deserved a good turn, please spare my young and impressionable son from that viper d'Effiat, who is to be appointed as his governor."

"It's too late, my dear," said the king, as his brother approached, looking expectantly at his wife.

The Chevalier de Lorraine was close at his heels. Liselotte groaned at the thought of their contemptuous gloating at her defeat, when the grande dauphine unexpectedly came to her rescue.

"*Komm, meine Liebe!* Do you fancy a stroll in the gardens to stave off indigestion?"

The duchess followed her with a sigh of relief.

◆

The panel opened onto a staircase, but once it had closed behind him the space was pitch-black, save for the dim light of Robin's lantern. Slowly and cautiously he felt his way down the spiral stone steps, worn with age. His steps echoed eerily in the hollow depths of what appeared to be a large circular dungeon. The air was damp and chill at the bottom and reeked of stale sweat. As his eyes adjusted to the gloom, he was startled at the sight of rusty shackles lining the wall at regular intervals and placed at various heights. To one side stood a half dozen large metal cages with straw mats covered by tattered blankets and stained sheets. To the other an odd array of objects covered a long rectangular table. A cat-o'-nine-tails spread its tentacles over the back of a chair. A large oak trunk was ajar and overflowing with other assorted whips and ropes. Carved wooden penises on a mounted rack were aligned according to girth and length. Among such finds, even a seemingly innocuous violin propped against a music stand looked menacing. Straight across from the entrance stood an oversize, ornately gilded throne covered in crimson velvet. It formed a grim and gaudy contrast to the bleakness of the predominantly gray stone interior. To one side, a series of sinister-looking Venetian clown masks with frozen grins challenged him to proceed. The air was saturated with evil, powerful and repugnant, as if the place had been drenched in it. Robin had to steady his nerves in order to fight off an instinctive impulse to bolt. He had to have one more look around.

Moving closer to examine the wall, he scanned the surface with his fingers. His torchlight caught a series of deep grooves and notches, here and there, mainly close to the shackles. It looked as if the limestone had been scored to mark the days. He wondered if the numbers might give some clue as to specific dates. In one area, he read *VI + VI + VI = LIII* carved not once, but three times, as if in desperation to get the message across. Taking mental note, he determined it was time to leave, but when he reached for the inside spring latch, he found nothing there. It had been so easy, too easy to get in, but getting back out was a different matter. To the right of the panel he saw a large iron hoop that held keys of various shapes and sizes. He fumbled around in a state of panic, hoping to find a keyhole. His lantern would soon go out and he would be left alone in the dark.

Somewhere here in this room lies the key to the enigma, he thought. For the first time in his life, Robin knew he would have to rely solely on his wits.

◆

Chrétien was a bit late returning to the kennels. To avoid his father's disapproving glare, he hurried about his duties grooming and feeding the hounds before letting them into their stalls, where beds of oak awaited them. Some of the stable hands preferred these accommodations to their own straw mats and would often spend the night with the dogs. Once he was done with his chores, he was suddenly overcome by fatigue and felt like curling up with the animals himself, but he knew there were still urgent matters to attend to.

Pretexting the need to search for poacher traps, he set off to return to Roussin's shack to bring food and water to the dying woman. From early childhood, Chrétien had roamed the woodlands and he was able to detect the slightest shifts in tension in his familiar stomping grounds. As he drew near the shack he noted the smell of stale scorched wood indicating that a campfire had recently been put out. He approached the campsite stealthily, moving silently through the underbrush. There he came upon a small clearing a short distance from the house, where the embers were still aglow, having been hastily covered with soil. The incandescent cinders under the loam shimmered ominously. Something was amiss. Chrétien took cover. From behind a small knoll he waited until at last the door to the hovel opened a crack. By the light of the full moon, he could see a man whose back was toward him, dragging what appeared to be a lifeless corpse. The man was coming toward him; he knew it as surely as if he could smell his scent, sharp and musky, curling in the air. The man had returned to his lair, thought Chrétien. Sure enough, an animal on the run returns for home. He watched as Roussin, pale as a ghost in the moonlight, heaved the deadweight of the woman onto a wobbly wooden cart and made his way laboriously through the brush. Chrétien wondered if the man had finished her off, or if she had died a natural death. At this point, it seemed immaterial. Her suffering had ended. The young woodsman followed silently until the other stopped and tilted the wheelbarrow, dumping the woman's body into a shallow grave, which had obviously been freshly dug for the occasion. Roussin then began to quickly cover her with soil and dead leaves. The sound of the shovel scraping the loosened rocks echoed in accompaniment to the flashing glint of metal. Chrétien hesitated as to his course of action. He would have the physical advantage in a confrontation, but tracking the man would lead to more reliable and perhaps more pertinent evidence. At this point, Yves could not be proven guilty of wrongdoing, nor linked to human trafficking. Margot had been his only witness, and she was no longer able to testify.

◆

The king was visibly in a state of ill humor. Even his dancing, of which he was very proud, failed to impress the Turkish envoys. Of course, he was no longer as young and agile a performer as he had been in his youth, but he could still display a well-turned calf. His irritation put a chill on the entire assembly. It was time for the final course of coffee, *digestifs*, exotic birds shaped out of fruit and almond paste, delicate spun-sugar flowers, rose-petal jam, and Turkish delights in honor of his foreign guests. From the veranda outside the open doors, Liselotte and Victoire observed an inebriated noblemen, wig askew, urinating clumsily but unabashedly against the marble columns lining the facade.

"Disgusting!" said the grande dauphine. "A vein of brutishness runs just below the thin layer of social veneer." Several other courtiers had come outside for a breath of cold night air. To the friends' surprise, Madame de Montespan joined them with a look of malice on her face.

"Good evening, mesdames! I see that you, too, are weary of the festivities. But there will be one more extravaganza before the evening is over. Louis has planned to bring in three giant floats, covered in pink and red rose petals, from which three lovely courtesans dressed in sheer red garments and feathered masks will spring. They'll shower the king's table with confetti and dance for his pleasure. I am sure that the Turks' interest will finally be piqued. As for me, I cannot wait to retire. I had hoped that the Marquis d'Effiat's handsome nephew might keep me company this evening, but he has begged off."

"A bit young for you, don't you think?" replied Liselotte, who was not one to mince words. A quality that won her a few admirers but more enemies at court.

Françoise-Athénaïs de Montespan took the slight surprisingly well. She was still a breathtaking beauty at the age of forty-two and sure of her effect on men. Despite her involvement in the Affair of the Poisons, it took the king a good decade, along with the persuasiveness of Madame de Maintenon, to pry himself away from her treacherous allure.

"I will need someone with vigor to fill the king's shoes, so to speak. A young buck would be just the ticket," she said spitefully.

"If you are trying to win the king back by making him jealous, that's the oldest trick in the book, although when it comes to women, he's clearly a fool."

Montespan ignored the sarcasm, having apparently come to join them for a different purpose. "Yes, indeed, he's certainly that. It may not surprise you then to learn what a strong sway his new lady love has over him. Maintenon is a devout Catholic and manages to keep the king dangling for her sexual favors, which she grants or withholds at will. It's been driving the man to distraction, for he's not in the habit of being refused. So much so that he is totally blind to her complete lack of feminine charm." The marquise's dark blond curls bobbed in indignation from beneath her turban.

"She *is* a homely bitch. I'll give you that."

"I thought it might interest you both to know that she's recently been harping on Louis to revoke his grandfather Henri the Fourth's edict," said the marquise.

"I hope that by that you don't mean the Edict of Nantes! That would mean the end of religious tolerance in France and would prompt the massive emigration of thousands of Protestants," cried the duchess. She had abandoned her reformed faith only by force of circumstance, and her sympathies for the Huguenots ran deep. "The persecution of Protestants could once again tear this country apart and harm France's economy through the loss of a thriving merchant class."

"Well, I have no mind for such matters, but I'm simply attempting to point out what harm a woman can do when she's mistress to the king of France. At least I never tried to meddle in politics!"

"Are you so sure, milady? Perhaps you don't consider your actions to have been politically motivated, but what of your association with the Marquis d'Effiat and the Chevalier de Lorraine? You seemed quite friendly with them over dinner."

"I'm not sure what you mean or where this is leading." The marquise was hedging, with an air of wariness etched on her brow. "We've never been enemies, if that's what you mean."

Madame reached into her satchel and pulled out the cross. "I believe your association goes deeper than that. Are you familiar with this amulet? I know that you commissioned an identical one or that one was commissioned for you."

The marquise's exquisite face betrayed only a trace of discomfort. She had quite clearly learned to mask her reactions by playing to the king's bidding for many years. Her voice came out stone-cold and sharp: "It was a gift from d'Effiat. I did him a favor once, and this is a token of his esteem. That's all you really need to know."

"What I want to know is why any woman would want such an emblem. The archangel Michael is trampling the devil in similar depictions. But here the devil has taken the shape of a woman."

"If it's so repugnant to your sensitivities, I'll be glad to take it off your hands," said the marquise, reaching for the locket.

Madame swiftly stowed it back in her pocket. "Finders keepers!" she replied.

"To many, the devil *is* a woman," replied the marquise. "La Maintenon is a prime example of that, but she's not the only one."

As are you, thought Liselotte. But she bit her tongue.

THE BROTHERHOOD

My *dearest Carllutz,*

You hope, as you claim, that my spirits can rise above the slander, and you add in your wisdom that the greatest displeasure one can cause one's enemies, is to ignore them. It would be easy to abide by your counsel, were my torment caused by distant relations. However, the greatest culprit of all is Monsieur, whose companions (my sworn enemies) have so beguiled him that he has more hatred for me than all the others combined. It is therefore impossible for me not to lose myself in sadness on occasion. Normally, when opponents loathe you, the prospect of a swift revenge can be of some solace, but then again my husband is the one person who is beyond my authority in such matters. However, even if I had the power to exact revenge on him, I would not wish to do so, for anything that upsets him falls back on me. Whenever he is prey to misfortune, I am the hapless target of his ill humor, and when fortune smiles upon him, he refuses to share it with me. As soon as he has money, he taunts me by lavishing it on his friends before my very eyes. He deprives me of my own fortune and gives me a pitifully small allowance, lording it over me the better to please the chevalier and d'Effiat. Had I some useful occupation or a kindred soul in whom to confide, like my good dark-skinned Théobon, it might console me, but they have removed her from my service and have made very sure that I dare not do or say anything in public without the dread of repercussions. When I innocently ask my people what time it is, Monsieur believes that I am communicating with them in some secret code and insists on knowing my meaning. You can well imagine how little respect such behavior commands among my servants. When I say two words to my children, I have to submit to a thirty-minute cross-examination by my husband. Such trials and tribulations have worn me down and made me a woman of constant sorrow. I would not have bothered you with such a boringly detailed account of my troubles (for you know how I hate to complain), were it not for the fear that you mistake my distress for pure whimsy.

Weird rumors abound here at court. They say that the son of King Charles the Second of England, the Duke of Monmouth, may have been involved in conspiring to have his own father assassinated. What is the world coming to? Meanwhile, in Vienna, the emperor is said to be able to see the advancing Turks from his bedroom window. This terrible news gives me hope, nonetheless, that all of our Christian rulers will finally unite to stop the infidels, which should put an end to war forevermore.

As for the sausages you sent along from Heidelberg, I am still wondering what became of them and their bearer, Monsieur de Morangis, who hopefully hasn't eaten them himself. I nonetheless thank you very humbly for the kind gesture. You know how much I savor them at lunchtime after an early-morning hunt! They remind me of my sweet homeland, and of you, dear brother. I do hope that your health is on the mend. You are with me every day in my thoughts and prayers.

Your loving sister, Liselotte

(Versailles, October 1, 1682)

. . .

Reading aloud, Madame paced the room in a great state of agitation, her heavy footsteps punctuated by tiny outbursts of vexation as she stopped now and again to correct an error. The grande dauphine listened quietly but intently to this written account of the escalating hostility between the duchess and the duke.

"How do you account for your husband's recent conduct?" she asked. "Surely, there has to be more to his mounting antagonism than would be warranted by his disinclination for the fairer sex."

"Everyone at court believes me to be obsessively paranoid and unjustifiably suspicious; my own brother, the prince elector Karl Ludwig, writes dismissively, advising me to adopt an attitude of resignation and endurance under pressure. Please don't tell me that you, too, now question my judgment," the duchess replied somewhat peevishly.

"I am your steadfast ally, and though I don't dispute the facts you've revealed, I entreat you to examine the possible grounds for this change from a more lucid perspective. Could your recent investigation into the significance of the locket have reached his ears? Would that not be reason enough for him to hate you?" The dauphine raised her eyebrows over her teacup.

"I wouldn't be surprised at all to find out that Julien de Grosménil, that blabbermouth of a silversmith, has decided to curry favor with the duke by betraying my interests. Madame de Montespan is another likely snitch. She seemed quite eager to have the locket, which doesn't necessarily mean that it belonged to her. But though I suspect collusion between some rather shady characters at court, and you know whom I mean, I have never once accused Monsieur of involvement in the suspicious death of his first wife, Henriette, as many others have done. I have been ever so careful never to bring up this delicate matter, as I believe her murder to have been executed by others, and unbeknownst to him." Madame rang the bell for Agnès. It was time for more tea.

"All I can say, *meine Liebe*, is beware of stirring up the muck that lies just beneath the surface. By the way, your account to your brother of the political situation and its possible aftermath, is nothing short of naive. Louis's rapprochement with the Turks, despite his obvious distaste for their ambassador during last night's festivities, is an overt attempt to weaken the powerful Habsburgs. There has never been any love lost between the king and the emperor, though they are cousins through Louis's mother, Anne of Austria. I'm sure the king plans to pledge to a policy of nonintervention rather than to defend a Christian Europe." The dauphine stood to leave and pecked her friend on the cheek affectionately.

Liselotte, who had been raised to speak her mind openly, was not offended by her friend's well-intentioned criticism, but she sent her letter off without any substantive changes and let the matter rest. It was time for her ablutions.

◆

Robin awoke shivering from a fitful slumber haunted by dark demonic images, to the sound of footsteps echoing on the stone staircase that led down to the dungeon. He had already unsheathed his hunting knife and grabbed an iron rod before his lantern had gone out and he had drifted off from exhaustion at the foot of the stairs. It was pitch-black in the chamber of horrors. He had no idea how long he had slept, but he presumed that it must be after midnight. He could take no chances with the intruder, unless of course it were his uncle. In which case there would be dire consequences if his identity were revealed! There was a click, and as the door opened, he caught a fleeting glimpse in the lantern light of a sallow face he had never seen before. Springing forward, he bashed the man in the head with his poker. The man crumbled to the floor and lay silent, unconscious. The lantern, remarkably, hadn't gone out in the brief scuffle, and with its light he studied his victim on the stones of the floor. As he reached for a pulse, he was struck by the stranger's pallor, his wispy, colorless hair, and a cloying, fetid odor of decay. The inanimate body blocked the exit, and Robin needed to remove it from the premises. Heaving the man's deadweight up the spiral staircase was a Herculean task but warranted by Robin's desperate need to keep his nocturnal visit a secret.

◆

The ark of the moon played hide-and-seek behind the passing clouds, as Chrétien lay in wait for Roussin outside the castle. He had followed the man through the woodlands with only a stray glimmer occasionally illuminating his prey, who halted once or twice at the snap of a twig. The young groundskeeper had kept his distance, for he was forced to begrudgingly acknowledge that Roussin seemed as sure-footed and familiar with the terrain as he was. At one point, he was sure that he had lost him, but a dim ray of light in the clearing betrayed the man's presence. It appeared to shine right through the ghoulish apparition, emitting an ashen glow. The path from the clearing led to d'Effiat's estate, at which point the man seemed to simply slip through the gated entrance, as if indeed he were truly a ghost. There was nothing further Chrétien could do but to wait for Roussin's reemergence, so he found a spot behind an ancient oak tree, from which to survey the back of the property adjacent to the hunting grounds.

He did not have long to wait. The faint clanking of the palace gate and a muffled rustling in the grass alerted him to furtive movement nearby. As the bustle approached, Chrétien realized that what he heard was the mingled sound of ragged breathing and the toilsome dragging of a heavy load through the dewy sward. Then the unmistakable odor of rank sweat he associated with Roussin and the dim vision of what appeared to be someone hauling a corpse. Chrétien could no longer remain hidden, watching passively as this fiend buried a second body in one night. He stepped out into the moonlight to stop the action, only to find that it was Roussin himself who was being towed, and by none other than the Marquis d'Effiat's nephew. Robin promptly dropped the body and lunged at Chrétien's shadow with his hunting knife, but having the advantage of the backlighting, Chrétien grabbed hold of the other's hand, forcing him to drop his weapon. Robin was lithe and fit, but he was no match for the taller, sturdier woodsman. Chrétien finally pinned his opponent to the ground.

"Sorry, milord. I mistook you for Roussin." He jumped off his opponent and extended his arm to help him get back on his feet.

"Who? Do you mean this fellow here? I've never seen him before in my life, but I caught him trespassing," said Robin, dusting off his jacket. The two young men eyed each other warily.

"Didn't I see you loitering outside the king's palace the other day with Catherine de Sauvignon?" Robin asked.

"I was there. I had some business to attend to."

The less information the better, thought Chrétien.

"And now here you are. What business did you have with this piece of filth?"

"I've been following him because he's been involved in some shady dealings, is all. Is he dead or just dormant?"

"Knocked out cold. I take it you've got no love for him, then, so you can help me dispose of him. He's a deadweight to lug around. He'll probably take some time to come to, given the

blow I dealt him. Where do you reckon we can ditch him?"
Robin kicked the inert body to check for a reaction.

"I know just the place," replied Chrétien, grabbing hold of
Roussin's ankles. "His shanty isn't far from here."

It took more than an hour for Roussin to regain consciousness. In the meantime, Robin and Chrétien had had an opportunity to coordinate their tactics regarding their treatment and
disposal of the man. Chrétien was well aware that the young
nobleman was on his guard and he himself was reluctant to
discuss what little he knew of Roussin because of his vested
interest in Catherine's welfare and his awareness that Robin's
social standing gave him a distinct advantage. But when, in the
course of their discussion, it became apparent that Robin and
Mathilde had a long-standing friendship, he reciprocated with
some limited information on Roussin.

They had returned to the fetid atmosphere of Roussin's
cabin. It reeked of illness, death, and decay, so they made a fire
and opened the door to chase what they could of the foul-
smelling air. In the process they debated the best way to question the man and his connection to the Marquis d'Effiat,
perhaps even the chevalier. Torture remained an option, but
they decided that the method most apt to loosen Roussin's
tongue was to subject him to mental terror. He did not seem
the type to become a martyr to a cause, or to sacrifice his own
interests to those of his master. They predicted he would not
take long to break. They streaked their faces with mud and
pulled their hoods over their heads. Roussin shifted in and out
of consciousness. Then his eyes gradually focused on their
presence, as they stoked the fire, heating an iron poker from
the hearth until it was red-hot. Roussin attempted to move,
only to find that he was bound and gagged. The fear
emanating from his body was tangible and rose as a strong
stench from his bowels, which he was unable to control.
Fighting an overwhelming urge to heave in the presence of

such degradation, Robin loosened the gag to begin the interrogation.

The prisoner stared at the two in bewilderment. He stammered silently, unable in his panic to produce even the slightest
sound out of the gaping cavity of his mouth. The sight of the
glowing instrument of torture and the ominous dark hoods of
the two men before him had seemingly rendered him mute.

"Pull down his breeches!" Robin ordered Chrétien. The
latter roughly tore open Roussin's soiled undergarments and
bent him over the wooden trestle table, shoving the rotting
food to the side. A loud guttural wail was the first sound to
escape the man's throat.

"What do you want from me? Have I not been a faithful
servant to my lords?"

As prearranged, Robin began the questioning. It would be
natural for Roussin to assume that his interrogators were in
some way connected to Robin's uncle, the Marquis d'Effiat, and
that they were questioning him on the latter's behalf.

"Yves Roussin!" The rogue began to tremble at the mere
mention of his name. "Have you betrayed our interests to
another party? Or have you been clumsy enough to be
followed? It would appear that certain inquiries into our private
affairs have revealed our clandestine activities and the location
of the underground chamber."

"I swear by the Sacred Brotherhood that I ain't ever squealed
on none of the members. I reckon I ain't ever been followed
neither, seein' as I only come and go to headquarters by night, and
it ain't possible for no one to follow me through the brambles and
the woodlands 'cause I'd hear 'em fer sure. Whoever knocked me
out was inside the dungeon all the while and took me by surprise."

It wasn't difficult for Chrétien to play the torturer, though
he had no intention of carrying through on their threats. But
his fury at the thought of young Gilbert Simon's fate gripped

his vocal cords and lent a terrifyingly guttural quality to his speech.

"Messenger, pimp, henchman, or traitor? Wasn't it you who were asked to dispose of the victims? You must have been followed at some point. Your hiding place has been discovered, and by a maiden, at that." He waived the iron rod as he spat out the words.

"A maid? That ain't possible! Just leave me to it, and I can make 'er disappear along with the others," Roussin pleaded. The youths looked at each other. He seemed to know nothing of the girls.

"Never mind," said Chrétien. At this point, it was obvious that Roussin was too unnerved to make even the feeblest attempt at holding back information. He was gambling for his life with no cards in his deck. If they let him go he would no doubt bolt for good, like a frightened rabbit. Should they get wind of his compromising admissions, Roussin's powerful backers would never allow him to come to justice; they would simply make him vanish. That would be one less lowlife to contend with.

"We want a full account of what happened to the others and how you managed to get rid of them."

"There was that one wee village boy about twelve years back. Name of Gilbert. His da' had been lookin' for him high and low. But the boy was found strangled, and I got rid of the body by burning it and stashing what was left in an old run-down shack, as the brothers asked me to."

Chrétien winced at the thought.

"Go on," said Robin.

"A few years later, the chevalier was accused of that little waffle merchant's death, 'cause he knocked him about. I hear it was an accident 'cause they took him to a brothel and the boy wouldn't give out none."

"Most people know about that one, even though he was made to disappear. Were you involved?"

"That one got a right burial in the well. It's true that the brothers like to play it rough, what with their handcuffs, chains, and whips, but I was only followin' orders, I swear!"

"Any others?" Chrétien moved forward menacingly, waiving the poker wildly.

"One boy died of an overdose of beetle powder, and another one, can't recall his name, died of bein' frozen to death on account of escaping naked through the woods. That was during the Lent, in early April of last year." Roussin was shaking uncontrollably.

"So you got rid of them, too."

"Those ones are in the well, too, seein' as it's all dried up. That's all of 'em, on my mother's head!"

The irony of the time of death did not escape Chrétien. "Lent's the time Christ spent forty days in the wilderness, resisting the temptation of Satan."

Despite his terror, Roussin couldn't avoid an involuntary shrug of the shoulders. Chrétien resisted a violent urge to belt him.

"All I ever did was to scout for the boys, sometimes with the help of Father Anselme, the village priest. I never laid a hand on them, 'cept to lure them in or cart them off! When accidents happened, I took care of things, nothin' more."

Realizing that there was nothing more to be gleaned from the man, Chrétien exchanged glances with Robin and advanced on Roussin. By this time, the man was shaking so mightily that the trestle table to which he was tied wobbled beneath him on uneven legs. His shock and relief were so great at being set free, that he nearly collapsed.

"You have ten minutes to gather your belongings," warned Robin. "Should we ever set eyes on you again, we will brand you with hot iron as the villain you are, tie you to a tree, and leave you to die in the woods, half devoured by wild animals, like one of those poor victims you abducted."

Roussin didn't bother to collect his things. He pulled up his trousers and scurried off like a frightened rabbit, as fast as his quavering legs could carry him.

◆

When Mathilde arrived at her lady's chamber with a carafe of water, she found her sitting for yet another portrait. To bide the time her mistress had been savoring more than a few candied chestnuts. The girl noted that half the box had already been consumed. On Madame's lap lay Tallemant des Réaux's scandalous new *Historiettes*, which had been making the rounds through clandestine circles. Mathilde had heard about it through her clique of friends, but no one had as yet had a chance to read it. Just as she was wondering how she might have a glimpse of it, the duchess's head slumped to the side as she nodded off to sleep, and the fascicule slid off her knees and onto the floor. The painter, Pierre Mignard, did not seem to mind the change of pose, as he was painstakingly concentrating on rendering Madame's feet, in an attempt to make them appear much daintier than they were. With nothing else to do, Mathilde eagerly began reading the collection of short, provocative, and often scathing biographical narratives under the disapproving glance of the painter. There was a particularly blistering account of Madame de Maintenon's relationship with the king, which no doubt accounted for the banning of the manuscript. However, it was the story of the present king's father, Louis XIII, and his ill-fated minion Cinq-Mars that immediately caught her attention. His name had come up more than once when Mathilde had eavesdropped on Madame's most recent conversations. She devoured the tale, largely based on hearsay, hoping to find information that she might later put to use.

Cinq-Mars

His Eminence the Cardinal Richelieu, seeing that he needed to provide some form of entertainment for King Louis XIII, cast his eyes, as I mentioned earlier, on Cinq-Mars, with whom the king was already infatuated. In the beginning, Cinq-Mars debauched the king: they danced and drank many a toast together. However, as he was an impetuous young man who liked his pleasures, he began to languish in a lifestyle that was not of his own choosing and that he had only taken up half-heartedly to please the cardinal. But Louis loved him to distraction. Fonterailles recounts that one day when he entered Cinq-Mars's chambers in Saint-German without knocking, he caught the young man having himself rubbed from head to toe with jasmine oil before going to bed. "It's cleaner this way," he said to Fonterailles, rather self-consciously. A moment later there was a knock at the door and the king entered. It would appear, said the man to whom this story was told and who repeated it to me, that Cinq-Mars was lubricating himself for "combat."

Mathilde did her best to suppress a giggle. Tallemant's lapidary style and scathing wit had hit a nerve at court because the accounts, true or not, were such a convincing depiction of the depravity of the previous and the present reign. The author's active imagination had undoubtedly filled in some of the gaps in the narrative, but all in all, its gossipy tone had an air of credibility. Mathilde was eager to read on, but a brief snort alerted her to her mistress's awakening. She quickly placed the manuscript back on the floor where she had found it and resumed her needlework.

After a fleeting moment of bewilderment, the duchess recovered her bearings and resumed her dignified pose with a loud yawn. Noticing the object on the floor, she said, "Mathilde, you should read the chapter on the old harpy. It's quite an eye-opener! It would appear that in her early days, Maintenon claimed to be a direct descendant of the house of Constantinople and would often drop the words *my grandmother, the Empress*, into the conversation. Hah! Grandmother, my arse! Françoise Scarron, as she was once known, always wanted to be the center of attention! The woman is believed to have worn out several lovers through her sexual ardor, and according to Tallemant, she could at one time be had for the mere sum of fifty *pistoles*. No wonder the circulation of the *Historiettes* is prohibited! It certainly tarnishes her image of moral rectitude, a charade she presents to the public and spoon-feeds to the king himself."

The artist grinned knowingly but kept his silence.

"I hear that there's also a scandalous account of Louis XIII's lover Cinq-Mars. I very much doubt that the king enjoys the retelling of his own father's debauchery," said Mathilde, hoping to prolong the discussion.

"And I hear that *you* are sweet on that scoundrel's grand-nephew! Remember that corruption runs deep in that blood-line. They are all bad to the bone. I am sure that Robin, though young, is no exception. Beware, my dear, beware!" In a rare gesture of affection, she laid her hand on Mathilde's cheek.

"Rumor has it that he's to be married to Madeleine de Noailles, so she'll be the one to bear that particular burden, Madame, not I." Mathilde turned away briefly so Madame wouldn't see her pain, but then turned back, stiffening her upper lip. "Now that you and the dauphine have had a chance to examine the locket, Madame, would it be too bold of me to ask for you to give it back?" Speaking of Robin had reminded her of her promise, and though she still had every intention of giving him a piece of her mind, she knew that the cross could serve her well in bartering favors. She wasn't sure how much Robin knew of his forebear Cinq-Mars, but he would certainly be interested in the account by Tallemant she had just read.

"I should not want it back, if I were you. It bodes ill fortune. However, what is fair is fair. Just leave it with me for a brief while longer. I have one more inquiry to make, and I'm awaiting Wendt's arrival to send him on a fact-finding mission. I should be able to return it to you in a few days' time and to report back to you on what I've learned by the eve of the masquerade." At the thought of the upcoming event, she added, "Incidentally, have you chosen your costume?"

"Catherine and I have shared some ideas, but we have yet to visit the cloth merchant," replied Mathilde unenthusiastically. She had lost all interest in the event.

"Ever since Louis's fashioned himself in the image of Apollo, it's become quite fashionable to impersonate the heroes and deities of Greek and Roman antiquity. Racine's tragedies, particularly *Phaedra,* which is all the present rage, have turned the fashion into a craze. I've decided, and not by chance, on the role of Demeter, Mother Earth—I certainly look the part—and my husband plans to come as Hades, the ruler of the underworld. What could be more appropriate? The two were at odds over the abduction of Persephone, Demeter's daughter. Do you know the story?"

Knowing how her mistress delighted in storytelling, Mathilde shook her head even though she was somewhat familiar with the myth.

"Persephone, the maiden goddess of spring, was captured by Hades, who raped her and carried her off to the underworld, forcing her to become his queen. In her desperate search for her daughter, Demeter's obsession and sorrow resulted in a blighted land and eternal winter. In order to preserve the world of the living, Hades struck a deal with Demeter, whereby the two would share the girl. Thus, the earth would again be fertile for six months during the time the mother and daughter were reunited, and barren the rest of the year. The analogy here is that the duke and his cohort the Chevalier de Lorraine are threatening to assign tutelage of my little Philippe to the Marquis d'Effiat. To me, this would be tantamount to the boy's abduction and would lead inevitably to his sexual exploitation, if not by d'Effiat, then by the chevalier himself. I can't think of a more appropriate illustration of the state of our marriage at this time. Should my son be taken from me, I will see to my revenge. I'll have the same courage as Demeter, born from despair."

Mathilde nodded somewhat absentmindedly, as the duchess continued, her voice taking on a sarcastic tone: "Still, I wonder if the duke won't view this as yet another occasion to dress as a woman, but no doubt he will leave that to the chevalier. The grand dauphin will look ridiculous as Ares, the god of war, but his wife, the Dauphine Victoire, will be well suited to her choice of Athena, goddess of wisdom. Madame de Montespan desperately wanted the role of Aphrodite, but that was already taken by that old bag Maintenon." The duchess's dimples showed, and her belly began to shake with bitter laughter at the very thought of such a preposterous mismatch.

"Given my rank at court, I should probably take on an unassuming part," replied Mathilde, with uncharacteristic modesty. "I thought the role of Hermione, the vengeful, jilted fiancée of Pyrrhus, son and heir to Achilles, might be appropriate. For Catherine, maybe that of Cassandra, the ill-fated Trojan prophetess, who predicted the fall of Troy and later Agamemnon's death. But lately I'm starting to think that the role of Cybele would be a better choice for my friend, who seems to have a penchant for the lower classes."

"This afternoon the Italian mask makers and the silk merchants from Lyon should arrive to display their wares under the colonnade. I will grant you a small sum to make the necessary adjustments to your formal attire." The duchess reached for her coin purse.

A knock on the door put a halt to the conversation. The painter, seeing that his subject was restless, was beginning to close up shop, folding his easel, rinsing and wrapping his brushes and paints, when Hermann Wendt entered the room. He bowed briefly, clicking his heels in Germanic style. The duchess felt a rush of relief at the sight of him. She had only a few people who were unconditionally loyal to her, and he ranked at the very top. "I count on your discretion in this matter, my dear Wendt. Have you made any progress with your investigation among Madame de Montespan's servants?"

"Limited progress, Madame. As you well know, it's very difficult to question people directly without arousing suspicion, and gossip at court travels swiftly. The one thing that seems to link Montespan to d'Effiat and his circle is the use of aphrodisiacs. It's still unclear whether the king's former mistress was involved in Mademoiselle de Scoraille's miscarriage and untimely death, but, as I mentioned, she was reputed to have had commerce with Catherine La Voisin, the notorious poisoner. It would appear that her aphrodisiac of choice was blister beetle powder, a sexual stimulant, which can be lethal when administered in excess. It also seems to be commonly known that your husband, the chevalier, and the marquis are members of a not-so-clandestine pederastic society, of which the logo on the cross represents a common aversion to women. Why Montespan would own a similar pendant remains a mystery. So far, that's all I've been able to learn."

The duchess pulled out the locket and wrapped it in a silk kerchief, knotting it at both ends. "I am going to entrust this to you for twenty-four hours, during which time you can see if the sight of it jars anyone's memory, but be careful not to display it too casually, and not to the wrong people. I have the feeling that Grosménil cannot be trusted, and that my husband may suspect that I am on to something compromising that involves him, if not directly, at least marginally. Most of all, I want the name of the secret society, a complete list of its members and its ringleader, and finally its meeting place. I need more than simple hearsay in my battle to discredit my adversaries." With those words, she dismissed her courier and returned to her box of candied chestnuts.

THE MASQUERADE

"Well, if it isn't Lully's little nightingale!" said Catherine by way of a greeting.

Since her performance at the Turkish festivities, Julie d'Aubigny's fame had spread like wildfire. And Lully had become her constant companion and mentor. Little did he know, as yet, of her alter ego, the chevalier de Maupin, and her formidable fencing skills. Mathilde looked her up and down to appraise her allure and her potential as an ally or a rival. The girl had a most definite androgynous appeal with a splattering of freckles across the bridge of a straight, narrow nose. Her high cheekbones and almond eyes gave her a distant, haughty air, but full, rather sensuous lips promised pleasure to those brave enough to kiss them. The total effect was crowned by sleek, deep auburn locks, so very different from her own bright red unruly curls. With a wig and a waistcoat, Julie's slender form and noble face could easily pass for those of a handsome adolescent boy. Today, however, she was in a creamy frock that brought out her feminine beauty. She was shopping for the accessories for her costume for the masquerade.

"So who's it to be: Julie Henriette d'Aubigny? Or the chevalier Jules Henri de Maupin?" Catherine asked.

Julie looked back and forth from Mathilde to her cousin, annoyed at the reference to her double.

"Don't worry! My friend won't reveal your secret. It might be of use to us in a venture where you'd play the leading role."

"At this moment, my best interest lies in my association with Lully. He's a powerful man at court, as he's the king's composer, dancing master, and occasional unofficial adviser." She reached for a bolt of crimson silk under the watchful eye of the Italian merchant.

"It's true that the two have been friends since Louis was a lad, but Lully may have fallen out of favor, or so I've heard," said Catherine from behind a feathered mask.

"I'm sure you're aware that the music and ballets Lully has written in honor of His Majesty have served to immortalize his image as the Sun King," said Julie defiantly. "Since you're so curious to know about my costume for the ball, I'm planning to dress as the siren Thelxiope, whose singing, it's said, was irresistibly sweet. It's Jean-Baptiste who came up with that idea to promote my budding career as an opera singer."

"Yes, but Thelxiope's voice was known to engross both body and soul in a fatal lethargy," said Mathilde with a wink to her friend.

"Jean-Baptiste, is it now? You seem to be on very familiar terms!" said Catherine.

"Not as familiar as he'd like them to be! The man is besotted with me, but I've managed to put him off so far, with considerable effort, I might add. So tell me, what's this proposed adventure that awaits me? I hope the two of you aren't trying to draw me into some risky scheme," she said with an impish smile.

It dawned on Mathilde that Julie's disturbing charm was the result of her unpredictable, untamed pluck. There was a wildness to her that came out in her mannerisms and even more in her musical performance. No wonder Lully wanted her so badly! She made a mental note to keep the girl away from Robin.

"Here's what we have in mind," said Catherine, summarizing their recent escapades, adding that Julie's newfound mentor Lully might be of some assistance in their search.

"So, effectively, you want me to spy on him to gain access to information on his group of consorts, who ostensibly include the Marquis d'Effiat and the Chevalier de Lorraine. But what's in it for me?"

"Don't forget that it's thanks to my intercession with the grande dauphine that you're here at Versailles!" said Catherine.

"I'll need better than that," answered Julie, turning back to the display of merchandise.

"Gratitude doesn't seem to be your forte," said Mathilde. "But perhaps a chance to further your ambitions with the help of my mistress the duchess, who has a vested interest in this inquiry . . . She is quite taken by your talent and has connections at the Palais-Royal opera in Paris."

This time Julie turned around and gave the girls her full attention. "I'll see what I can glean from Jean-Baptiste first, as I already have him under my spell. It might warrant getting a little too close for comfort, but then again, he is a strikingly handsome and supremely intelligent man, though a bit old for my taste.

"Should that prove unsuccessful, you can change genders at will. The other two have probably never noticed more than a fleeting resemblance between Maupin and yourself."

"Hold on a minute! Aren't you getting ahead of the issue? One step at a time! I have no interest in compromising my bright future with Lully for the sake of some vague assurances. A bird in the hand is worth two in the bush. I'll see what I can do, but no guarantees." Julie punctuated her words with a nobleman's bow, displaying her penchant for theatrical flourish. She then turned to examine a bolt of emerald-green silk, rubbing the fine fabric between her fingers. Holding it up to her face, she asked: "How does this color suit my complexion? I plan to bring a lyre to complete the effect."

"Bellissima!" said the silk vendor, holding up a mirror to capture her reflection.

"Ravishing!" added Catherine a bit sardonically, knowing that Julie had no lack of self-regard. "As for me, I've decided on the role of Hector's sister Cassandra. I'm working on the train of my frock, which will be embroidered with a cascade of tears. I've also ordered a mask with one eye open, and the other closed. Mathilde here is still pondering over how to best portray the madness of Hermione, and I think the key is to backcomb her hair into a wild, blazing mess."

"Yes, and her mask should show passion and fury. I think blackened eye sockets with lightning bolts running down her cheeks would do the trick, don't you?" Julie, who had been sorting through the display of masks, wigs, and props, lifted up a Gorgon's head. "Maybe the Medusa would a better choice," she added wryly.

"That sounds a bit melodramatic, but why not? I guess I won't be the belle of the ball, but my love already has a heart of stone. On the other hand, the dress will have to display my physical charms so that Robin might be both attracted and repelled by the sight of me." Mathilde pulled the wig over her head, tucking in her curls, while the obsequious merchant attempted to adjust the serpentine coils of gray felt to full effect.

"What a strange idea! You shouldn't allow yourself to cater to any man, worthy or not," said Julie with a contemptuous smirk. "I'm two years younger than you, but I'm already practiced in the art of detachment and self-control when it comes to matters of the heart."

"Perhaps it comes with playing the field on both sides," said Catherine, handing a few coins to the Italian.

"I'm an excellent performer, as you may have noticed. Wearing a mask comes naturally to me, and I've a good sense of what it must feel like to be a man. Perhaps I should go to the masquerade as a transvestite after all," said Julie, contemplating Mathilde from head to toe. "I could ask for the favor of a dance with Mathilde."

"In that case, the role of Narcissus, who fell in love with his own reflection, would suit you quite well," added Mathilde wryly.

◆

The wet cobblestones glistened bluish gray in the evening mist, as the horse-drawn carriages began to arrive for the ball. One by one, each coach delivered its passengers to the Cour de Marbre, where they were greeted at the main entrance by a doorman who led them into the central staircase. Every chandelier was lit, and the palace glowed from within its darkened shell. Through the haze, one could discern an occasional flash of color: a carriage door emblazoned with a vivid coat of arms, a bright waistcoat, or a magnificent plumed hat. Madame de Maintenon had chosen an uncharacteristically flamboyant, flouncy crimson gown with heart-shaped ruby earrings to portray Aphrodite. She nearly lost her golden arrow as she slipped on the pavement, narrowly missing a steaming pile of horse manure. Fortunately, the Duke de Guise managed to spring forward and steady her before the fall. As the duchess watched the endless parade of vanity from her window above, she blinked to make sure she wasn't hallucinating, for suddenly a piglet on a diamond-studded leash, which had managed to escape its owner's grip, ran amuck through the courtyard in a panic, squealing loudly. It took several coachmen to capture the slippery creature and to return it to none other than Madame de Montespan.

"Would you look at *that*!" exclaimed the grande dauphine to her friend. "That woman always has to be the center of attention, but this is unfathomable! I know she wants to play the part of Circe, but I hope the king won't allow that animal into the ballroom!"

"Maybe it's one of her former lovers, transformed like Ulysses's companions into a pig. She *is* known to have that effect on men. I've known many courtiers who are less worthy than that poor animal of attending a royal function," said the duchess with a snort. Her own gown was made of green taffeta embroidered with a spray of vibrantly colored appliquéd flowers in the front, but the back was fashioned of plain black cloth. She wore a two-sided mask: the back of which displayed a frown. It was disconcerting to watch her move about from behind, as she seemed to be in constant retreat.

"I don't normally enjoy these festivities," said her friend, whose sober white attire gave little evidence that she had chosen the role of Athena. She wore a half mask and the silver scales of justice were painted across the top. "But I have to admit I would not have missed tonight's display. Do you see the Chevalier de Lorraine? His costume is simply outrageous!"

Liselotte turned her head toward the entrance and shook her head in exasperation. "How predictable! I was sure that once he'd found out what costumes Monsieur and I were planning to wear, he would have to make just such an unsubtle allusion to our mutual dislike."

The forty-year-old chevalier had donned a pink organza gown embroidered with bloodred flowers, a blond wig, and a bit too much rouge. His lips were a slash of scarlet under his black mask. The effect, nonetheless, was of a striking, though somewhat aging Persephone. Only his Adam's apple gave him away. As he ascended the Ambassador's Staircase with his entourage, he chanced to look up at Madame as she stared down at him. A flicker of sheer loathing passed over his countenance, but he managed to conceal it a moment later, as he greeted his nemesis with an exaggeratedly deep curtsy. He hurriedly turned away to take his place by the man who loved him unconditionally, and who staunchly protected his every move.

"Hades's protégé belongs in the underworld beside his lover. And I shall see that he gets there," Madame whispered to Victoire.

Meandering through the upstairs galleries, the crowd slowly flowed into the great Hall of Mirrors. Some of the ceiling frescoes were stilled unfinished, but the effect was breathtaking nonetheless. Each guest stopped in wonderment and silence for a moment at the magical vision. Every facet of the room had been designed with the intention of heightening and reflecting the honeyed radiance of a thousand candles. Glittering shards of shimmering light danced on gowns and jewels, masks and swords, bounced off mirrors and chandeliers, and onto the gleaming parquet. And in the midst of the splendor stood a statue of the king, covered in gold from head to toe, a radiant burst of sunrays crowning his head and his scepter. In the parallel mirrors his image appeared to be reflected indefinitely. The diminishing layers had a hallucinatory effect. Ever the master of the spectacular, the king had engineered a vision of the eternal.

Each of the ladies of the higher nobility had received a precious gemstone corresponding to the month of her birth. Montespan gave a contemptuous sniff when she set eyes on her opal bracelet, noting to her companion that Maintenon had received a diamond tiara rather than a topaz, which was the birthstone for November. Circe's piglet was nowhere in sight. It had been escorted out the door, much to the merriment of the crowd.

The musicians were tuning their instruments, and the discordant notes drawn on the stringed instruments, accompanied by an occasional burst from a horn or a flute, heightened the crowd's anticipation, as they lined up against the walls to leave room for the dance. In the center stood a movable raised platform bearing the king's throne. A trumpet blared and a martial beat announced Louis's arrival as he moved toward the center stage. The courtiers bowed in unison, like stalks of wheat in the wind. He gently kissed his diminutive wife's hand as she tottered off to the side and he ascended the throne. Lully, the master of ceremonies, stepped forward to announce,

"Tonight, let us cast aside our fears and our rivalries, and celebrate the peace and harmony that reign in our great nation and that bring us here together as Frenchmen under Louis the Great, the living embodiment of God's will." The crowd applauded politely as it waited restlessly for the fun to begin.

The King then signaled the Marquis d'Effiat to step forward with his nephew and Madeleine de Noailles. It was a true mark of royal favor to be asked to do so, and d'Effiat could not conceal his pride at the honor of announcing Robin's engagement to the entire court during a major celebration such as this one. It did not occur to him at the moment that the personal donation he had contributed to the future construction and ornamentation of the royal chapel might have more to do with this mark of esteem than any affection on the part of the king.

Mathilde and Catherine stood beside their respective mistresses during this ordeal, clenching each other by the waist. Madame glanced over at the bobbing snakes of her lady-in-waiting's Medusa head, feeling sorry for anyone so unwise as to become the target of the girl's turbulent disposition. A single tear from beneath Mathilde's mask had left a telltale streak on her powdered cheek. Having satisfied their fickle curiosity, the rest of the crowd resumed their conversations, except for a group of young men, presumably Robin's mates, who stared at him with undisguised derision. The latter shifted his weight uncomfortably from one foot to another, eager to leave the festivities and the mocking scrutiny of his peers, but he knew better than to think that he might escape the ball without a dance or two with his betrothed. He and Chrétien had made plans to slip out during the fireworks to meet with Mathilde and Catherine in the groves at the edge of the Grand Trianon, at the intersection of the Allée des Hâ-Hâ and the aptly named Allée du Rendez-Vous. He felt enormous trepidation at the thought of his encounter with Mathilde. He had no defense to offer for having put off the moment of truth, and now the cat was out of the bag.

Thinking that he might as well get his ordeal over with, Robin stepped up to his bride-to-be, and bowed slightly by way of an invitation to dance the gavotte. Madeleine greeted him with a smirk and a nod, not quite the demeanor he had expected. Perhaps she was not the docile fiancée everyone thought her to be. The woman was not an accomplished dancer—far from it—but her stiff posture belied the lustful look in her eyes. As Robin performed the courting ritual with a perfunctory smile etched on his face, he was acutely aware of Mathilde's penetrating stare, sharp as a dagger, directed at his back.

Having fulfilled his obligation, he turned toward Mathilde in an effort to appease her, but she abruptly turned away and left the room. Catherine was left chatting with a newcomer, an auburn beauty, whom he had never seen before. As a measure of spite, he interrupted their conversation to ask the girl to dance, barely acknowledging Catherine's presence. Unlike Madeleine de Noailles, Julie was a lithe and supple partner. Those standing about the room could not help gawking at the accomplished pair. What drew Robin to her the most power-fully, however, was her unwavering poise and her brazen stare. She appraised him from top to bottom with a complete lack of discomfiture, despite the fact that she was several years younger than he. Robin couldn't help imagining what she would be like in the throes of passion, as he lingered by her side. This reverie came to a sudden halt when his uncle abruptly appeared before him to remind him of his social duties.

Robin was again mindful of the hour and the need to leave the party at the appointed time. It would not be easy to escape unnoticed, as a cluster of well-wishers, who seemed to relish his mortification, had sidled up to him. He looked around to see if he could spot Catherine, but it seemed that she, too, had disappeared. As he was determining what to do next, he heard a loud thud followed by a squeal and stifled guffaws. Somehow, Madame de Montespan's pig had strutted back into the room. Surrounded by frenzied movement and noise, the animal had panicked and had darted across the ballroom floor, finding shelter beneath the ample crimson skirts of none other than Madame de Maintenon, who bellowed an unladylike curse as she tumbled to the floor. All heads were turned in her direction. Robin needed no further prompt to slip out of the room and into the night.

◆

Chrétien had been waiting for him by the terrace, beneath the windows of the Hall of Mirrors. He had been staring up at the resplendent ceiling and chandeliers on the first floor, which was all he could see from his vantage point. He was wondering if Robin would be able to make their rendezvous, considering the announcement of his engagement. Hearing the crunch of gravel on the walkway, he moved behind a pillar, unwilling to draw attention to his loitering. It was not Robin, but Madame's messenger Hermann Wendt, who stopped for a moment to check his timepiece by the glow of the windows.

Having waited a respectable amount of time, Chrétien gave up, muttering to himself, "If punctuality is the courtesy of kings, as they say, then Robin is certainly no gentleman!" The fog had gotten denser since his arrival at the palace, and he made his way with caution down the alleyway, following the vague ethereal glow of sparsely scattered lanterns lining the road like sentinels of the night. The muted crunch of carriage wheels on the pavement and the muffled sound of farewells marked the early departure of several, no doubt elderly, guests. In the distance he could distinguish the approaching steps of someone loping along, stopping occasionally to make his way in the dark. When Robin's face finally came into view, it was no more than two feet away, beaded with sweat, black curls matted down against his skin.

"Careful, there! You almost ran me over!" whispered Chrétien.

"I didn't bring a lantern, either, for fear of being seen, and I nearly twisted my ankle running in the dark. It was hard to slip out unnoticed, but I managed thanks to Circe's piglet," said Robin, gasping for breath.

"What the . . . ?"

"Don't ask! You wouldn't believe it anyway. So here I am! Let's hope the girls are still waiting. The weather isn't fit for man nor beast." Robin pulled his cloak tighter to his chest.

"I doubt whether they'll have turned back. They're quite the intrepid damsels from my experience! Caught them out in the woods in the middle of a downpour when first we met."

"Too intrepid for their own good, perhaps, or for mine for that matter. I'm afraid that tonight I'll have some explaining to do. Mathilde is in a frightful state, judging by her costume alone." Robin removed the Venetian bird beak mask that he'd pushed atop his head and cast it into the bushes.

"Be a good chap and leave me out of your domestic quarrels, mate," said Chrétien with uncharacteristic familiarity. He normally kept his distance from the upper class, but despite their differences, the two youths had formed a bond in their joint venture, like two complete strangers who sense a surprising, yet undeniable connection. Robin's arrogance had been bred in the bone, but strangely, he was not condescending toward the gamekeeper. He spoke to him with deference, as if to an equal, and Chrétien was sensitive to this treatment.

Tonight there would be little danger of being spotted by lovers seeking shelter and playing the two-backed beast in the labyrinth of bushes. The weather would have discouraged even the most arduous couples. Mathilde was the first to come into view by the light of a tiny lantern set on the ground along the path. She was fretfully pacing back and forth with knotted fists anchored to her slender hips. Catherine's soothing tones preceded her apparition in the dimly lit haze as the youths approached the designated spot. The girls seemed rather surprised to see them together.

"I see you've made great haste to be here on time!" said Mathilde spitefully. "We were about to give up hope. You must have had your hands full with your lovely bride-to-be. Congratulations are in order, no doubt."

"Mathilde, you've got to understand! I kept hoping my uncle would respect my wishes and break the engagement to Madeleine de Noailles. But the king's seal of approval and the public announcement tonight were the final blow. There's no going back now. You know I'm fond of you."

"Fond? I guess that says it all. I've loved you my whole life it would seem, and I've been your trusted companion throughout the years. When were you planning to tell me? My only consolation now is the social ridicule cast upon you by such a mismatch!" Tears welled up in Mathilde's eyes. Her mask was gone, but the wig was still in place.

As always, Mathilde's distress left Robin speechless. His

carefully prepared excuses seemed petty and shallow in the wake of the girl's devastating grief.

Chrétien and Catherine exchanged an apprehensive glance, eyeing each other with mutual understanding. The meeting was rapidly, though predictably, getting off track.

"Come now, let's accept the unavoidable. Robin was bound to be married sooner or later. I'm surprised his uncle put it off for so long. At least you've got nothing to fear in terms of Robin's affection for that wet noodle," said Catherine in an attempt to reconcile the two. She drew her arm around Mathilde's shoulder.

Chrétien knew better than to interject his humble opinion on the matter. He was well aware that his own father had ambitions to find him an acceptable match within the higher ranks of the palace servant staff in the not-too-distant future. And Chrétien was indeed a great catch with a promising future as head gamekeeper. He shuddered at the mere thought of being shackled to the likes of Sylvie with her brash ways and opulent bosom. His mind lingered on the memory of the exquisite taste of Catherine's parted lips and the willowy grace of her svelte body.

"All right. So be it! We've got business to attend to tonight, so let's get to it," said Mathilde finally, breaking the palpable tension. "Madame has sent her messenger Wendt on a fact-finding mission regarding the connection between Montespan and your uncle's circle of friends. It's been confirmed that the image on the cross is the conceit of your notorious forebear the Marquis de Cinq-Mars and a symbol of his debauchery. However, since the common denominator between the other owners of similar pendants seems to be a loathing of women, no one appears to understand why a woman might be in possession of one as well."

"Let's not forget the locket's inscription *Qui m'aime me suive*, which suggests a leader and his disciples. In short, a relationship of domination and submission. Montespan doesn't seem the type to submit to any man, whatever his orientation. During her prime she had the king in her power and used every means available to retain control of him," added Catherine.

"That's right. She used her connection with La Voisin to obtain aphrodisiacs, and it's even rumored that she poisoned her rival Mademoiselle de Scorailles, who was pregnant by Louis at the time. She only narrowly escaped the gallows by currying favor with the king." Mathilde appeared to have temporarily lost her bad humor, and Robin seemed visibly relieved.

"So let's assume then that she did the chevalier or d'Effiat a favor, for which she received a token of his gratitude. You might say the locket indicates an honorary membership in their group..."

"The Sacred Brotherhood of Glorious Pederasts, you mean," said Robin.

The girls, who had been exchanging ideas, now turned their heads in interest.

"It seems that you know a great deal more than we thought. We want your information, but first let's explore Montespan's role in all this. I don't believe she's bisexual, but she's suspected of murdering a woman she hated. I fail to see, however, how poisoning Scorailles, whose influence at court was limited to her fashion sense, would be perceived as a favor by your uncle's entourage," said Catherine, who had not acknowledged Robin's presence until then.

Chrétien finally spoke. "Wendt may be the only one with the freedom to come and go as he pleases, while remaining virtually invisible. Let's see where his investigation takes him. Speaking of the man, I saw him outside the palace this evening, checking his timepiece, while I was waiting for our friend here to disengage himself from the crowd."

Chrétien then told them how his own inquiries had led him to a dying woman on the edge of town, who had exposed Yves Roussin for the blackguard he was and the part he had played in the disappearance of several young boys.

"This gets more and more baffling as we go along," said Mathilde. The truth, if found, won't be simple. Maybe none of these things are connected. Do you assume then that the remains we found might have belonged to the victim of a child prostitution ring? Or might they be those of Roussin himself, whose usefulness had come to an end?" She shuddered, but not from the cold.

"Certainly not those of Roussin, who, as we speak, is probably miles from here," said Chrétien.

Or so we hope," Robin added. "I'll take it from here. As you know, this is a delicate matter that involves my family's reputation. I realized there was some connection when my mind was jolted by the resurgence of a childhood memory. I count on your discretion." He looked around the circle for the group's tacit consent.

"But matters are now in the hands of two of the most powerful and high-ranking women at court," said Catherine.

"And who happen to have a visceral hatred toward my uncle and the chevalier. By handing them the locket, you girls have handed the duchess a powerful weapon in her struggle to discredit them."

"What do you care? You've never been close to your uncle," said Mathilde, removing her wig and shaking her curls loose.

"I care little for his fate, especially in light of these horrid revelations, but I fear my own reputation will be tarnished through association if the matter ever gets aired. That's why I need to be kept informed every step of the way."

"Your reputation?" said Mathilde. "Your only reputation at Versailles is that of a lady's man and a dandy." Her tone was rising again to a higher pitch.

"Now, now! Can you two simmer down for a moment? Chrétien, do you have anything to add?"

"Well, the next day I came upon Roussin when I went back to the run-down shack to bring food and water to Margot Ledoux. In vain, because the man was digging her grave. I later managed to follow him through the woods and straight to the d'Effiat estate, where he slipped through the back gate. I'd been waiting for him for less than a half hour, when I witnessed none other than Robin emerge from the building dragging an unconscious Roussin in his wake. That is how we met and agreed to pull the worms from his nose, so to speak. Robin, you can take over from here."

Chrétien stepped back tactfully, closer to Catherine. He realized that his alliance with Robin was fragile and that the marquis's nephew had little knowledge of the people of the working class. Considering Catherine's active dislike of Robin, and Mathilde's emotional instability, he might easily be asked to back off from helping with the investigation.

Robin now came forward and after having sworn his coconspirators to secrecy, he recounted, with some reluctance, his venture into the dungeon, mentioning the enigmatic inscription, $VI + VI + VI = LIII$ on the wall, and a layout similar to the one depicted in Catherine's etching.

"The fifth day of the third month, *le cinq mars*, or rather five three, is inscribed on the throne in the etching, and seems to be a common denominator in both scenarios, since fifty-three inscribed in roman numerals could be an oblique reference to my great-uncle. But the rest of the equation escapes me."

No one noticed a rustling in the bushes, so intent were they on deciphering the coded mystery.

"Six, six, six is the devil's sign! Cinq-Mars is the devil," said Julie, who startled them all by popping out of the hedge. "Some secret meeting *this* is! It isn't hard to overhear you from twenty meters away. Especially you, Mathilde! I see you really do need my help. Just to explain my presence here, my cousin Catherine and her friend have enlisted me, in view of my special talents, to find out what I can from Lully."

"And so we meet again," said Robin.

Mathilde did not like the seductive undertone in his voice.

"Though I can't see what business it is of yours. There are already too many people involved in this investigation, and the danger of exposure increases with each additional person."

"My cousin can pass quite easily for a youth, and her fencing skills probably surpass your own. She's got enough courage for four grown men and is willing to serve as a spy, should that become necessary. Furthermore, she's well situated to do so, because her singing talent has already made her Lully's protégée and we all know of *his* involvement with the duke's entourage."

"Well, how can I refuse such an offer? Now that she, too, knows everything!" said Robin grimly. "But I feel like my attempt to keep this matter a secret is doomed to failure. You may think this is some kind of game, but if you'd seen the dungeon, or met Yves Roussin, you'd understand the risks you're taking. Mathilde and Catherine, you two can keep informing us about the duchess's findings on Montespan. Chrétien and I, who have more freedom to roam, will see what more we can learn about the activities of the brotherhood. Somehow, somewhere, we'll find the connection. As for Mademoiselle Julie, she can serve as a go-between and report back to me." Robin could not suppress a smile at the thought of future close encounters.

"Since when are you in charge?" asked Mathilde.

"Since I'm the only one with access to the dungeon," said Robin cavalierly.

As the church bell sounded one in the morning, the group decided it was time to disband before their absence at the ball became too noticeable. Julie left alone, as quickly as she had appeared. Robin and Mathilde lingered on to bicker a bit. As Catherine turned to leave abruptly, she almost collided with Chrétien, who was standing right behind her, a hair's breadth away. He slid his arm around her neck and deftly tucked a folded note under her bodice strap. She was too startled to utter a word, but by the time she had removed and unfolded the message, the young man had vanished into the woods.

WHO'S WHO?

$\mathcal{L}$iselotte awoke later than usual the day after the ball. She had a splitting headache and every joint in her body creaked as she heaved herself out of bed. She groaned as she rose onto her aching knees, steadying herself on the bedpost for balance, and waddled over to the washstand. Through swollen eyelids she scanned the tapestry on the wall opposite her ruelle, which featured the myth of Leda, whom Zeus had seduced and ravished by turning himself into a swan. The swan's beak was pulling at a translucent, gauzy cloth that barely covered the queen's well-rounded, rosy buttocks. The duchess sighed, almost inaudibly, at the thought that such passion would forever elude her. At that moment, Mathilde entered to announce the arrival of Hermann Wendt. Flustered by this unexpected visit, Madame summoned the girl to fetch her pink moiré morning gown and satin slippers while she hastily slipped on a wig. She was still fidgeting with the loose strands of hair jutting out from underneath the net when the courier was ushered in. Wendt's presence always had an unsettling effect on her, making her feel like a blushing schoolgirl. Knowing that this morning she was not at her advantage made her fumble all the more. Her voice, still hoarse from slumber, came out like a croak:

"Have you anything new to report, Herr Wendt?"

In lieu of an immediate answer, the servant held out his arm to her and opened his hand. The abruptness of the gesture startled her, but she gathered her wits when she realized he was merely returning the cross. Her imagination had gotten the better of her.

"Madame, I've made certain discreet inquiries, and I've had to listen to a great deal of idle gossip in the process. Sometimes it's hard to separate the truth from the abundant rumors. So far I have nothing new to report on Lorraine, aside from what we already know of his salaciousness and unsavory past."

"He seems to play his cards close to his chest. What a shame!" said the duchess.

"True," echoed Wendt, "but we all know of his alliance with d'Effiat and their mutual loathing for Monsieur's first wife, Henriette. I do have something new to report on the marquis, though, which dates back to the day before your predecessor's death, twelve years ago."

"But you've already told me of the suspicions surrounding her untimely passing and their presumed suppression, to which the king himself seems to have consented for the sake of preserving the peace." The duchess stuffed the pendant in the pocket of her dressing gown and patted it once or twice.

"Well, the devil's in the details. Henriette became ill only a few days after she returned to Saint-Cloud, following her journey to Dover with Louis to help negotiate a secret treaty with her brother, Charles the Second. Their objective was to return England to papist control, which thankfully for us Protestants, never materialized."

"I dare not imagine what kind of carnage would have ensued among our English neighbors!" said the duchess. Her chin quivered with indignation. "We'll have to stand by each other if we are to weather Catholic fanaticism in France, for which the chevalier's ancestors are largely to blame. The persecutions and the massacres of innocent Protestants by Guise's Catholic League have not been forgotten."

It was a great relief for the duchess to be able to confide in someone about her faith. Converting to Catholicism had not been easy for her, but at nineteen she had not been given a choice in the matter. Hermann Wendt had been at court several years before her arrival and had witnessed the scandal of Henriette's death. He had been a priceless adviser on the ways of French nobility and had eased her transition into the French way of life. She was thankful to her aunt Sophie for having recommended him to the king. Louis even trusted him with his most sensitive correspondence.

"If I may say so, Madame, you have the ill-advised habit of speaking your mind on such matters. But circumstances I've uncovered would require more caution and certainly more discretion. Allow me to advise you to cease your inquiries immediately. Perhaps my account will persuade you to do so," said Wendt stiffly. The many years he had spent at the French court had not affected his bearing or behavior.

"We shall see about that!" said the duchess sharply, a bit too sharply, she thought. Tempering her voice, she added, "Forgive me for the digression and please continue."

Wendt stood there woodenly, like a soldier, moving barely a muscle as he continued his account. "You may be aware that Henriette's initial fatigue the day after her trip quickly worsened, and that she drank a glass of chicory water as a remedy. That seems to have been the final straw. Although she insisted she had been poisoned, her doctors ruled it out and refused to administer the antidotes to arsenic."

"I've heard that her stomach problems had begun three years prior to her death and about a year after the chevalier had joined Monsieur's household. She was known to drink large quantities of milk, the common antidote for slow poisoning, which she suspected at the time. Nothing new there." Madame's voice was raw with disappointment.

"Perhaps not, but what I did learn, is that about an hour before she fell fatally ill, Henriette's valet had caught none other than the Marquis d'Effiat pottering about in her drinks cabinet. When her valet let his suspicions be known to the king, one of d'Effiat's stewards, a ruffian and a scoundrel named Yves Roussin, was taken into custody and put to the question. Although he confessed that he, d'Effiat, and Lorraine had poisoned Monsieur's wife, that confession, which was made under duress, was later fully retracted. The whole affair was hushed up, and the doctor who performed the autopsy ruled that Henriette had died of a perforated ulcer. What's highly suspicious is that the circumstances of her death were almost identical to those last year of your lady-in-waiting Marie-Angélique Scorailles de Fontanges, for whom Louis abandoned Montespan."

Madame slapped her forehead with the palm of her hand. "*Natürlich! There's* your connection! Hell hath no fury like a woman scorned! That she-devil is capable of anything! But do you believe that there might be some tangible proof of her involvement, aside from idle gossip, or that my husband had anything to do with his former wife's death?"

"Roussin swore, even under torture, that he did not. However, the king must have had his doubts, as his brother seemed totally unaffected by her untimely passing at the age of twenty-six."

"I doubt whether he would shed a tear at my funeral, either. And I know some who would dance on my coffin." Madame tapped a quick dance step to illustrate her point.

"That is why I urge you to beware, Madame! We certainly know of what your enemies are capable. As a cautionary tale, I've learned that when Henriette's stomach, which had swollen in the most extraordinary way after her death, was cut open for the autopsy, such a foul stench arose, that everyone in attendance had to step back and apply a mask against the evil odor. Long-term arsenic poisoning leads to liver breakdown and putrefaction, and is accompanied by stomach odor, green bile, and yellow vomit. A mere teaspoonful of arsenic would have been undetectable in Henriette's chicory water and could have killed her in a matter of hours, particularly if it wasn't the first time she'd ingested it."

"Yes, but if Monsieur's first wife's death was cause for suspicions, my own death would confirm them, would it not? D'Effiat and Lorraine would want to avoid reigniting those rumors at all costs."

"Are you willing to take that chance, milady? You have a son and a wee daughter to raise. And poison is not the only way to get rid of someone."

"That's why I need to be sure that peritonitis was not the actual cause of death. I can't accuse my enemies without grounds. My husband's protégés are very powerful men and they've already joined forces to cause harm to my reputation and to pressure me through my son. Montespan seems untouchable, but perhaps her former companion and purveyor of love potions might be persuaded to wag her tongue since there's no love lost between them. For a price, perhaps?"

Hermann Wendt let out a reluctant sigh. "I see, Madame, that you're bound and determined to pursue this matter against my strongest advice. Claude des Œillets has become a woman of independent means, and I rather doubt that any sum you would have at your disposal could persuade her to take such risks, even for the sake of revenge."

"This information is still all circumstantial. We have an eyewitness, quite possibly a coconspirator who recanted, a physician who pronounced natural causes and collusion between those closest to the king," said Madame with exasperation.

"Yes, and the lead physician was given a noble title a few months after the event, while the Chevalier de Lorraine was not only allowed to return to his residency at court but was also appointed to serve in the army at the rank of field marshal!"

"There's no rest for the wicked! What total disregard for the feelings of Henriette's brother King Charles! He was known to be very close to his sister and they both wept bitterly when she left England after her last fateful visit. Did she have a premonition of things to come, I wonder? Sometimes I feel like I'm walking in her shoes, but unlike the lovely Henriette, I have a tough hide." Madame put her fist to her chest and pounded it twice.

"Most likely she did. Right before she died, she asked her lady-in-waiting, Madame de Bordès, to send her letter case and her diaries to her brother Charles. But the documents in question mysteriously disappeared after they were seized by Monsieur."

The duchess scratched her earlobe. "We need to pursue two lines of inquiry, as I see it. First, we'll have to continue our investigation into the connection between d'Effiat, Lorraine, and Montespan, though they've covered their traces well, and second, we must find the alleged accomplice, Roussin."

"Of course, Madame de Montespan is quite capable of having acted alone, out of sheer spite. She had set her sights on the king way before his affair with Henriette or with his sister-in-law's lady-in-waiting, Louise de La Vallière. She was suspected of having hired a paid assassin to climb through La Vallière's window at the Palais-Royal. Fortunately for the intended victim, the Swiss guard on duty thwarted the assailant and saved her life. Because the aggressor lost his life in the skirmish, it was impossible to obtain any information as to his employer. Her involvement in the Affair of the Poisons and her death threats against the king and Fontanges later on, when his interest in her began to wane, make her our prime suspect."

"That's why it's vital to establish Montespan's connection with d'Effiat. Your findings are of utmost importance, because they confirm a tie that will lead us to Lorraine. I'm sure of it. However, it's the king who needs to be convinced beyond a doubt, or he'll once again be pressured into dismissing the charges." She rubbed her chubby hands together, as if preparing with relish for the fight ahead.

"I'll see what I can do to locate d'Effiat's steward, and I'll be sure to report back to you, Madame. But once again, I must urge you to beware for your own safety."

The duchess was deeply moved by the look of distress in Wendt's eyes. Despite their difference in rank, their bond went far beyond the ties of nationality and religious belief. It was one of those rare instances of authenticity in the midst of the perpetual masquerade at court and it gave her an occasional glimmer of faith in mankind.

Following Wendt's departure, Madame gazed a moment at her reflection in the mirror. She had regained her composure during her courier's visit, but now she was dismayed to see how ridiculous she looked with her blotchy skin and the strands of wispy hair that had escaped the postiche. She summoned Mathilde, who scuttled in from the antechamber, where she had been eavesdropping once again, under pretext of polishing the duchess's silver jewelry. Madame made a mental note to be more careful. The girl always seemed to be conveniently within earshot when sensitive matters were being discussed. As Wendt had reminded her, the walls had ears. Nonetheless, she trusted the girl and was not used to keeping secrets from her. The greatest service of a lady-in-waiting was, after all, that of confidante. Life at court was very lonely indeed, despite the constant hubbub. One had to be on the defensive all the time lest one's smallest gesture or comment be misinterpreted. She had certainly learned that from the gossip surrounding her reputed relationship with the Chevalier de Saint-Saens.

"As promised, I'm returning this cross to you for safekeeping, my dear," she said to Mathilde, as she pulled the object from her pocket. "But I forbid you to give it to Robin. It was never his to begin with, so he has no claim to the object. Losers weepers, as they say. It may be an important piece of evidence, but it would also appear that there are many facsimiles. One way or another, its primary value has been to further the investigation. I trust you overheard my conversation with Wendt."

Mathilde nodded unabashedly, hedging her bets. It would have been futile to dispute the fact that she had been listening in.

"I've made a discovery of my own," said Mathilde. "But I was reluctant to mention it in front of Wendt. He seems worried about your safety and might not appreciate the extent of my involvement, not to mention that of my friends. The fact is, though, that I've heard of this Roussin as recently as yesterday evening."

The duchess's eyebrows nearly rose up to her hairline. "How is that possible? I can't believe that even my lady-in-waiting appears to know more than I do. Do you know of his whereabouts? He is by all accounts the key witness to Henriette's murder. If he could be persuaded to testify once again, I would offer him a handsome reward."

"But he seems to have powerful protectors, Madame, and if he was directly involved in her poisoning he'll have d'Effiat and Lorraine to fear. In fact, I'm surprised that he hasn't already met with some accident." Mathilde had removed her mistress's wig and was skillfully rearranging the disheveled locks.

"It may be that his usefulness to them outweighs the threat of any revelations. And those two fiends no doubt feel emboldened by Monsieur's protection and their impunity thus far. They consider themselves invulnerable and above the laws of commoners. It'll be up to me to find their Achilles' heel." Madame looked at herself in the mirror. She looked frightful with only a hairnet.

Mathilde fumbled nervously with her bodice laces, twisting them around her index finger. "Things aren't that simple, Madame," she said. Her words faltered as she searched for the most tactful way to inform her mistress of her consorts and their bold initiatives. "By all accounts, he's fled the area in the interest of personal safety. However, like a bad coin he does seem to keep turning up. I am not sure that we've seen the last of him."

"You've proven to be very useful, Mathilde, but I wonder where you got your information."

Mathilde was saved from revealing her sources by the sudden entrance of the grande dauphine. Victoire barely waited for the doorman to usher her in. Her normally pallid cheeks were flushed with exertion, as she interrupted the conversation. "A word, my dear!"

Mathilde let out a sigh of relief. It was in her interest to avoid mentioning Robin's involvement, and the interruption would allow her to compose an adequate but evasive response. Madame wouldn't be pleased by the number of people involved in the investigation.

Madame's attention was for the moment concentrated on her compatriot. "What's the haste, Victoire?"

"I rushed ahead to warn you to prepare yourself. You've been summoned to a private audience with the king. Or should I say, semiprivate. Your husband and the chevalier will be in attendance." The dauphine beckoned Mathilde to finish coiffing the duchess.

"It's an evil wind that bodes no good. Do you have any idea what's afoot? This reeks of a conspiracy."

"That's why I hurried over. I know it's got something to do with your son Philippe, but that's all the information I could gather. In light of what you shared with me about your refusal to support Lorraine's cause, I fear that there is more mischief brewing. Arm yourself with fortitude, my friend. As I have not been summoned, I will not be allowed to attend the meeting and provide you with support. You'll be outnumbered and at a distinct disadvantage, especially if d'Effiat shows up."

"The thought of those two snakes makes my skin crawl," said Madame with a shudder. This is an ambush, and I may not have adequate preparation, nor enough ammunition for a decent counterattack. Mathilde, fetch me my gray silk dress with the ivory collar. No frills. I need to look the picture of gravity and self-restraint, despite the inner turmoil. Appearances are a form of armor."

A rap at the door announced the arrival of the king's messenger in full livery. His uniform bore the official emblem of the sun, and in his hand he carried the staff of Mercury. Madame reflected once again on the sovereign's affinity for ostentation and panache as she eyed him from head to toe.

"The king requests your immediate presence in his private cabinet, Your Highness."

By the time Liselotte had made it through a succession of vestibules and passageways to the Salle du Conseil, underarm sweat had formed dark circles beneath her armpits. Was it her imagination, or were the eyes in the portraits shifting to follow her down the hallway? She stopped a minute to wipe her brow and upper lip, gritted her teeth, braced for battle, and made her entrance. She steadied her eyes on the king as she made her reverence, then rose to stare down her opponents with the boldness she was known for. D'Effiat had indeed joined Lorraine, and the two flanked the Duke d'Orléans like bookends. Her husband looked small and vulnerable between them. She was itching to swat a barely concealed sneer right off the chevalier's face.

The king betrayed no emotion as he invited his guests to sit down. He himself preferred to remain standing. "I have sent for you to today to make the peace between you. I've heard certain allegations against the chevalier, and I have entertained the possibility of his guilt, but I have yet to pronounce myself on the charges against him, which are of seducing my legitimized son by Louise de La Vallière, Louis de Bourbon, Count du Vermandois. Louis has refused to incriminate you directly, Lorraine, but has admitted to relations with a certain Claude Puzin, the son of a minor officer. I have therefore determined to send my son into combat in Flanders, effective immediately. That should make a man out of him, if all else fails! Should he acquit himself honorably of his military duties, I shall consider rescinding his banishment from court. As for the chevalier, his fate is yet to be determined. But that is not what we are here to discuss today."

Once again, the chevalier had maneuvered a stay of execution.

But how? she wondered. And for how long?

At that moment Madame de Montespan was ushered into the room, to the duchess's great surprise. As usual, the woman made her customary grand entrance, fussing, gushing, and fanning her opulent bosom.

The king greeted her with pomp and led her by the arm to a seat strategically reserved for her next to the marquis.

"Now that all the interested parties are present, I have an important announcement to make. I am counting on your approval and support in this matter, which has been of concern to me for some time. My friends d'Effiat and Lorraine have urged my dear brother to consider a beneficial alliance between our royal houses. As you know, Madame de Maintenon was once the governess to my children by Madame de Montespan. She still harbors deep affection for them and ardently supports my desire to marry them off to their advantage."

Madame braced herself, for she suspected where this was heading. Despite their legitimization, she considered Louis-Auguste and Françoise-Marie de Bourbon to be well beneath her station. She caught a fleeting complicit smile that passed between the marquis and the king's former mistress in the corner of her eye.

"Madame, your husband has given this matter due consideration and is prepared to support the betrothal of your son Philippe, age eight, to my daughter Françoise-Marie, age five. Furthermore, he is willing to entertain the prospect of a further alliance between your daughter, Elisabeth Charlotte, age six, and my son by Madame de Montespan, Louis-Auguste, age twelve. As you know, he is my favorite, and I have appointed him Duke du Maine and d'Aumale, Prince de Dombes, and Count d'Eu. Such a marriage can only be to your daughter's advantage, though at this point your husband and I are still disposed to entertain an offer from the Duke de Lorraine on behalf of his son Léopold, currently residing in Vienna. Especially because my son has shown little enthusiasm at the prospect of such an arrangement." The king smiled stiffly.

The nerve! she thought.

All eyes now turned toward the duchess, as she spoke with as much dispassion as she could muster. But her inner fury made her forget all sense of self-preservation. Her nails dug into the palms of her clenched hand, nearly drawing blood, as she cleared her throat.

"You all look to me for my consent, so it would seem that I am the last to know of this arrangement, which is the latest in a series of conspiracies against my good name. It pains me to witness how little regard my husband has for our children's reputation. Of course, I know he has been biased against me by his cohorts, who've evidently been working behind my back to curry favor with you, Your Majesty. You ask my opinion, for what it's worth, which is very little indeed. I know that my role here is purely *pro forma*, but if I had my way, such a mésalliance would only happen over my dead body! The only ones to gain from such a mismatch would be Madame de Montespan's illegitimate bastards. There, I've spoken my peace."

"May I remind you that they are my children, too! I could have you placed under house arrest for disloyalty," replied the king, as her adversaries gloated in silence.

Madame knew she had crossed the line when she saw the scowl on his face and heard the rage in his voice. Her devotion to her children was her supreme *raison d'être*. Even through her clouded judgment, in the back of her mind she was aware that she should have held her tongue. To regain the king's favor would require an act of extreme self-abasement.

"I beg your forgiveness, Your Majesty." The words seemed to stick to her throat. "Please allow me to withdraw from the present company for reflection on the matter. I hope that we can discuss this in private at your earliest convenience."

"Very well, this meeting is adjourned," the king replied abruptly, and turned away.

Madame flew to her chambers in a state of utter distress. The grande dauphine, who had been waiting in an adjoining salon, could barely keep up with her.

"Slow down, Liselotte! Such haste will get you nowhere. Tell me what happened in there! I can only presume that you didn't heed my advice to proceed with caution?"

"I will tell you by and by, but first I must write to my aunt Sophie. The letter must go off within the hour."

Once alone, Madame took out her fountain pen and began chewing nervously on the wooden tip, as was her habit, before putting it to paper.

My dearest Aunt Sophie,

My trusted Wendt has been sent for regarding a family inheri-

tance matter. He is leaving for Paris tomorrow, there to meet his uncle Harling, who has traveled here from Germany. I seize the opportunity to inform you in secret of my latest misadventures here at court. One can never be too vigilant when it comes to such affairs. Now, more than ever, discretion is advised.

I must admit, my dearest auntie, that I have suffered considerable torment for some time now, which I try to hide as best I can. I have finally understood why the King suffers the presence of d'Effiat and Lorraine, despite his rather transparent dislike of the men. They have by all appearances agreed to convince my husband to humbly beg His Majesty to marry his two bastards by Montespan to our own son Philippe, and daughter, Elisabeth! I am afraid that my response to this was rather undiplomatic, to say the least, and I fear that I have abruptly fallen out of favor with the great man. Not that my credit with him was abundant in the first place. That Saint-Saens rumor still haunts me and my attempts to avoid the presence of my imputed lover have only backfired by fueling even more tongue-wagging. Anyhow, it will take eating a lot of humble pie to set matters right, if all my bridges haven't already been burned. But I cannot bear to be humiliated in front of those two fiends and their ally Montespan. If the king has his way, my poor daughter will have to marry that hideous gimp the Duke du Maine, and my son, who is fourth in line to the throne, the illegitimate Françoise-Marie de Bourbon, who is better known as Mademoiselle de Blois. Everyone conspires against me, including that old crone Maintenon, who for once sees eye to eye with the king's former mistress. Don't forget that when she was still Madame Scarron, she raised those bastards of his, and she loves the vicious little come-by-chance Louis as if he were her own son.

So you can well imagine my worried mind at the thought of my daughter marrying far below her rank, while Montespan's girl is to marry a prince of the blood. But I can tell you that even if he were of legitimate birth, rather than the issue of a double adultery, I wouldn't want the little duke as my son-in-law, nor his sister as my son's wife, because Maine is so horribly ugly and handicapped, with one leg shorter than the other. And his physical defects are not even remotely redeemed by his character, for he has so many less visible flaws. Although only twelve, that spoiled brat is as self-centered as the devil and generally of a sour disposition. His sister, though much more pleasant and gracious, suffers from poor health, and her eyes are so weak that I fear she will soon go to blind. Moreover, they are both the offspring of the most mean-spirited, evil, and debauched bitch the world has ever known. I leave you to imagine how little I desire such a marriage.

Liselotte stood up for a moment to stretch, in an effort to relieve the tension that had built up inside her since her meeting with the king. Her favorite portrait by Pierre Mignard was suspended above her writing desk. It represented the duchess in her favorite brown velvet hunting gown with light blue sleeves. Her two children were at her side, Elisabeth in blue brocade gently leaning her cheek on her mother's lap, while her son Philippe, standing to her left in a red taffeta dress and cap, could have easily been mistaken for a girl with his lovely locks. She wiped a tear from her eye at the thought of her beloved firstborn son, Alexandre-Louis, who had not lived past his third year, and at the visceral dread of her surviving children's possible fate. In the painting, the duchess was reaching for a flower from a lush arrangement of roses, peonies, and lilies in a blue enamel vase on the table to her right. A sword in an ornate cloisonné sheath on top of a book—a Bible perhaps — rested on a cushion at her feet. Copies of the portrait had been given as gifts to a few loyal friends, despite her self-critical references to its depiction of her "bear-cat-monkey" face in her correspondence. But she had little time to spare before Wendt's imminent departure, so she sat back down to resume her outpouring of woe.

. . .

The worst part is that I dare not speak of these matters to my husband, for whenever I utter the slightest complaint, he turns around and tattles to His Majesty, exaggerating my every word, thereby incurring the king's displeasure. I have no recourse in the matter and I am wrought with inner turmoil and anguish. Every time I see those little bastards, my stomach turns and my blood boils. Imagine, my dear, how loath I am to see my only son and daughter be the victims of my cruelest adversaries, who seek to harm me daily with their evil gossip. Rumor has it that d'Effiat has been promised a dukedom, and the chevalier a rather handsome sum of money. At present, of course, I know why. Meanwhile, they are praised to the heavens and treated with respect, whereas I should consider myself fortunate to be allowed to exist. These grievances are not the result of my humors or my spleen but of very real essential concerns. What could be more distressing than to witness your own poor children being sacrificed to your enemies' ambitions? It is the most painful thing one could ever experience! My insolent response to the king today makes me fear that I may be exiled, for my husband has already alluded to such an eventuality in the past.

Fortunately, I have my compatriots Wendt and Marie-Anne Victoire as steadfast allies. I know that you and I both had other ambitions when we tried to negotiate a match between your daughter, Sophie Charlotte, and the grand dauphin when he came of age. However, now I see that her betrothal to the future king of Prussia is much more advantageous to her (if somewhat less prestigious) and she won't have to suffer the hypocrisy and the xenophobia of the court of Versailles. Furthermore, the king's legitimate successor is an infantile half-wit, whose grandparents, Louis XIII and Anne of Austria, were as closely related as half siblings. The inbreeding at this court is simply outrageous. My friend Victoire, though ugly as sin, is highly intelligent and a breath of fresh air here at Versailles. Her son Louis, who was born two months ago, seems for the moment to have no congenital defects. As for your own son, Georg of Hanover, there is the remote possibility of his succession to the English throne, providing, of course, that the country remains Protestant.

What else can I tell you? I don't really know. This court has become so dreary with its continual religious hypocrisy and pretense of Christian devotion that it's downright unbearable. People are pestered, maddened, and exhausted to the bone marrow by attempts to lead them down the path of righteousness. And who better to lead them there but the most malevolent miscreants such as d'Effiat and the like. As for Maintenon, I can assure you that the king has never in his life had a passion equal to the one he has for her. It's quite curious to observe them when they're together. Should she be away for a moment, he cannot stand to wait more than fifteen minutes before hastening to her side to whisper some sweet nothing in her ear, even though they are practically joined at the hip all day long. That woman is a niggardly she-devil, fawned over and cajoled by all, but liked by few. She will find any opportunity to disparage and lash out at the grande dauphine, whose character is beyond reproach, in order to assert dominion over the poor woman, who has tried time and again to ingratiate herself with her. Such is the current dismal state of affairs at court. I'll stop there, so as to have time to remit this letter into the trusted hands of Herr Wendt.

Thereafter, I am summoned to the chapel to listen to Les Ténèbres by Charpentier. It has got to be the most profoundly tedious and insipid piece of music in existence!

But that's all for now, except to assure you that wherever I may be, and however I may feel, happy or distressed, dead or alive, I remain your loving and devoted niece, Liselotte.

(Versailles, October 4, 1682)

Madame quickly folded the letter and sealed it. She rang for Mathilde, who had been busy in an adjacent chamber removing a stubborn splotch of ink from the sleeve of one of her mistress's gowns.

"Make haste, my dear, and bring this to Wendt before his departure for the city. But then hurry back. Immediately after the church service and those long-winded chants of lamentation, I need to see you about this man Roussin you mentioned earlier."

The duchess picked up her breviary and made her way to the door, almost tripping over one of her terriers.

A SHOT IN THE DARK

*M*onday morning brought rays of filtered light streaming through the windows. Mathilde was almost happy again, going about her morning tasks. For some irrational reason, she had renewed hope at the thought of her ties to Robin. She had managed to accept the inevitability of his engagement with the knowledge that she would have no true rival in Madeleine de Noailles. She went downstairs to fetch dried lavender and warm water for Madame's ablutions. As she turned the corner to the kitchens, a hand reached out and grabbed her. Startled, she wrenched her arm away, only to see it was Robin.

"Ouch! How dare you manhandle me!"

"Come with me. We need to talk!" he replied tersely.

Mathilde's heart skipped a beat. The opportunity for a private meeting with Robin outweighed all commonsense considerations. They hastened through the labyrinthine under-belly of the palace, until they came to an exit leading to the park. The warmth of daylight radiated down the maiden's head and shoulders, and Robin turned to rediscover her sun-drenched beauty. Her ginger hair sparkled in the light and her freckled skin seemed to glow from within, opalescent and enticing. Once they had reached a secluded spot, Robin pulled her toward him slowly, draping his cloak around her. He removed her shawl without a word, taking his time to unlace her bodice. Shock waves ran up and down Mathilde's body, while Robin licked the moisture off her neck and breasts, inhaling the scent of her skin. The air seemed so charged with electricity that it felt opaque, almost too heavy to breathe in. As the couple fell to the ground, Robin positioned Mathilde on top of him, thrusting gently at first, then, as she opened her legs to receive him, with greater urgency. Mathilde cried out as waves of pleasure took hold of her body, until she collapsed on Robin's chest, her tousled hair tumbling around his face. Autumn leaves of gold shimmered through the russet veil. He had the presence of mind to pull out before he came, since Mathilde was still in a trancelike state of euphoria.

Once she had stopped trembling and was better able to gather her wits, the girl wondered how she and Robin could be at odds one moment, and, once a certain physical boundary was crossed, drawn together by a seemingly irrepressible magnetic force. She was intuitively aware that Robin felt the same, and it soon became apparent that the reason for his visit had not been, at least initially, to make love to her. He extricated his arm from beneath her shoulders and propped himself up on one elbow.

"So I've come once again to ask you to return the cross," he said, in a gently persuasive voice, pushing a stray strand of hair behind her ear. Although basking in the afterglow of their embrace, Mathilde reminded herself of Madame's admonition and of Robin's recent erratic behavior to summon all the strength she could muster at this moment of weakness and tender affection.

"I'm sorry, Robin, but although it has been returned to me, I have strict orders to keep the pendant until further notice."

Robin's dark eyes became darker yet, and his hooded gaze instantly returned, transforming his demeanor. The distance between them opened up again like a giant chasm, but his voice was more disappointed than angry this time.

"How dare you go back on your word, Mathilde!"

"Unfortunately, I now realize my word was not mine to give," she replied defiantly. She stood up and began brushing off her skirts. "I owe allegiance to Madame."

"And what do you owe me? Don't I count for something? Doesn't our long-standing friendship count for something more than that?" There was an unfamiliar ring to his voice. Was it an admission of defeat?

"Stop, Robin! Don't try to make a case! You yourself know what it's like to be subject to your family's will. I've forgiven your engagement because I know it wasn't a matter of choice. You, too, owe obedience to your uncle."

"I can't understand why in the world you had to go blabbing, first to Catherine, who can't be trusted to keep a secret, and then to the duchess," said Robin grudgingly.

"Catherine is my best friend, and she's extremely loyal. She was concerned for my safety, as you would be, too, if you had any true feelings for me," she replied.

"Perhaps you deserve better than me, Mathilde. I may not have the makings of a faithful lover, and this may be of little consolation to you, but one thing I know for sure is that our bond is stronger than any feeling that will ever tie me to another woman." Robin secured the laces of his britches and adjusted his waistcoat while checking for any unexpected observers.

"It's better than nothing," replied Mathilde with a sigh. "But now it's high time for me to return to service. Madame requires my presence. She fell asleep during the Lamentations last night and will want to see me first thing this morning. She has questions on Roussin."

"Best not to mention my name. Have Chrétien be the one to inform her of the encounter. He's a neutral party in this affair, and if anyone has the ability to sniff Roussin out of his lair, it's the groundskeeper. That is, providing that vermin is still lurking in the vicinity."

"A neutral party? He most certainly has an eye for Catherine, and she herself seems to be suspiciously on the defensive whenever Chrétien's name is mentioned. I'm worried that she's fallen for a commoner."

"He's a good man from what I can tell. But that doesn't justify a breach in convention. You may have to make sure that they stay away from each other."

"Like you and I should do?" replied Mathilde with a smile, as they headed off in opposite directions.

◆

"You're late! Do I have to remind you that you're *my* lady-in-waiting? I shouldn't be the one to wait on *you*," said the duchess with vexation. "I am far too indulgent a mistress, and were it not for my affection for you and your dear deceased mother, I would have replaced you with Agnès, the chambermaid. At least she does something useful from time to time, such as feed my pups." As she spoke, Madame extended her arm to be licked by her darlings. They gathered around, hopping up and down, and hoping for some dainty morsel to fall from her hand. Mathilde had the urge to kick them aside, but restrained herself under the circumstances.

"I regret, Madame. I was detained by a matter of urgency." She smiled at her own private joke.

"Well, I can't think of anything *more* urgent than to locate this man Roussin. I do apologize for falling asleep last night. What do you know about that scoundrel? And how did you come about this information?"

Once Mathilde had delivered a truncated account of the previous night's revelations, she ended by explaining Chrétien's vital role in hunting down Roussin, as well as the possibility of the latter's escape.

Madame frowned as she asked, "And how do we get our hands on this Chrétien? Who is he, anyway?"

"He is the son of Jean Desforges, the head groundskeeper, Madame."

"You mean that strapping young man with the golden locks? I've noticed him at the hunt. He looks like a Nordic god!"

Mathilde reflected on the relativity of taste, as she answered, "Yes, that's him. And wherever you find Catherine, he's certainly not far away."

"Really, now? You astonish me! He has excellent, if inappropriate taste. Wendt is in Paris for a day or two, so I'll have to ask Catherine to bid Chrétien to come to me. That is, if what you say is true. As soon as possible. Now hop to it!"

"Of course, Madame. I'll ask her to send for him." Mathilde curtsied and rushed out, her ruffles catching and rustling through the doorway. She was relieved not to have had to mention Robin's involvement in the whole affair, knowing that her mistress would have certainly disapproved. Nonetheless, she felt like her half-truths were a betrayal she would soon regret.

Once outside, Mathilde stopped for a moment to reflect on the fragile alliance that bound the young people together. She didn't trust Julie one bit, despite Catherine's confidence in her cousin's extraordinary pluck and her talent as a chameleon. As for Chrétien, she would not have given that upstart the time of day were it not for his usefulness, and she was increasingly suspicious of his intentions toward her friend. And on what, she asked herself, did she base her allegiance to Robin? She certainly wasn't blind to his mercurial volatility. For reassurance, she dug her hand into her pocket to fondle the cross, only to find it wasn't there. Seized with panic, she checked the satin pouch at her waist, which seemed intact. Her thoughts immediately turned to Robin. Had he somehow managed to fumble through her pocket during their lovemaking? Had the amulet fallen to the ground? She ran back to the bower and fell to her knees to inspect the ground, frantically combing through the fallen leaves.

"What in the world are you up to now?" To Mathilde's relief, it was Catherine's voice, filled with gentle mockery. "I saw you suddenly take to your heels, just when I was on my way to see you."

"It's a catastrophe, Catherine!" said Mathilde, looking up at her friend. Madame finally returned the cross to me and ordered me to keep it safe. But it has almost immediately disappeared into thin air!"

"Calm down, my dear. Let me help you try to think back to what you've been doing and where you've been since your mistress gave it back."

Mathilde blushed down to her roots, and Catherine immediately understood the meaning of her discomfort.

"So you've been at it again with Robin? And out here, practically in the open! Have you lost your senses?" Catherine shook her head in disbelief.

"May she who is without sin cast the first stone! I've seen how you look at Chrétien."

"So you think Robin's missed his vocation as a pickpocket?" said Catherine smugly.

"It's possible, but he's not quite devious enough to do such a thing and how would he have known it was in my pocket?"

"Well, I presume he was fondling you and may have simply had the dumb luck to chance upon it. Because otherwise, you're right: he isn't smart enough to be conniving. I've rarely met someone as transparent."

Mathilde shrugged off the slight to her lover. In some ways her friend was right, Robin wasn't duplicitous.

"When and where did you get hold of the cross? Try to remember with whom you've stopped to consort since then . . . not in the biblical sense, of course," said Catherine with a smirk.

"Yesterday, once Madame had returned it to me, she sent me off hastily with a letter for Wendt to take to Paris. Once it was in safe hands, I had dinner in the dining hall, and came back to prepare her bedclothes. She was so done in from those dreary Lamentations that I had a hard time dragging her to bed. She didn't even want to eat the candied orange I'd brought to her from the table for a light collation. As soon as she'd nodded off, I joined you and the grande dauphine in the library. This morning Robin was the first person I saw, and he practically dragged me outdoors . . . well, you can guess the rest!"

"And you were all too willing to follow!"

"All right, that's enough with the high-and-mighty tone, Catherine. I may simply have dropped the cross in my haste to find you, and I'll have to retrace my steps. Anyway, Madame has a mission for you and one that I dare say you will find to your liking. She has orders for Chrétien to attend to her immediately, and I suggested that you might be better able to find him than I."

"You'll have to explain yourself first. Why make that assumption? And what in the world does she want with the groundskeeper?"

"*C'est un bon orateur, qui se convainc lui-même!* You're more skillful at convincing yourself than me! I won't dignify the first question with an answer. Your interest in Chrétien has been all too obvious. Even Robin has vaguely taken notice, and as you say, he's not the most discerning person in such matters."

Mathilde's face broke into a huge grin that revealed a slight and very sensual gap between her two front teeth.

"You have an awful lot of nerve!" said Catherine, without much conviction. On some level she blushed to think that even the mention of Chrétien's name was pleasurable. "And your mood swings are wildly out of control these days. I never know which Mathilde I will be dealing with from one minute to the next. The jealous, jilted lover; the childish prankster; or the loyal friend? I would pity Robin if he deserved it."

"All right, let's bypass the coy objections and diversions and get to the point! The duchess wants your friend to find Roussin. His tracking abilities should serve him well, as he knows the lay of the land. Chrétien and Robin frightened him off, and he'll have to try to lure him back if he's still in the area. Madame wants him questioned regarding some information that Wendt recently shared with her. She thinks that Roussin was somehow, directly or indirectly, involved in the poisoning death of Henriette, Monsieur's first wife. He was apparently questioned at the time of the murder and confessed to aiding and abetting d'Effiat and Lorraine, but later he recanted and the whole affair was hushed up."

"The plot thickens! Well, I'll see what I can do, but if you think that I go loitering around in the hopes of catching a glimpse of Chrétien, you're sorely misguided. Unlike someone I know who goes mooning around the palace in search of d'Effiat's nephew."

"I'm sure that you have some idea where to find him, so I'll leave you to it! Have fun, my dear!" said Mathilde teasingly. And off she ran. Little did she know that Catherine knew exactly where to find Chrétien.

When Mathilde got back to Madame's chambers, her mistress was pacing the floor.

"How long can it take to find your best friend? I am still not dressed and I need to attend court so that people don't spread false rumors behind my back any more than they already do! Especially under the present circumstances I'll need to present a placid countenance. This is the second time today that you've been tardy. You had better have a good explanation!"

"I apologize, Madame," said Mathilde with an exaggerated curtsy, bending deeply to hide her discomfiture. "I had to track down Catherine, who'd been sent on an errand by the grande dauphine." The girl knew that the truth in this case was not an option.

"Very well! As long as you managed to give her my orders."

"I have, Madame. As I said, it shouldn't take her long to find the groundskeeper's son.

"*Ausgezeichnet!* In the meantime, the hunting party this afternoon will be an opportunity to bend the king's ear in the aftermath of our disagreement. The man doesn't take lightly to being challenged, but I've learned that he's more accommodating in a *tête-à-tête* than in public. Thank God that his meddlesome ex-mistress and that old shrew Maintenon don't hunt, due to their 'delicate' constitutions. Even so, it isn't easy to keep up with him, let alone speak to him in relative privacy." Madame looked out the window toward the forest and the sunlight captured her profile and chased shadows into the furrows of her brow.

"What does Madame wish to wear for the occasion?" Mathilde went over to a stack of clean linens that Agnès had not yet tucked back in the armoire.

"The weather is cloudless and bright, but there's a brisk undercurrent in the wind. Why don't you bring me my light blue woolen cape? It brings out my eyes and I'll need to use every asset within my limited range to persuade the king," said Madame with a slight grunt of satisfaction.

◆

Catherine kept repeating to herself that she needed at all costs to keep a safe distance from Chrétien. In the absence of temptation, she had always been what was known as a virtuous maiden. But she was beginning to seriously question her own merit. The idea that she suddenly not only had free rein but actual orders to seek him out, had her in a state of bewildered turmoil. If people could read her so easily, why couldn't she read herself? And if they disapproved of an attachment to a commoner, why send her in harm's way? Her heart pounded and her blood rose at the mere thought of her eagerness to search out Chrétien. Naturally, he would assume that she'd read his note, and of course she had done so. It would have taken a superhuman effort not to. He had asked her to meet him at three in the afternoon, during the hunt, in the labyrinth by the fountain of the Council of Rats, were they had first kissed. She had resolved to withstand the pull of his presence, but this excuse to see him, seemed like a gift of fate. She removed her jewelry and laid aside her lace collar and head-dress, so as to appear guileless in her simple black satin dress. Although she did this so that Chrétien would not mistake her intentions, she felt as though she were preparing for a sacra-ment. She tied her hair up in the least seductive manner she knew how, unaware that this simply exposed the curve of the downy nape of her neck. Then, when the time was right, she set out on her assignment.

By the time she reached the fountain her cheeks were flushed and her brow was moist. No one was there to meet her and her stomach sank with disappointment. Could Chrétien have been toying with her? It only took a few minutes for humiliation to replace anticipation, but as she prepared to leave, a rustle startled her. Chrétien had been there the whole time, hidden behind a column. He seemed even more hand-some than before, colored, she thought, by her own desire.

"I was wondering whether you'd come, or even bother to read my message," he said gently.

"Before you get any fanciful ideas, it's the Duchess d'Orléans who sent me to find you. She wants you to track down Yves Roussin so that she might question him herself." Catherine's tone was terse, in an attempt to conceal any emotional response to the young man's presence.

"So you're not here for me?" he said with that grin of his that could disarm even the most hostile listener. "Come here a moment. There's no harm." He drew her near and the two felt no further need to speak. They simply stood there, wrapped in each other's presence, savoring the stolen moment, the forbidden contact.

Catherine was surprised by her own boldness, as she reached up to caress Chrétien's face, her other hand lingering on his shoulders, then venturing down his torso toward his belt. He pressed himself up against her and she could feel he was hard. He bent forward, touching his lips to her forehead, then parted her lips with his tongue. She was caught up in the heat, all of her resolve melting as she lost herself in her wanting.

A sudden commotion in the distance brought the lovers back to their senses. It seemed to come from the depths of the forest, growing louder and louder.

"Something must have happened at the hunt," said Chrétien. He grasped Catherine gently by the waist and looked at her with a smile. "To be continued, my lovely, or so I dare hope." With that he adjusted his waistcoat and shirt, and darted off.

"Don't forget your orders!" Catherine called after him.

"How could I, given the messenger?" he called back.

Catherine found herself standing alone in wonderment. She felt no guilt at all, to her great surprise. She lingered a bit by the fountain and started down the path toward the castle. As she approached, she saw people running from all directions and converging at the garden-side entrance to the château. Her own mistress, the grande dauphine, stood there barring the entrance to the curious. As she sidled up to the door, she was ushered in. At the same moment Mathilde came running up, out of breath.

"What news of my friend?" the dauphine asked.

"A minor graze, milady. She's in a foul temper, but not much pain. The king's physicians are in attendance."

"That may do her in yet!" replied Victoire. "I must go to her side and see to her safety. You two stay here to keep out the riffraff until I send my personal guards to the door." She scurried off as fast as decorum and her ample skirts would permit.

"What the devil?" said Catherine.

"Where indeed have you been? You've missed all the action!"

"I was simply attending to the errand you sent me on, so don't blame me!"

"I don't know how you managed to find Chrétien so quickly, but it's your affair, after all!"

"Stop it! What's been going on?"

"Well, Madame was nearly killed during the hunt. According to Saint-Saens, the only witness, she tried to corner Louis so as to garner his attention. She was eager to discuss her son's fate with the king. The king, however, was distant and unmoved by her pleas. Madame de Maintenon and Madame de Montespan had cautioned him not to speak to Madame in private. They'd given strict orders to Louis's entourage not to allow the duchess to approach him under any pretext."

"I can't see her being deterred by that!" said Catherine.

"Of course not. She's a skillful rider, and she managed somehow to ambush Louis a second time when he was in a clearing by edging her way into the gulley between His Majesty and the other members of the hunting party."

"So how was she injured? Was the king involved?"

"Saint-Saens claims that Louis ordered her to let him pass. As she was backing away, an arrow grazed her arm and got stuck in the tree behind her. There's little doubt that it was intended for her, unless, of course it was a stray arrow or shot by a very poor marksman. They're searching for the culprit right now."

"If it was unintentional, I pity the poor bastard who misfired. He'll no doubt be put to the question. I'd confess to anything under torture." Catherine shuddered at the thought of such a fate.

"Madame, of course, will suspect the chevalier and his coterie. It's nigh on impossible to snoop around incognito at this court. I'm quite sure that the battle lines have been drawn."

"She's lost the king's protection and is now quite vulnerable. She may have to rely more and more on us and on her dear Wendt, as we're of little interest to gossipmongers. This means, ironically, that she'll also be relying indirectly on one of her worst enemies' nephew. Are you sure of Robin, Mathilde? He may do more harm than good."

"He may not love me as I do him, but I trust him not to want to harm me or my mistress. I'm the only one who knows his tender side. He's selfish, but not a monster. He's also the only one to have free reign in his uncle's estate. He's a very useful ally, but Madame would probably have her reasons to suspect him. She mustn't be informed of his participation in the inquest under any circumstances."

The girls' muted conversation was interrupted by the arrival of the grande dauphine's guards, who crossed their halberds to bar the growing throngs of onlookers. Relieved of that duty, they rushed to Madame's chambers, where they managed to press through the crowd of courtiers assembled to watch the physicians carry out their duties. And the two doctors were doing that with all the dignity and composure of their station, aware of the auspicious opportunity to display the full extent of their erudition. The elder, hence supposedly the wiser of the two, solemnly unscrewed a jar of leeches and pulled one out with deliberate flair, like a priest unveiling the host to the congregation. Madame, whose wounded arm was resting on a pillow, revealing a nasty scratch, was shielding her brow with the other in an overly dramatic pose. She shuddered as the leech was placed on her inner arm. The second physician, whose long, pointed beard hadn't yet acquired the whiteness of wisdom, was bending over Madame's plump ankle, scalpel in hand. A small amount of blood spattered into the white porcelain bowl. Both men approached to sniff and taste the sample. They looked at each other with an air of cryptic understanding and nodded to the crowd. A few members clapped politely at the performance, and began to leave as soon as the spectacle had come to an end.

Victoire remained at her friend's side, holding her hand and whispering to her in the deep, comforting tones of their mother tongue. The king had already left, putting in a perfunctory appearance of support to his sister-in-law, but Maintenon had waited for him at the door impatiently, glaring at the duchess and watching Louis with a hawk's eye. The duke, Madame's husband, had brought along d'Effiat and a gaping Chevalier de Lorraine, a real slap in the face to his wife. Fortunately, they, too, seemed in a rush to leave.

"Don't just stand there, Mathilde!" said Liselotte gruffly. "Bring me my pups, my sweet little companions."

"But, Madame, are you sure? Won't they be a nuisance? You've been ordered to rest."

"Don't question me, girl! *Gott im Himmel!* What a defiant attitude you have."

Mathilde returned with the dogs. They jumped and tumbled all over the bed to the duchess's great delight. She seemed to have forgotten her injury momentarily.

The dauphine's voice brought her back to reality. "My dear,

if this mishap was no accident but an intentional act of aggression, we need to discuss additional safety measures. Without Louis's protection, you'll be a sitting target. Just take cover for a while and don't attract attention with your inquiries. You know that word is out of your attempts to discredit your husband's entourage, and maybe even the duke himself."

"Where is Wendt when I need him?" complained the duchess, grasping her friend's hand in the manner of an overly dramatic supplicant.

"He should be back from his day trip to by now. But despite appearances, the man is in no position to help you in any way against a powerful enemy."

"What I do know is that I'm on the verge of proving the chevalier's involvement in the murder of Monsieur's first wife, Henriette, and I won't give up until I do. Those fiends know that I'm onto them, and they're trying to blackmail me into submission by threatening my children. Poisoning me would be too conspicuous a solution, although I have my tasters on high alert. The hunting incident shows their desperation. It was very risky, and a second such attempt would again point a finger to their obvious involvement. They'll have to regroup, but in the meantime, I'll make it appear that I have given up out of fear of reprisal, while my younger allies continue to investigate in the shadows. One thing I swear by all that's sacred, however, and that is that I shall never capitulate. It's not in my nature." Madame looked like a bulldog as she set her jaw and her jowls in grim determination.

"Please get some rest, Madame!" said Mathilde, as she plumped up her mistress's pillows. Agnès appeared from the kitchen with a cup of warm milk sweetened with honey. Mathilde removed it from the silver tray and brought it carefully to her lady's lips, which she then dabbed with a linen kerchief. The duchess was unusually docile, but just as she began to nod off, she suddenly sat bolt upright.

"The key is Roussin! We need to smoke out that rat, but if I'm the one to question him, he'll go straight to d'Effiat. I'll have to leave that up to your friend, the groundskeeper's son. Have you managed to transmit the message, Catherine?"

"Yes, Madame," said the girl, blushing from ear to ear. "He assured me he'd see to the matter without delay."

"I have it on good authority that young Desforges was sent out with the search party to look for your assailant. His tracking skills should stand him in good stead," said the grande dauphine.

"So much the better! He can kill two birds with one stone," Madame replied. "It'll give him the very excuse he needs so as not to attract attention to his other search. Now as for you, Mathilde and Catherine, you'll be my eyes and ears at court, as well as the liaison between Chrétien Desforges, that ne'er-do-well nephew of d'Effiat's, and myself. You'll report back to me regularly with even the most insignificant details. We need to strike while the iron is hot!"

With that she laid her head back on the cushions, drew the covers around herself and her brood, and turned her back to her visitors, signaling their cue to exit. Mathilde extinguished the candles one by one, closed the shutters, and drew the heavy brocade curtains. A musty odor permeated the air.

There was a damp autumn chill in the darkened room, despite the bright orange flames licking the logs in the fire-place. The flickering light cast ominous shadows over the bust of the Sun King on the mantelpiece. His facial expression seemed oddly mobile in the glow, smiling one moment and sneering the next.

DIVIDE AND CONQUER

*M*y Dearest Aunt Sophie,

It is with a heavy heart that I write to you today from my convalescence. It is bad enough to be the constant target of ridicule at court, but to be hated so for being German is wearing me to the bone. Bad news travels fast, they say, and by the time this letter reaches you, you may already have become aware of the fact that yesterday I was the victim of an attempted assassination. I was fortunate enough to get away with nothing more than a painful flesh wound, which is being treated by a pair of obsequious charlatans who bleed me night and day. Louis is dismissing the incident as a mere accident, a misfired arrow at the hunt, but I know better. I have recently ventured a bit too close to the truth on the misfortunes of my husband's first wife, Henriette. I must be more circumspect in my investigations in the future and go undercover by delegating my inquiries, so to speak. My big mouth has gotten me into trouble on more than one occasion and I have fallen out of favor with the king.

I know that as a staunch Catholic Henriette was not your favorite cousin, as her attempts to reconcile her brother Charles II of England with the Roman faith would have changed the line of *succession to England's throne. The turmoil in the British Isles has not abated much since the execution of your mutual ancestor, Mary Stuart, or that of her unfortunate grandson, your uncle Charles I. There seems to be a dark cloud over the family line and the present king's adherence to our faith I suspect to be in name only. This political and religious instability could someday lead to the Hanover branch of Stuart descendants taking over the succession to the crown of England and Ireland, but it would require a series of unlikely events for that to happen. Most of all, the country would have to remain Protestant.*

Very little can distract me from my melancholy, but your letters offer some measure of relief. They remind me of happier times in my homeland. Think how fortunate it is that your daughter was able to avoid my fate, though at the time you thought otherwise. Your ambitions for her at the court of France would have been her undoing, but how were you to know what evil lurks behind the shining surface? I would tell you more, but I must be wary lest my words fall into the wrong hands.

Speaking of my lovely cousin Sophie Charlotte, there is no need to alarm her by informing her of my recent misadventures, in view of her tender age. You ask me for news of the latest fashions at Versailles on her behalf, and though I pay little attention to such matters, I will do my best to satisfy her curiosity. It should provide a brief distraction from my daily preoccupations.

The king's absolute power extends far beyond the realm of politics into the private sphere of couture. On the one hand, he signs edicts against extravagance, when on the other he promotes it with his continual fetes. Fashion has become a matter of courtly etiquette, and Louis reigns supreme. Courtiers obey his every fancy and the town follows suit, as much as possible, and more than is reasonable. The most extravagant sums are paid for dresses that go out of fashion almost as soon as they've been worn. Every lady at court wants to impress, and has but to appear in some striking costume, than every lady of rank immediately endeavors to imitate her the next day.

Scarcely has one fashion usurped the other, when it is succeeded by a third, which in its turn is replaced by some newer fashion, not by any means the last. And not only women fall prey to the tyranny of "la mode." A tailor recently made a claim of 300,000 francs against Le Grand Condé. Of course, you know that my husband and his cohorts spend lavish sums on their attire, while I am left with next to nothing to spend on my own or my children's apparel. I have had to have our garments mended and altered on more than one occasion.

As to the details, let me quote a recent article from the Mercure Galant, which chronicles all the goings-on at court, salacious or otherwise. "At a recent masquerade Mademoiselle de Montpensier, Mademoiselle de Villeroy, and Monsieur [yes, indeed, my own husband] wore cloth of silver and rose-colored braid, black velvet aprons, and stomachers trimmed with gold and silver lace. Their dresses were cut like those of the Bresse peasants, with collars and cuffs of yellow cloth in the same style, but of somewhat finer quality, and edged with Venetian lace. Their black velvet hats were entirely covered with crimson, pink, and white feathers. Monsieur's bodice was laced up with pearls and fastened with diamonds, and had diamonds all about it. The three of them carried bright red shepherd crooks ornamented with silver." Imagine the affectation! Peasants and shepherds indeed!

Here is another description from the same scandal rag: "The famous author Madame de Sévigné gave to Madame de Montespan a gown of gold upon gold, embroidered in gold, bordered with gold, above which was a band of gold, worked in various gold alloys, with a transparent overlay, and forming the most divine material that can be conceived." But you can't make a silk purse out of a sow's ear!

Many women still wear masks occasionally but must remove them in front of a person of consideration. Hair is often worn down and curling about the neck and shoulders, or piled ridiculously high "à la Fontanges" after the fashion of the king's late mistress Mademoiselle de Scorailles. The fontanges is supported by a wire cage, tied up with ribbons and bows into a topknot, and adorned with lace and trimmings. These are elaborate creations that are guaranteed to give you a stiff neck, of which I am well aware, having had to pose with one for hours for my most recent portrait.

I am greatly fatigued from my many bleedings, and I must now rest my pen. I hope that I have satisfied your curiosity regarding the fickleness of fashion. I beg you to keep me in your prayers and to write to me as soon as you are able. Please give my love to your husband, Ernst Augustus, Elector of Hanover, and may God protect and bless your children, Georg Ludwig and Sophie Charlotte.

Your doting niece, Liselotte
(Versailles, October 5, 1682)

Madame reached wearily for the bell cordon by her bedside to summon Mathilde.

"My dear, I am depending on you as usual to deliver this directly into the right hands. Do not dillydally about, as this is a matter of great urgency. Once you have done so, check with Catherine on the groundskeeper's progress. Has he been able to discover the whereabouts of that scoundrel Roussin? I will need to know immediately once his mission is complete. In all matters be circumspect. There is reason to believe you are being watched."

"Yes, Madame. I shall be careful not to attract attention."

"Before you go, I have another request. I have been reluctant to make use of your friendship with Robin until now, because I don't want to encourage you to consort with that fiend d'Effiat's associates or family members. However, it may be the only manner to get close to the marquis. He chooses to reside at his own estate, as it is adjacent to Versailles. That makes his devilish machinations with the chevalier difficult to detect," the duchess said with a snort.

"What would you have me do, Madame? You are aware,

aren't you, that Robin is now engaged to Madeleine de Noailles?"

"That bag of bones?" she replied with a shrug. "One should never underestimate the power of a beautiful young woman such as yourself. Use your charms judiciously, but cautiously. Robin has a weakness for the fairer sex. Need I say more?" The duchess waived her fan in the direction of the door.

Mathilde nodded with an air of complicity, curtsied, and slipped out, scanning the hallway right and left for an inopportune observer. She was well aware that her mistress's request was far more complicated than it seemed. Robin had already demonstrated extreme reluctance to share sensitive information about his uncle, though he liked him not. Furthermore, she knew that where Robin was concerned, her seductive powers were somewhat limited by her own willingness to please him. It dawned on her that Julie d'Aubigny was far more likely to beguile Robin, primarily because she had shown so little interest in him. And Mathilde had not been blind to Robin's attentiveness to Julie's charm.

She found Wendt in the guard room, conversing with several other domestics. She walked past him with a brief nod and walked out into the courtyard. He joined her a short while later, as expected. Along a pathway lined with boxwood she slipped him the envelope discreetly, making sure they could not be observed.

"How fares Madame?" he asked with a tone of deep concern in his voice.

"She is quite shaken by yesterday's ordeal, which has taken a greater toll mentally than physically. For now, she remains confined to bed and feels abandoned by all, save the grande dauphine and yourself, Monsieur Wendt. Please make haste to post this letter to Sophie of Hanover and do not let it fall into the hands of the court censors."

"You can rely on me, milady." Wendt slid the sealed missive beneath his vest.

"Before I go, I have a question. Is there any chance you might have laid eyes upon the cross Madame returned to me? It was in my pocket when I last saw you the other morning."

Wendt looked startled. "I have not, milady, and I hope you harbor no suspicions concerning me in that regard!"

"Naturally not, however I am trying to retrace my steps in the hope that I find it again. Madame would not be pleased and would assume that I had turned it over to Robin. I would prefer you not mention this incident to her until I am able to locate the pendant."

"Of course, mademoiselle, you can count on me to remain silent. However I will not tell my mistress a lie, should she ask. That is the most I can guarantee." Wendt's countenance remained inscrutable. "Does Madame require my presence in any way?"

"Not at the moment. She is still quite shaken, I would say, but the damage is more to her pride than to her physical well-being. Madame was never a shrinking violet, and this incident will not deter her inquiries."

"Much against my most urgent pleas, but she is too head-strong to heed my advice."

"Nor that of her doctors. She plans to attend the king's fete this very evening. She knows that her absence would foster more plotting and gossipmongering among her enemies."

Wendt shook his head in dismay, and left the room with a perfunctory bow.

Mathilde knew that the time had come to prevail upon Robin to break the silence regarding his discovery of d'Effiat's dungeon, but she had lost the pendant, which might well have been a bargaining chip. Madame would need more than mere rumors, which always abounded at court, more than the testimony under duress of a ruffian like Roussin, to establish the collusion between d'Effiat, the chevalier, and Montespan, or their involvement in the untimely death of Henriette of England. No, they needed physical proof, and if Robin's account was to be believed, the dungeon told a tale of horror.

As Robin's longtime friend and recent lover, Mathilde was acutely aware of his barely disguised attraction to Julie d'Aubigny, and she wondered whether she could trust the girl, whose promiscuity had already been established. Her own plea would fall upon deaf ears. Another possible consideration was Julie's recent bond with Lully. There was no doubt that the girl was skilled in deception. Her first appearance as the Chevalier de Maupin, and her subsequent transformation into Lully's protégée was seamlessly executed and their resemblance was barely questioned, despite the scandal it might have caused. With that in mind, she set out to the music room, knowing that wherever Lully could be found, Julie was never far behind.

As it happened, the dulcet tones of the court composer's latest songbird came floating out of his private study on the ground floor, next to the queen's chambers. Julie waited patiently, biding her time until the lesson came to an end. Mathilde stopped outside the heavy double doors dripping with gilded serpentine figures. Strange, she thought, how easily one becomes used to such lavish displays. In the end, they become familiar, commonplace, and unmemorable. Quite contrarily, the muted harmonies that were streaming forth from the room had an exquisite strangeness about them that stirred her soul. She waited outside reverently, as she listened to the pure timber of Julie's vibrantly confident voice. Once the music had subsided, to be replaced with playful banter, she hazarded a brief knock on the door. Muffled laughter and the rustle of silk, a small cry of indignation, and a low sigh could be made out behind the door before it opened just a crack. Long enough to offer a view of the handsome musician adjusting his waistcoat and wiping his brow. A resplendent Julie, dressed in several shades and layers of bronze silk trimmed by pale blue lace of Bruges bid her enter the room.

"How do you like my new dress, Mathilde? It was a gift from Jean-Baptiste!" She performed a pirouette to display her finery and her figure.

Lully shot Mathilde a withering look of dislike and discomfiture. It was obvious the interruption had displeased him.

"It's lovely, Julie! I wish Madame would open up her purse strings and buy me a new garment from time to time, but she has no interest in fashion, and that would be her least priority on her meager allowance. Watch that you don't make Montespan envious!"

"Old Maintenon will probably wag her tongue with disapproval, and Monsieur the Duke d'Orléans will have a copy made for himself!" She laughed with delight at her quip.

"The first rule at court is that one should never laugh at one's own *mot d'esprit*. Of all people, you should know that!" replied Mathilde with a smile.

"Enough mischief! Off with you girls!" said Lully gruffly. "I need to get back to my new opera, *Phaëton,* before Maintenon censors it. Since she's been sharing the king's bed, the arts have fallen into disfavor."

"So has homosexuality," whispered Julie to Mathilde with a complicit dimpled grin. The two made their way down the hallway lined with armored statues and coats of arms.

"You see that I have taken some initiatives on my own," she declared. "Lully will soon be eating out of the palm of my hand. I've given him just enough of a 'down payment' so to speak, that he believes surrender to be imminent."

"This is all just a game to you, isn't it?" said Mathilde. She suddenly thought better of asking her rival to exert her influence on Robin. What had she been thinking?

"What if it is?" asked Julie. "Don't worry! I promise not to touch your precious Robin. Not necessarily for your sake, but simply because I do not find him interesting in the least. He's a spoiled and pampered brat with very little determination. As with most men, I can get more out of Lully by leading him on than by giving in. I'll see if I can get him to show me the dungeon. He may see it as an opportunity to impress and seduce me, and if he should try to take advantage of me, I have unarmed, or should I say, unmanned, more than one with my trusty sword." She tapped her thigh as she spoke, to reveal an oblong shape protruding beneath her petticoat.

"But can't you hurry things along? My mistress is most anxious for results."

"Haste makes waste! I am waiting for him to mention his association with the brotherhood, and it won't be long before he tries to draw me into some shady affair. But asking too many questions will awaken his suspicious nature. I believe that he will prove to be an excellent source of information if I play my cards right. But what's to be my reward for taking such risks? You don't really believe that I would do this for no payment, do you?"

Mathilde realized that this was indeed unlikely, for Julie had no allegiances at court.

"Well then, name your price! And I'll see if it's negotiable with Madame."

"No, dear, it's not money I had in mind," whispered Julie, drawing close to Mathilde. She slid her hand around her waist and pulled her quickly and firmly to her breast. Mathilde was too surprised to resist, and Julie kissed her full on the lips, lingering there until neither one could breathe. Mathilde finally had the presence of mind to push her away, but there was an undeniable electric current running through her, which made her momentarily lose her grasp of reality. The stirring was unfamiliar, quite unlike the feeling she had with Robin. Without a word, she darted back along the corridor and up the stairs to safer quarters.

◆

Chrétien had lost no time in coming up with an evasive excuse to extricate himself from his daily chores. Madame's orders would naturally supersede those of his father, however he was unable to reveal the exact nature of his mission. His father eyed him with suspicion.

"This had better not be some fabrication to indulge in a petticoat chase! I know your weakness for the so-called fairer sex."

"I hope to have proven myself to be responsible and hard-working, father," the young man replied solemnly.

"Very well, but see to it that your chores are finished before you turn in tonight," the older Desforges replied sternly, but not without a hint of fatherly affection.

Chrétien unchained Goliath, who pounced on him, slathering his face with saliva. "Down boy, down! It's time once again to show your worth."

They made their way through the brambles and down to the village, and from there on to the crumbling shacks by the swamp. The stench of rotting flesh inside the cabin was overwhelming. Chrétien wondered if Roussin had found Margot's lifeless body and buried it, or if he had finished her off in her misery. Either way, death was in the air, and he wondered if the smell would mask their quarry's trail. He found a pair of soiled and tattered trousers under the bed and held them out for Goliath to sniff. The mastiff immediately put his giant nose to the ground and tugged on his leash, absorbed in the chase. The trail led first to the site where, ten days earlier, he had witnessed the unceremonious hauling and disposal of Margot's lifeless body. Goliath looked up, temporarily disoriented, and seemed to hesitate between taking the path leading to d'Effiat's estate or heading into the woods. Chrétien led him away from the castle, as he knew that if Roussin had, quite improbably, sought shelter there, he would be unable to lay a hand on him. After a while, the terrain became familiar again. They were approaching the boundary to the palace grounds, when Goliath began to forge ahead with greater urgency. They passed by the ruins where Chrétien had first caught sight of Catherine. The hound lingered only briefly by the hearth, and then continued deeper into the woods to the abandoned well. Once again, Goliath leaped up on his hind legs, haunches heaving, stretching his bulky neck into the void. Once again, the young man lowered his lantern into the darkness. He recoiled in horror. For this time, it was not a skull glaring back at him from the depths but the glassy-eyed frozen stare of Yves Roussin, lips recoiled over rotten gums, mouth gaping in an eternal silent howl.

Chrétien steadied himself against a tree, lowered himself onto the ground, and sat with his head bent forward, cradling it between his knees. Roussin may have gotten his just deserts, but the sight of his final agony and the terror etched on his face were deeply unsettling. By the smell of things, Chrétien deemed that the body had been there several days, but it was early autumn and the nights had been cool. Otherwise more decomposition would have occurred. Had it not been for the immediate prospect of reporting to Catherine, the sight of human misery would have put him in a much more somber mood. But he found his step lightening and his heart lifting as he got closer to the palace.

Upon entering through the side door under the western arcade, Chrétien caught sight of a page dressed in the livery of the Orléans branch of the royal family. He beckoned him over and told him to fetch Catherine de Sauvignon, lady-in-waiting to the grande dauphine. It was a glorious day and he stretched out on the ledge of the fountain of Apollo, where he had had his first meeting with Catherine several weeks earlier. The warmth of the sun on his head, spread down to his neck and shoulders, lulling him into a pleasant torpor and stilling his thoughts for a while. When Catherine finally appeared, she stopped for a moment and stood stock-still to admire her lover at rest, eyes closed, his blond locks shining like a halo of spun sugar around his brow. He stirred and she cleared her throat, embarrassed that he might have witnessed her blatant gawping. But Chrétien was too self-conscious himself at having been caught with his guard down to notice her discomfiture. He pulled her toward him to sit beside him on the fountain's ledge, but the place was too public for any further display of affection.

So close, and yet so far away, he thought.

Struggling to resume a more official tone, Catherine said, "What have you to report to Madame? Any leads on Roussin?"

"Indeed I have, mademoiselle," said Chrétien, mimicking the girl's formality with a slight grin on his face. "No disrespect, but I believe the duchess will want to hear it first."

"Very well, I shall take you to her." She led him through the extensive suite of corridors and vestibules connecting the private chambers of the very highest peers of the realm. This was new territory to Chrétien, who tried hard not to gape at the gold moldings, the heavy damask, and the oil paintings adorning every wall. His muscular frame seemed to take up too much space in this world of miniatures. He kept his arms to his sides, afraid of knocking over some odd priceless bauble or a delicate side table teetering on slender legs. Catherine rapped discreetly on Madame's outer apartment door. The knock was immediately followed by the muffled sound of barking dogs and scratching paws. Mathilde silently opened the door and a small hoard of frisky miniature pups rushed at Chrétien, sniffing his trousers and boots. He knelt down good-humoredly to pet them as they romped and cavorted at his feet. Mathilde eyed the scene with indignation but held her tongue.

When Madame entered the sitting room, she chuckled

deeply. "I see you are a dog lover like me, my boy. Mathilde here has little use for my brood and would normally have kept the little beasts in my bedroom, but your visit was unexpected."

"Please do not concern yourself, Madame," said Chrétien, bowing deeply. Most of my life is spent in the kennels, and I often prefer the company of the hounds to that of my siblings."

"So I've heard. I know your father by reputation as a man of character, and I have been given to understand that you are a trustworthy fellow in your own right. Let it be understood as well that what we discuss here today should remain between a chosen few. In this palace the walls have ears." As she spoke, she looked around the room apprehensively.

Chrétien bowed his head in deference.

"I assume that you have come to me to report on the whereabouts of Yves Roussin."

"I have indeed, Madame. But I fear that my findings will not be to your liking if you're looking to question him."

"Has he fled the country, as might be expected?"

"No, but well he should have. Today I found his body at the bottom of a well bordering on d'Effiat's estate. It must have been disposed of in haste, as no care had been taken to disguise its identity by reducing it to ashes."

"I assume that this is the very same abandoned well where previous discoveries were made . . . ?" The disappointment was obvious in Madame's voice, as it trailed off to a sigh.

"Yes, Madame, the very same. As in the past, any foot- or hoof prints can only be traced back to Versailles and not to d'Effiat's estate."

"That leaves us with four thousand suspects," said the duchess ill-humoredly. "I guess it's back to the drawing board, or have we reached a dead end? Roussin's death confirms our suspicions, or should I say our knowledge, that he knew too much. I'm frankly surprised that he survived as long as he did, but that itself is a testimony to his usefulness. The problem is that we are left without proof of any sort of the chevalier's involvement, yet I feel it in my bones." Madame clenched her hands together, interlacing her stout fingers tightly.

Chrétien caught a glance of complicity between Catherine and Mathilde. He knew what they were thinking. It was time to persuade Robin to give evidence, but it would take some convincing. He wondered if he might once again prove useful in that regard.

"I will do what I can, Madame, and should I discover anything further, I shall contact Catherine," he said with a sideward glance at the girls and a slight grin at his inner joke. Catherine blushed under Mathilde's scrutiny and with a quick curtsy, ushered Chrétien out the door.

"How dare you!" she said once they were out of earshot. "If you think that your little game has gone unnoticed, you are sorely mistaken. Mathilde has been ribbing me unmercifully, and Madame has picked up on it as well."

"I can well imagine how your snooty little friend feels about it," he countered, with some irritation. I would venture that even Madame harbors kinder thoughts about me."

"Mathilde only has my welfare at heart," Catherine said defensively.

"Am I, then, such a threat to your well-being? Perhaps I should make myself scarce," and with that, Chrétien turned on his heels and left.

He immediately regretted his impetuous outburst but had too much pride to turn back. Catherine could only look on in disbelief. By the time he reached the courtyard, he was utterly disheartened. The two had rare enough occasion to meet, so why make such a mess of it? He realized that he had reacted out of apprehension. For the first time in his life he felt the weight of public opinion and the harm it could do to Catherine's reputation. He had no right, he knew, to pressure her into a romantic entanglement, yet the bond was already too deep to sever. He would rather cut into his own flesh than see her hurt, but he knew he didn't have the willpower to break it off. Faced with such insurmountable odds, he suddenly felt too weary to face his family, so he turned back toward the park to reminisce a while by the fountain of the Council of Rats, where he and Catherine had first kissed. A slight rustling of leaves followed by the faintest of treads made him turn his head, just as she reached for his face, cupping it in her hands. An uncontrollable shiver raced down his spine and into his groin as he drew her near. He knew in that moment that their fate was sealed, no matter what the cost, to him or to her. They would go down in flames together.

"I cannot let you go," he said. He held her close to hear every breath, to feel every vibration of her body. With a swift movement he picked her up as if she were a child and carried her into a small glen where he laid her down reverently on the soft moss. Somewhere, in the distance, they heard the moans of lovers, or was it merely the echo of their own muted sounds? They didn't know; they had lost all sense of time.

◆

Meanwhile, Mathilde made haste to send a note to Robin, hoping he would meet with her the next day. His courting obligations would require him to be at Versailles, in the company of Madeleine de Noailles, but he would have to disengage from his fiancée's presence without seeming discourteous. She knew it would take more than her longstanding friendship with Robin to convince him to disclose the dark secrets of his uncle's dungeon. Certain guarantees of nondisclosure would be required of the duchess, but beyond that, though Mathilde was loathe to admit it, she would not hesitate to use Catherine's beautiful cousin as a lure. She no longer feared losing her lover to the mysterious newcomer at court, since she already knew that what Julie really wanted was something only she had the power to grant or withhold. And the kiss had been a tantalizing promise of unknown pleasures to come. Suddenly, that thought prompted a flash of inspiration.

◆

Chrétien found Robin in the stables of the d'Effiat estate, tending to his prize horse. He was brushing down the flanks of the steed, whose muzzle was half buried in his oats. Sarrasin lifted his head with a snort and shook his mane when he heard Chrétien's approach, then turned his sleek neck to observe the young man with a wary eye. Robin swung around on cue, and greeted the groundskeeper with a friendly wave. "How are you, mate?"

"Well enough, but there's mischief afoot, and I've been at Madame's beck and call, these past few days." Chrétien reached out to the magnificent animal to let him sniff his hand before stroking him gently behind the ears.

"What's that to do with me?" replied Robin.

"Everything, if you will, or nothing at all," said Chrétien cautiously, knowing it was not his place to pressure the future marquis. "I suspect you may soon receive a call from her lady-in-waiting."

"All right, then, out with it! I would rather have the news from you than from a hotheaded beauty who knows how to manipulate me," said Robin with a grin.

"Madame is on the warpath, or should I say a holy crusade, to discredit the Chevalier de Lorraine. You know most of the story, but recent events are forcing her hand. The king seems to have aligned himself with his brother and his allies against the duchess. Since her children's future is at risk, she will stand her ground, whatever the cost. But she must lie low to avoid another attempt on her life, or so she sees it."

"So she sends you to do her dirty work," Robin said grimly.

"She doesn't know I'm here, however she did send me to scour the forest in search of our friend Roussin. I rather suspected he had left the area, but apparently not soon enough."

"So you found him?" said Robin as he closed the gate to the stall.

"In a well, that is. With a broken neck. He wasn't the sharpest tool in the shed, and his greed must have gotten the better of him."

Robin did not seem too surprised. "Well, his fate must have been sealed, and it was only a matter of time. He was bound to come to a bad end and lucky to have lived as long as he did, although it's hard to see that as a life."

"Perhaps. But now Madame has lost a potential witness, however disreputable he might have been. She is desperate to establish a link between the chevalier, his coterie, and the death of Henriette of England. One potential piece of the puzzle she lacks is the knowledge of your uncle's dungeon."

"What interest have I in revealing that little house of horrors to my uncle's enemy? You are forgetting the predictable blot on my family's reputation."

Chrétien bit his tongue in an effort not to say the obvious. So instead he appealed to Robin's gallantry.

"If Mathilde's safety means anything to you, it would be advisable to give her mistress the necessary ammunition to contain her enemies. The girl's life is potentially at risk, and the duchess won't hesitate to employ her as a spy if she has to."

"I have indeed considered the matter. My uncle is no friend of mine, and I am his only heir. Were he to be banished or stripped of his title, I would be next in line. The title doesn't mean nearly as much to me as my freedom. The freedom to marry the woman of my choice, for example. . . ." Robin's voice trailed off as he weighed the consequences of his decision. "On the other hand, should he get wind of my betrayal, there'll be heavy consequences to pay."

"When Madame finds out, she'll no doubt take that into consideration. Remember that your uncle has no idea that you know of his dirty little secret. It'd be easy for her to point the finger elsewhere, hinting at some type of betrayal within his own entourage."

"It's a dangerous game you're asking me to play. But I can see my own advantage in it. My uncle wants me to marry Madeleine de Noailles for her fortune, but as the saying goes, *Ne vous mariez point pour de l'argent, vous pouvez emprunter* à *meilleur marché*. Don't marry for money, it's cheaper to borrow it!"

Chrétien let out a laugh. "Your point is well taken. Shall we shake hands on the matter?"

"Before we do, let me see if I understand correctly. The idea would be to create suspicions among the members of my uncle's secret society, dividing it from within, while I would remain above suspicion. I think Madame would agree that driving her enemies apart would be to her greatest benefit, not to mention mine." Robin held out his hand.

AN UNEASY ALLIANCE

*R*obin awoke early the following morning to a discreet knock on his bedroom door. The twisted sheets bore witness to a restless night. He had managed to find sleep in the wee hours of the morning, and his eyes were still clouded with slumber when he answered the door. His servant apologized for the intrusion, while handing him a note that bore the inscription *Urgent* on the envelope. He tore open the seal, to read the succinct message.

I must speak with you immediately. I shall be waiting for you in the gardens at your earliest convenience. Julie d'Aubigny.

Robin was suddenly fully alert. He pulled on his attire hurriedly, without waiting for his valet to bring him his wash-basin. On his way out he glanced at his reflection in the mirror, not without a certain degree of satisfaction. The disheveled curls and the shadow of stubble on his chin gave him a roguish look that worked to his advantage. The very sort of thing that would appeal to Julie. He imagined she must like it rough.

It took him a good five minutes to find her. *The little vixen is playing hard to get, already!* he thought with a sense of anticipation. But his excitement at the prospect of seeing her alone was soon dampened at the sight of Mathilde at her side. Julie scanned him coolly up and down with a complete lack of self-consciousness. He felt she was measuring every inch of his body, as her defiant gaze focused on his crotch. Her left arm was resting loosely on Mathilde's slender waist and despite his discomposure, he could not help but admire the alluring vision. As she turned toward Mathilde, he was shocked to see that her right hand had a firm grip on the hilt of a rapier hanging at her side, which was partially concealed by the folds of her ample skirt.

"What's this all about? Are you trying to provoke me to a duel?" he said as he stepped back from striking distance.

"Just a precautionary measure for two damsels out walking alone on the d'Effiat estate," replied Julie.

"But why come on foot? Besides, it's early morning, and I'm scheduled to be at Versailles this afternoon. Could it not have waited?"

"We knew you would be all tied up," said Mathilde with a grin. At which point, Julie raised her hand to Mathilde's forehead to sweep back a wayward lock of hair. The tenderness of her gesture left little doubt as to her feelings for the girl.

"We have an enticing proposition for you. Take it or leave it! But you'll have to decide right here and now. The early bird gets the worm!" said Julie. Was it Robin's imagination, or was she taunting him by stroking the rounded pommel of her sword with her thumb?

"So what's your offer?" said Robin, trying to hide his confusion by returning her stare. "This must be good for you two to have ventured onto my turf."

"Simply put, I am well aware that you and Mathilde are lovers, but how would you like to make it a threesome? I've noticed your poorly concealed interest in my person."

A huge grin spread across Robin's face. "I would certainly

be so inclined," he said, advancing toward them without the slightest hesitation.

"Not so fast, my friend!" said Julie, sliding her rapier halfway out of its sheath. "In return we require that you help with Madame's inquiries. We have so far kept your secret to ourselves, as promised, but she is at her wits' end when it comes to her investigation. She needs to know about the dungeon in order to go forward. Are you willing to inform on your uncle in exchange for a tryst with two fair maidens?"

Robin smiled at the irony of his own luck, for the girls were as yet unaware that he had already agreed to come forward after Chrétien's visit, knowing that as long as the source remained anonymous it would be to his advantage to do so. The idea of marrying Madeleine de Noailles had become increasingly repugnant to him, but the only way out was to strip his uncle of his authority. Nonetheless, he thought it in his interest to pretend to be hesitant.

"This is risky business you're asking me to engage in," he said. "May I ask for an advance on your favors?" Ignoring the rapier, he wedged himself between the maidens, hooking his arms around their shoulders with an arrogant familiarity.

"Not now, but once you've completed your assignment, you can count on us to fulfill our part of the deal," said Julie. Promptly disengaging herself from his embrace, she turned her heels on him, leading Mathilde toward the exit.

"I shall announce your imminent visit to Madame. Be there between five and six, or I'll consider our agreement null and void," added Mathilde, before hastening out the door.

By the time Robin had returned to his room for the key and had reached the dungeon, he was in a total state of bewilderment. He knew that the girls had gotten the better of him, and that their offer was far too enticing to turn down. Despite the fact that he had made up his mind the day before to entertain the idea of giving up his secret, he still felt that the final decision was his and his alone. He now resented the feeling of being a pawn in the girls' game. His free agency had somehow fallen prey to overwhelming lust. As he opened the heavy door to look again upon what he was about to divulge, he considered for a brief moment the downfall of his great-uncle Cinq-Mars. Had he, too, like the long line of infamous ancestors who went before him, inherited the predisposition to abandon all caution and succumb to his sexual appetites?

A brief glance convinced him that very little, if anything, had been moved since his last visit. The lurid display of instruments of sexual torture and abuse were still there, leering at him in the lantern light. He could hear the moans rise from the deathly silence, as if conjured up by some demonic presence. Surely he had nothing in common with such monsters. His own demons were harmless by comparison. Or were they? He shuddered as he shut the portal to the underworld, and headed upstairs to a different reality, one in which appearances mattered. And it was time to make just such an appearance at the court of Versailles. Once there, however, his first stop would be at the palace library, to secure the engraving that might well serve to support his claim.

◆

Mathilde appeared in the nick of time to attend to Madame's toilette. She had slipped through the door so quickly and quietly, that her sudden, breathless presence quite startled the duchess. "Why, girl, you nearly gave me a heart attack! What's with you, these days? You seem flustered and distracted."

Mathilde blushed and curtsied deeply to hide her embarrassment. Her mistress had the unnerving ability to see right through her. But she had no time for excuses and no choice but to come straight to the matter. "Robin d'Effiat requests an interview to discuss a matter of grave importance, Madame. He'll be in attendance this evening at the *fête galante* in honor of Madame de Montespan's birthday and wishes to see you in your private chambers before the event."

Liselotte eyed her suspiciously. "You'll owe me an explanation later, my dear. I presume you've used your feminine wiles to our advantage. But for now, please inform me what extraordinary circumstances have prompted the young lord's visit? I trust that arrogant wastrel no further than I can shake a stick, but he's our only lead."

"Madame, I did my best, as you instructed," Mathilde said with the slightest hint of a smile. "However, I believe it would be better for Robin himself to provide you with an accurate account of what he knows. In the meantime, let me apply a new dressing to your scratch."

"Humph! It's more than a scratch!" Madame held out her flaccid arm docilely. "Very well, then. Have him meet me in my parlor around five, when most of the courtiers are resting, in preparation for this evening's festivities. Be careful not to draw attention, and if you notice any form of surveillance, be sure to abort the mission."

"I'm sure that Robin is well aware of the need for discretion, Madame, but if not, I'll see to the matter," she said as she applied a dab of tea tree honey to the wound.

As Mathilde was letting herself out the door, she nearly backed into Hermann Wendt, who was waiting in the hallway to speak to her mistress.

"The grande dauphine has sent me to ask if the duchess can spare the time for a brief *tête-à-tête* this afternoon. Catherine is apparently nowhere to be found."

Mathilde looked thoughtful. It wasn't like her friend to be negligent of her duties.

"It'll have to be soon. I believe that Madame is expecting an important visitor later in the day," she replied enigmatically.

Then she hurried off before she could be pressed for more information, wondering if she had said too much. But Wendt was, after all, the most trusted member of Madame's inner circle and was responsible for all her confidential correspondence to Germany, she reasoned.

She met up with Robin at the appointed time outside the library. He drew her into an alcove and pressed himself up against her. "This is neither the time, nor the place, Robin. I see that our little negotiations have got you all hot and bothered," she said, boldly cupping his crotch, then releasing her grip and pushing away from him. "Madame expects you around five. I've brought a long hooded cape and a wig for you to wear. If you were clean-shaven we might have passed you off as a proper maiden, but this will have to do. Any sighting of you entering Madame's chambers would arouse suspicion and the gossip-mongers would go into a feeding frenzy."

"I realize there is no need to alert the public to any commerce between the duchess and me," he said. "However this cloak-and-dagger game is a bit ludicrous, don't you think?"

Instead of answering, Mathilde simply secured the garment around his neck.

"I came on foot, so as to avoid announcing my visit, and slipped in with the gawking commoners." He tried again to land a peck on Mathilde's cheek, which she ignored.

"Stay here for now and pretend to read. I'll let you know when the coast is clear. The Grande Dauphine Victoire requested a brief meeting with Madame this afternoon, and I'll have to make sure that she's left the premises by five."

"Well, hurry along, then. You know that reading bores me to tears." He patted her bottom familiarly as she turned to leave and received an angry glare in exchange.

When Mathilde got back to Madame's private quarters, she found Catherine sitting on a bench outside the massive doors, working on a piece of embroidery. "This is why we're called ladies-in-waiting," said her friend, with some degree of ill humor. "I feel that I spend half my life waiting for something to happen."

"You'll have to make your peace with the fact that our primary function is for the sake of appearances. It wouldn't do for a lady of rank to do anything for herself, or to be disturbed by the slightest inconvenience."

"True, but deep down, I suspect it's to keep our ladies from feeling alone. Life at the top is solitary, despite being constantly surrounded by obsequious courtiers."

"Speaking of that, where were you today when your mistress was looking for you? She had to send Wendt to request a meeting with Madame."

"Yes, they're in there now," Catherine replied evasively, glancing down at her work. She looked particularly fetching in a gown of wine red velvet with deep folds revealing glints of gold embroidery.

"You haven't answered my question, dear. What have you been up to? You look finer than your own mistress, who is the second-ranked woman at court. Beware that she doesn't become jealous!" Mathilde lifted the skirt an inch or two to examine the elaborately embroidered hem.

"She has too sweet a disposition and is too unassuming to concern herself over such matters. And unlike the duchess, she's liberal with her purse strings. I'll loan you a dress for the party this evening, if you like."

"I'd love that! The lavender silk would do quite nicely, thank you! Julie's all done up in a stunning confection that was given to her by none other than Lully. And she insists that she's so far managed to avoid 'paying for it.'" Mathilde felt a begrudging admiration for Julie's impenitent self-confidence.

"You've certainly been chumming around with my cousin these days. I'd assumed that you had some misgivings about

Robin's attentiveness to her." Catherine seemed eager to turn the attention away from herself.

"You let me handle that! I've got him at my beck and call, and Julie, too, for that matter," said Mathilde with a certain degree of smugness.

Catherine looked at her quizzically, but Mathilde continued her train of thought.

"To get back to the matter at hand, I can tell you that I've noticed your poorly disguised interest in Chrétien. For a while you fooled me into thinking that the attraction was purely one-sided. But now I'm convinced that you've been deceiving every-one, including yourself."

"Oh, Mathilde! If only you knew what I'm going through! I never thought that love could be so bold. . . ." Catherine's face crumbled with worry.

But just then the door opened and Victoire was ushered out. Her cheeks and eyes were puffier than usual from recent tears, that she dabbed away as she walked. "Come along, Catherine. I have imposed on my friend long enough." Catherine had no choice but to follow.

It was now Mathilde's turn to be curious, but it was nearing the appointed time to fetch Robin for his audience with the duchess. She found him where she had left him, but he had been cornered by Madeleine de Noailles in her absence. He hadn't managed to put on the wig in time to avoid his fiancée, to his obvious chagrin. He was trying his best to be civil and attentive, but he looked like a squirming eel. Robin was visibly and audibly relieved to be summoned by Mathilde, who received nothing more than a contemptuous nod from his betrothed.

"Where are you off to, darling? I expect you to sit beside me this evening and to dance with no one but me. Am I making myself clear?"

"Crystal clear, my dear," said Robin, with an abrupt about-face.

"You've never been much of an actor," said Mathilde, bursting into laughter when they were out of earshot. "She has you by where the hair is short, and you're not even married yet!"

Robin scowled, but now was not the time to argue. His future was in the balance, and it was time to act. As anticipated, the halls were deserted and they made their way to Madame's apartments unobserved. Mathilde ushered him in, just in time to avoid being caught by the Chevalier de Lorraine, who appeared as if from nowhere as she closed the door and headed off toward the staircase. She couldn't help but wonder where he was headed, as Monsieur was back in his own castle of St. Cloud for the week.

Madame's glare was openly hostile when she greeted Robin, and his was no kinder. They sized each other up and down, as if preparing for combat. Madame's girth was formidable, and a physical reminder of her power. Although everyone knew that she had recently fallen out of favor with the King, there were certain forms of entitlement that even his Royal Highness would have difficulty defying without undermining his own symbolic authority. Robin had the arrogance of youth and the privilege conveyed by his uncle's immense fortune in his favor. Neither one chose to sit. She stood her ground by the mantle, stirring the ashes in the fireplace with a poker. The gesture looked more threatening than intended. Meanwhile, Robin gripped onto the back of a chair, as if it were a shield. Finally, the duchess broke the silence.

"I hear that you have some news of importance to share with me. Pardon my misgivings, but nothing would suggest a reason for your sudden cooperation. You'll need to convince me first that you're not a spy operating under orders from my enemies, most notably your uncle d'Effiat and that mongrel Lorraine."

"My uncle and I have little in common. He has no heed for my happiness, as has been recently demonstrated by my forced engagement. He's only interested in expanding his own sphere of influence through my marriage of convenience. We rarely communicate, and as for the chevalier, he is a loathsome swine."

"Yes, but you stand to inherit a vast fortune from the marquis someday. It would not be in your interest to betray him." There was a razor's edge to her voice.

"Yes, it's a huge risk. He quite naturally wants the fortune to remain in the family and I'm the closest male relative, although whatever affection, if any, he may have once had for my departed mother, did not extend to me. That's why the information that I'm about to give you needs to be attributed to a different source. It's only with such a guarantee that I will agree to talk."

"It would be relatively easy in this gossip-ridden court, to spread false rumors. . . ."

"But will you vouch for me? I need your personal assurance that what I'm about to tell you won't lead back to me. Your reputation for integrity is well-known, as is your hatred for my uncle and the Chevalier de Lorraine. You have the power not only to be my uncle's undoing but mine as well." Robin twisted the signet ring on his finger nervously.

"If the suspicions were to be deflected onto one of their inner circle, it would serve to spread distrust among them. That would be to my political benefit. But what's in it for you, young man?" said the duchess, eyeing him skeptically.

"Quite simply put, freedom from my uncle's tyranny and the right to marry the woman of my choice. Madeleine de Noailles pleases me not. Neither in appearance, nor in character. But in order to annul the engagement, which has the king's stamp of approval, I'd need to establish that my uncle is either of unsound mind or a person of moral turpitude. I believe that's the legal term. I have the means to prove that." Robin paused to measure the effect of his words on his interlocutor. She dropped the poker into the fireplace and seemed to let down her guard, stepping forward.

With that, Robin opened his satchel and removed the book. Madame smirked as she read the title. "What edifying material! *Maxims for the Foundation of a Christian Marriage.* I see that you're avidly preparing for the trials of matrimony."

"Yes, the text is educational in every way," he said, turning to the back of the volume, where the engraving was concealed.

Madame bent over her ivory-handled magnifying glass to inspect the document, only to be jolted back by the macabre scene. But not being one to be easily unsettled, she soon gathered her wits about her and said, "You gave me quite a shock, there, my boy. But I fail to see how this can advance my cause."

"First, pay careful attention to the details. You may note the inscription in roman numerals on the throne."

Madame peered again, this time more carefully. "Of course, there is some form of ceremonial ritual going on, which almost certainly involves the abuse of young boys. But the number fifty-three has no significance to me." She looked up expectantly.

"Does the name Cinq-Mars mean anything to you?"

"Of course! I hadn't made the connection! Your great-uncle who was executed on grounds of treason!"

"It would appear that he was the first to wear the locket Mathilde and I found near the ruins on my uncle's grounds, a facsimile of which is now worn by those, like my uncle, whose perversions extend to violence and sexual enslavement."

"Cinq-Mars was obviously no lover of the fairer sex!" said the duchess, narrowing her eyes. "The amulet depicts an angel of death trampling the life out of a woman. I've done some research of my own, and it would appear that the replicas were ordered by your uncle. He distributed them to his 'friends,' who appear to be members of some secret society."

"You mean the Sacred Brotherhood of Glorious Pederasts, Madame."

"I see that you're well-informed. But how will this engraving serve as proof? Your inglorious ancestor is long dead, and his guilt can't be transferred onto his family and allies, as would have been the case in ancient times."

Robin spoke in measured tones. "What if I were to tell you that I know the exact location of this octagonal vault? I've seen it with my own eyes and was nearly trapped in it myself."

Madame was now keenly alert. She had thought that the information might be of little value, but here was some hard proof. "Where is this place, and who may know of it?"

"I found it while mucking about in the estate's wine cellars. I was originally on the outlook for the portrait of Cinq-Mars, which has been stored out of public view. While there I discovered that the painting conceals a passageway leading to the dungeon. Of course, it took a while for me to obtain a copy of the key," he said, pulling it out for inspection.

"My lad, I see that you're somewhat smarter than I'd given you credit for. And braver, too. Can you describe the premises?" She reached for the key, but Robin was not yet ready to hand it over. He stashed it back in his vest pocket.

"It was empty except for an array of instruments of torture and sexual abuse. I was trapped in there for several hours, and if it hadn't been for the arrival of an unsuspecting Yves Roussin, I might have met with an untimely death."

"All roads seem to lead back to Roussin! Are you sure that no one remotely suspects your discovery?"

"The only witness, Roussin, never saw my face. I attacked him from behind in the semi-lit entrance to the cellar. When he regained consciousness, Chrétien Desforges and I frightened him into revealing his dealings with the secret society, but we wore masks and hoods. He acknowledged his role as the procurer of young boys who were sequestered and sexually abused. We let him go, but he's met with a bad end, I hear."

"I did hear that Chrétien had been following the man, so I take it you met by chance."

"He thought I was Roussin as I was dragging him out the back entrance and nearly knocked me out. He proved himself very useful during the interrogation, though." Gradually Robin's nervousness subsided. His impression of the duchess measured up to her formidable reputation.

"I'm having a hard time digesting all this information. I don't want to get my hopes up too high, but I may now have the evidence I need. Nonetheless, I'll have to use extreme judiciousness in revealing it to the king. He's very protective of my husband, who in turn protects the chevalier. I'm also not sure to what degree the duke may have been involved."

"Since Roussin didn't heed our advice to leave the area immediately, there's reason to fear that he may have had the time to alert the marquis or someone else to the presence of an intruder in the vault. If you don't move quickly on this matter, it may be cleared out."

"If it isn't already. . . ."

"As yet, the evidence is still intact. I was there today." With that, Robin dug the key back out and handed it to the duchess.

Madame looked at Robin thoughtfully. "Beware not to double-cross me! Hand me the engraving, too. You never know when it could come in handy."

Robin complied and made to take his leave.

"One more word, young man! Is it Mathilde you wish to marry, then?"

He turned toward her and said, "That, Madame, is no one's business but my own."

◆

Mathilde ambushed him as he was heading toward the gaming parlor to meet with Madeleine and pass the time gambling until the evening's festivities.

"Well met," he said, pulling her toward him. "The meeting was a success! Please tell your friend Julie that I intend to collect on my little reward as soon as possible. In the meantime, I need to hasten to the side of my betrothed so as not to arouse suspicions until the moment is right. Spare me your bouts of jealousy for the moment, my sweet!"

"I've just come from a brief visit with Catherine. According to her, Chrétien had already proposed a similar strategy, to which you had already agreed last night. His charms must be greater than ours!"

"My, my, doesn't my little blabbermouth have a sharp tongue! If by some stroke of good fortune I manage to back out of my engagement to Mademoiselle de Noailles, I may have to reconsider my idea of marrying you!" he said teasingly.

His words left Mathilde speechless, but she soon regained her composure. "And here I thought Julie was the current object of your desire."

"Let's say that it hasn't escaped my attention that I might get two or more for the price of one. Your display of lust for Julie is not just an affectation."

"How can *you* tell? I am much more adept at acting than you, although I have to say that when it comes to acting you're the worst! No one's fooled by your feigned affection for Madeleine, least of all Madeleine herself."

"We're more easily fooled by our own vanity than by others," replied Robin with a laugh.

"Well, if you insist on quoting La Rochefoucauld, here's another maxim to ponder," said Mathilde combatively: "'The surest way to be cheated is to think oneself more cunning than others.' I'll leave you with that thought as you go off to play whist with your sweetheart."

"I love you," whispered Robin under his breath, as Mathilde ran off to attend to her duties. The words had escaped without warning and had taken him by surprise, because it suddenly occurred to him that in that moment he did.

◆

Madame was in a tither when Mathilde rushed in. "Late again! Oh, for the love of God! Hurry to dress me, you foolish girl! All of this anguish has caused me to break into a rash. We'll need to apply a rather thick coat of powder and rouge to hide my complexion."

Mathilde looked at her mistress dolefully. She wasn't sure it was in her power to perform miracles.

"We need to put our heads together before this evening's festivities, my dear. Robin was very informative today, and despite certain misgivings that I may be rushing into a trap, I have to reveal what I know to the king before the evidence can be disposed of."

"I believe I can vouch for Robin's honesty in this matter, and he has his own reasons for wanting to discredit his uncle."

"Yes, there's the matter of Madeleine de Noailles. I know that you fancy the boy, but were it his decision alone, do you believe he would choose you over a more advantageous alliance?"

"Robin has enough money to afford the freedom to choose, although I'm not entirely sure that I'd be the one. Material possessions interest him far less than the senses, but there are so many more beautiful women at court who wouldn't object to marrying him." Mathilde preferred not to mention that Julie might have tilted the balance in her favor.

"Perhaps, but you and Robin have been close friends for years. This might be an advantage, particularly if you're willing to overlook his future dalliances, an unescapable fact of life here at court. The reason, however, that I bring this up, Mathilde, is that you're almost as dear to me as my own daughter, and I wish for your happiness, to the extent that such a thing might be possible with young Robin. D'Effiat is a slippery eel, and should our little stratagem not succeed in toppling his influence, I believe that it may still be in my power to free Robin from his engagement."

"How so, Madame?" Mathilde was startled.

"Thanks to a person of trust, I happen to know that Madeleine de Noailles has some skeletons in her closet. She may look like a spineless fool, but her reputation for virtue would crumble under close scrutiny. Nonetheless, I'd hesitate to do her harm unless it were absolutely necessary."

"That's very good to know. One should always have several irons in the fire."

The duchess reached out for Mathilde's hand. "Beware, my dear girl! Marriage is like a city under siege. Those outside want to get in, but those inside want out."

Mathilde burst into laughter.

Madame, however, still looked perplexed. She unlocked her writing desk and pulled out a scroll. "I promised Robin that I would divert the king's suspicions onto another source. It would have to be one of the members of the chevalier's inner circle. Here is the list of medallion owners, provided to me by Grosménil, the court silversmith. They would all appear to be members of the brotherhood, with that baffling exception of Montespan. I would have no trouble hinting at a betrayal, but it needs to seem credible. How about placing the blame on the outlier?"

Mathilde took no time to answer. To her, the person to take the fall was obvious. "Jean-Baptiste Lully, Madame!"

"But he's the court composer and one of the king's favorites!"

"You mean *was*. He's earned the wrath of Madame de Maintenon and in her efforts to turn His Majesty toward a life of devotion, she's condemned Lully's dissolute lifestyle. The king is said to be particularly revolted by his homosexual encounters, and has bestowed royal favor on Marc-Antoine Charpentier instead."

"That old witch!" said the duchess with a scowl. "At least this time her influence on the king may prove useful." She placed the scroll back in her writing desk, locking it with care, then stuffed the key securely between her breasts, where no one would dare to venture.

"At the moment, Lully's attention is taken up by Catherine's cousin, Julie d'Aubigny, who'd like nothing better than to gain fame as an opera singer." There were some things Madame didn't need to know, thought Mathilde uneasily, as she omitted mentioning the morning's events.

"Well, she certainly has the voice of a nightingale! Do you think she can be induced somehow to help point the finger at Lully, without necessarily mentioning him by name?"

"Madame, I do believe that she can be persuaded, provided it proves to be in her interest to do so. In return perhaps you could help to further her career in Paris . . . ?" Mathilde smiled at the thought of killing two or three birds with one stone. Things were falling into place.

"Whatever I do, things will have to move quickly. Well, that's all for now," said Madame, making some final adjustments to her attire, and caking another layer of powder onto her face. "I believe you've done all you could to make me look presentable. Oh, by the way, is the locket handy? I'd like to tender it to the king tonight, along with the key to the dungeon and the engraving Robin gave me. One can never have too much ammunition!"

The smile on Mathilde's face suddenly disappeared. "I am afraid that I have lost it," she said with a sigh.

THE DEVIL IN THE DETAILS

*D*earest Carllutz,

First of all, I want to thank you for your kind wishes for a quick recovery after my unfortunate "accident" in the woods. In the fortnight since I last wrote, there have been a number of interesting new developments. For a brief time, things seemed to be looking up, but I was soon to be disappointed once again. Will my enemies always have the upper hand? It would seem so, but I shall let you judge for yourself. And since you complain of ennui at the Court of Heidelberg, I shall regale you with my tales of woe. They should take your mind off your own misfortunes, and help you appreciate the virtues of a peaceful existence away from the turbulence at Versailles.

You may recall that I have no affection for the king's former mistress Françoise-Athénaïs de Montespan. But those feelings pale in comparison to the loathing I feel for Françoise de Maintenon. Although the former's shady dealings and dabbling in magical spells and aphrodisiacs would have led her to the gallows, but for the king's pardon, she is still very much a presence at court. So much so that Louis threw her an extravagant birthday party last week, much to the displeasure, and despite the vociferous objections of his current *mistress. Nonetheless, as you know, the king has a vested interest in marrying off his bastard children by Montespan to their stepcousins. The engagement of Françoise-Marie to your nephew Philippe is by now a foregone conclusion. However, I categorically refuse to have my beautiful daughter marry that hideous gnome, the Duke du Maine, even should he someday become heir to the throne of France because he is his father's favorite. I have my doubts as to his claim to royal lineage and have long suspected the Maréchal de Terme of having spawned that evil seed! I have been stockpiling my arsenal of griefs against his mother, as a means to prevent such a mismatch. In so doing, I have discovered a somewhat nebulous link between Montespan and a group of sadistic child abusers. Two of the main culprits are none other than d'Effiat and Lorraine. Jean-Baptiste Lully, the court composer, well-known for his deviant ways, is apparently also an associate. Because I finally have physical proof of their unholy alliance, I thought I should bring the matter to the king's attention. Unfortunately, Louis has been avoiding me, and his harpy has seen to it that my requests for an audience are categorically denied. So the party was a rare opportunity to corner the king.*

The duchess laid down her pen for a moment and rested her chin on the palm of her hand. Her head slumped forward as she dozed off for an instant but was suddenly startled awake by the sound of her pen falling to the floor. She picked it up and mulled over the previous week's events, wondering how much of the story to convey to her brother, who wasn't keen on detailed accounts....

On the evening of Madame de Montespan's birthday party, when she and the grande dauphine made their entrance, the festivities were already in full swing. The menu consisted of, among other things, beef madrilene with gold spangles, pureed chestnut soup with truffles from the Italian court, scallops with oyster liqueur, smoked eel, hare stew, morel soufflé, and, to top things off, edible candles! These courses were followed by an interlude of dancing and music, arranged and conducted by none other than Lully. Once the food had settled and the spirits were high, a gargantuan layer cake was wheeled in, lavishly decorated with crème de Chantilly and candied fruit. The duchess's stomach rumbled at the thought of it. She reimagined the guests' cries of wonder when out popped the king's jester, who then proceeded to entertain the crowd with somersaults and magic tricks. The stunt was well-received, even better than the belly dancers in honor of the Turkish dignitaries. Louis was in rare spirits and he even joked with Montespan, bidding her to lay with the dwarf. The duchess frowned at the memory of the remark, which she felt was in very poor taste. No use bothering her brother with such drivel, she thought. She dipped her pen back in the inkwell, and continued her letter.

While everyone's attention was held by the entertainment, I risked slipping the king a sealed note, which contained an incriminating engraving that happened to fall in my possession. I looked around and was relieved to see that Louis's guard dog Maintenon was engaged in conversation with the queen. I had no idea whether he would simply disregard the information, or whether it would end up in the wrong hands, but I was gratified to be summoned the next morning into Louis's private chambers and to see that he had taken the matter to heart.

We discussed the situation at length, and I revealed more of the sordid details, without disclosing my sources. Although I have yet to establish a proven connection with Montespan and Lorraine, many of my revelations rang true to the king, who does not trust his former mistress. Of course, he questioned me as to the source of my information. I did vaguely mention a name or two, including that of Lully, while claiming uncertainty as to the reliability of rumors at court.

Since His Majesty no longer has any love for that man, he readily
believed me. Without further ado, he sent his personal guards to the
Marquis d'Effiat's estate the following day. The lord of the manor was
absent, but they were able to search the premises and they found
evidence of sexual abuse in a secret dungeon, to which I had provided
the key. It remains to be seen what will become of d'Effiat, and more
important, the Chevalier of Lorraine. I can only hope that their
connection to Montespan will be revealed and that at least one unfor-
tunate marriage can thus be avoided. Furthermore, I am hopeful that
their depraved society will be shattered by the members' suspicions of
betrayal from within. Should that not occur, I can honestly say that I
should fear for my life. There are indications that those disciples of
Satan were in some way involved in the death of Henriette, my
husband's first wife. I am sometimes led to wonder how our dear,
departed father could have sent me to such a den of iniquity.

In the earnest hope that my next letter bears news of my enemies'
defeat, I remain your constant, loving sister, Liselotte.

(Versailles, October 11, 1682)

Liselotte folded and sealed her letter absentmindedly, then
rang for Mathilde as soon as she decently could. Anxiety had
left her sleepless that night and she had written to her brother
while waiting for daylight to come. While awaiting her atten-
dant, she cast a mournful, bloodshot eye over the landscape
outside her window. It was shrouded in a bleak blanket of gray
fog that had been lying on the ground persistently since the
early-morning hours.

"Madame?" said Mathilde. "You are already dressed! And at
such an unseemly hour! It's barely half past nine."

Madame thought she detected a slight tone of maternal
reproach in her lady-in-waiting's voice and was moved by her
concern.

"Hush, child! Don't worry on my account! Now go fetch

Herr Wendt for me without delay! The contents of this letter are so sensitive that it can't be entrusted to anyone but him. God forbid you should get caught handing it over and implicated in this whole sordid affair. They'll dismiss you the same way they did my good Mademoiselle Théobon. Once you've summoned him, I'll need to speak to Julie d'Aubigny. I want to fuel the king's suspicions regarding Lully in order to steer them away from your friend Robin, and I may be able to make use of her relationship to the man." The duchess knew that her actions were being fueled by sheer nervous energy and that soon she was bound to collapse from exhaustion.

"If Robin is accused of conspiring against his uncle, there'll be no place safe for him to hide. He must want to free himself from his shadow very badly," said Mathilde. It was more of a question than a statement.

"I am not sure of his intentions toward *you*, but I do know that Robin wants to choose a wife according to his own inclination. He stands to inherit enough of a fortune not to be concerned about the dowry, but he is indeed treading a fine line. The king has yet to decide on a course of action regarding the marquis and the chevalier, but he'll want to avoid angering his brother. I am afraid he seems to have a soft spot for my husband. The longer he hesitates, the greater the danger that he'll do nothing at all. The problem is, that I don't have the clout to pressure him directly. Well, enough dillydallying. Off with you, then!" She pulled her shawl around her, reclined as best she could against the stiff back of her armchair, and rested her feet on an outlandish leather ottoman that had been a gift from the Turks.

Mathilde curtsied and the duchess fell back into her reverie. The gilded, plastered walls could not, despite their splendor, conceal the dank, musky smell of the dampness rising from the bowels of the palace. She felt she was walking on a knife's edge. A false move could be her undoing. She had set the machinery in motion that might crush her in its cogs, along with those dearest to her, but it was now too late to retreat.

A knock on the door announced Wendt's arrival.

"What tidings, mein Herr? Is there anything current to report regarding Louis's intentions?"

"Yes, Madame, and some of it will be welcome news. The king sent for your husband yesterday, and they conferred for several hours. It's rumored that the duke was in a black mood when he left. Thereupon, the marquis, who had been summoned from Paris, arrived in a flurry of agitation, to be joined by the Chevalier of Lorraine. Court gossip has it that Louis was considering permanent exile for Lorraine, but upon his brother's beseeching, commuted the punishment to a monetary fine of an undisclosed sum and a temporary banishment from court."

The duchess's face slackened at the news.

"Once again, the dastard gets off with a slap on the wrist!"

"True, but on the other hand, you will be relieved to know that he has at least removed the guardianship of Robin from d'Effiat. And he's stripped the marquis of the position of your son's future governor as well. Louis doesn't want either one of those devils in a position of authority over young men. This should no doubt please Your Ladyship."

The duchess let out a sigh of relief. "It does indeed! Was anything mentioned about my children's betrothals?"

"The king stands fast in his desire to marry his illegitimate daughter to your son. His bastard, the Duke du Maine, however, seems to have a preference, despite his tender age, for Mademoiselle de Charolais, given the choice, and your daughter may be spared the ordeal of marriage to an invalid."

Madame raised her eyebrows in disbelief. "Imagine the arrogance of a twelve-year-old! I can't fathom the idea that such a wretch could consider himself above my daughter, Mademoiselle de Chartres! If only I could find the connection between his mother and those two devils, it might still be possible to prevent both mismatches...."

"All in due course, Madame. Be wary and do not attempt to overspend what little credit you have with the king. You've accomplished a lot, but His Majesty is not a patient man. There are many, including your own spouse, who would gladly see you removed from court and far from the inner sphere of influence. But I am sure that isn't news to you."

"Do d'Effiat and Lorraine suspect me in the slightest?" asked Madame with trepidation.

"They know that inquiries have been made about the cross. I believe the silversmith is a collaborator, as you suspected. However, they've turned their suspicions toward Lully for some reason. Could that be your doing? They apparently had an altercation with the court composer minutes after leaving the king's chambers yesterday." As always, Wendt's countenance was inscrutable.

"Lully will protest his innocence and may attempt to divert the accusations onto me or d'Effiat's nephew Robin. I need to tidy things up by hammering another nail in his coffin." In her anger, Madame went so far as to actually brandish an imaginary hammer.

Wendt seemed somewhat taken aback by this gesture. "Whatever you do, Madame, I beg you once again to exert extreme caution. Many powerful people, including some you don't suspect, may have interests at stake in keeping things quiet." With that, he handed her an envelope. "I was on my way to deliver this when Mathilde found me," he added.

"And I have something for you as well . . . this letter to my brother, Karl Ludwig, contains extremely sensitive information. See to it personally! Discretion is, as always, of the utmost importance."

Madame smiled as he left. His protective presence always

gave her the inner strength she needed to persist in the minefield that was the court of Versailles. But her smile faded as she examined the envelope more closely. She was always vigilant when it came to her correspondence, and she had a fifth sense when it came to tampering. The seal was indeed that of the House of Hanover, but it appeared to have been overlaid, for underneath there was the slightest trace of a faintly darker layer of wax. She set the letter down and began to pry at the seal with her paper knife. Indeed, it seemed as though the letter had been opened after sealing, but with the utmost care. Had her aunt broken the seal to add to her note, she would no doubt have paid little attention to tearing the parchment. It was also unlikely that she would have used wax of a different color. Could the court censors have been up to their usual mischief? But the seal was definitely that of her aunt Sophia. Royal seals were difficult to duplicate and guarded with the utmost care, as they were guarantors of authenticity.

As she unfolded the brief, she instantly recognized the slant of her favorite correspondent. Even the seemingly random ink spot on the upper-right-hand side of the signature page, which the two women used as an additional security code, indicated its authenticity. The letter was bona fide, but she suspected it had been read by someone in possession of the Hanover seal. Was her imagination playing tricks on her? She knew she was prone to occasional bouts of paranoia. The message, she saw, was uncharacteristically brief.

Geliebteste Neffin,

Please forgive the brevity of this message, but I write to you today with a matter of great urgency. I beg you to cease and desist at once in your efforts to bring down your enemies at court, however much you may desire to do so. Though I am far away at the court of Hanover, I have eyes and ears at the palace of Versailles. You and those you love may be in grave danger by exposing the skeletons in the closet, in particular regarding the sudden death of your unfortunate predecessor. Heed my advice, my headstrong girl, and no harm will come to you.

Your loving aunt Sophie

Liselotte let the letter rest on her lap as she considered the warning with mixed emotions. She felt for a moment like a naughty child who had been chastised by a disappointed parent. But contrition and remorse were emotions that were mostly foreign to her. As a child in Heidelberg, she had more often than not been given free rein and had thus developed a rather audacious and impenitent disposition. She loved her aunt, who had taken her in when her mother's jealous tantrums disrupted the children's education, but she was unshaken in her determination to connect the dots between the Sacred Brotherhood, Madame de Montespan, and Henriette of England. Of course, she knew that she was taking on a powerful enemy. The recent attempt on her life, which the king had dismissed as a mere accident, was a vivid reminder of that. Again, she wondered who might have tampered with her aunt's letter. And how did Sophie know so much about the intrigues at court? Hermann Wendt came to mind, and she made a mental note to find out if he knew more than he was willing to let on.

◆

Her musings were interrupted by the sudden appearance of Mathilde, who had managed to track down Julie. She pushed her fears aside and composed herself as best she could.

"Come in, my dear girls. Please have a seat." The duchess

waived them into her sitting room. "Julie d'Aubigny, is it now? Or the Chevalier de Maupin?"

Julie didn't flinch at the mention of her alias. The news of her *Doppelgänger* had finally made the rounds at court.

"I hear you have ambitions to make a career as an opera singer. I attended your performance at the celebration in honor of the Turkish ambassador, and I have to admit that your voice is indeed divine. You have every right to entertain high expectations. But your promise must be accompanied by audacity if you're to make your way in the world as a woman alone. You will need powerful protectors."

"Monsieur Lully has confidence in my artistic promise, Madame. And he is well-connected and not without means." The girl's self-confidence was almost impudent.

The duchess smiled as she said, "A few months ago, I would have agreed with you, however, the king has turned his favor elsewhere, and the Italian is on the way out. Marc-Antoine Charpentier will no doubt step up as the royal court composer. And don't forget that Lully will expect certain favors in exchange for his protection."

"I have managed to stave him off for now, and I have resources of my own," replied Julie with a tone of satisfaction.

"So I've heard, but he'll lose patience by and by. And you'll be left to fend for yourself. Don't be so proud, my girl. What would you say to laying your future in my hands? My sponsorship would be of much greater benefit to you than that of a has-been composer, and there would be only one small favor that I would ask of you in return."

"I had already assumed that there would be a price to pay, Madame."

"So young, and yet so cynical! You'll go far indeed, my dear. I also hear that you're handy with the sword." Madame sized up the girl approvingly.

"My father was a fencing master, and in the absence of a

son, taught me his trade. I've handled a foil since the age of three. But what would you have me do?"

Mathilde stood by in silent awe.

"Let's hope you won't need those skills. It's a simple task, really," said the duchess, casually. It requires someone who has access to Lully's notes, letters, and general correspondence."

"Lully is notoriously disorganized. His desk is strewn with musical scores, operatic lyrics, visiting cards, and his personal correspondence. In that regard he's an open book. My guess is he believes he's above the law because of his longtime friendship with the king, and the king's love of music and dance."

"So much the better! He'll be the first to be surprised at my cards, if I play them well. Right now, however, he's busy dealing with the consequences from the other day, no doubt protesting his innocence to his allies. This is the perfect time for you to visit his chambers to gather any snippet written in his own hand that could be interpreted as compromising his loyalty to the Brotherhood. Should you be caught *in flagrante delicto*, you can pretext the desire to rehearse a particular arrangement and the need to find the score."

"I doubt it will come to that, Madame. I come and go as I please in his private quarters."

"Perfect. And you shall have your reward, my dear. When you get to Paris, I'll see to it personally that you are lodged and provided for in the Palais-Royal, where my husband once resided with his first wife, Henriette. I myself prefer our castle of Saint-Cloud, but it's located inconveniently far from the center of Paris. But beside that, the Palais-Royal has the important advantage of housing the Opéra de Paris." The duchess looked at Julie triumphantly, knowing that she had played her trump card well.

◆

The two maidens left the duchess's chambers and were making their way down the Galérie des Hommes Illustres, paying no attention to the stately portraits of high-bred lords frozen in time. As they approached the working quarters of the artists of the academy, which were located, somewhat ironically, right beside Madame de Maintenon's private drawing room, Robin popped out from the vestibule of the staircase leading to the top floor of the royal chapel, which was still under construction. Placing himself between them, he grabbed each of them firmly around the waist, with an affable smile on his face:

"Miladies, I believe we have some unfinished business to attend to."

Julie appraised him impudently. "As agreed, we intend to deliver on our part of the bargain, even though we've been led to understand that you were planning to squeal on your uncle before we shook hands on the matter. It's more than likely that I'll be leaving for Paris shortly, so it's up to you to name the place, and Mathilde and I will determine the time."

"I have just been informed that my uncle is planning to return to Paris, due to the mounting tensions here at court. The situation is too precarious for him, and he plans to make himself scarce by retreating to his private residence in the Marais with his current lover. In the meantime, he's left me in charge of his country estate. He'll be gone in a few days, at which time we can enjoy ourselves unhindered in the seclusion of my private chambers." Robin flashed them a wolfish mouthful of white teeth.

"Very well. We'll meet on the fifteenth of the month at midnight. There'll be a full moon rising. Have a carriage waiting for us outside the palace gate," said Julie in a sober voice.

"I shall count the hours and the minutes until next we meet, mesdemoiselles," said Robin with a gloating grin.

When he was out of earshot, Julie turned to Mathilde and said, "I don't know what you see in him! I'd like to knock that smugness right off his face, and I think I know how. He's not the only one who can deal in half-truths."

◆

Chrétien was toiling in the royal kennels, throwing scraps of entrails to the hounds as they snarled at each other, their breath coming out white clouds in the cold. Robin stood by for a while, leaning against the post, observing the youth's powerful frame. When the head groundskeeper's son looked up, he became self-conscious and hastily wiped his hands on his leather apron.

"What brings you here, milord?" he asked.

"I've come with an offer that you'll no doubt find attractive. You may have heard that my uncle has left me in charge of his estate, as he prepares to leave for Paris by the end of the week. The king has discovered his chamber of carnal delights, and the Duke d'Orléans has urged him to flee his country home while he pleads the marquis's case with Louis. It would appear that this may become a permanent situation, as the king's mistress has an increasingly tight grip on censoring licentiousness at court."

"So what's this to do with me?" said Chrétien briskly. He wasn't quite sure what tone to take with Robin. Their past adventure had put them briefly on equal footing, but he was well aware that his junior was his superior.

"I want to employ you as my head groundskeeper. You're young and strong, and you come with the necessary experience. You know the woods as well as anyone, how to chase off poachers, and how to train hounds for the hunt." Robin bent down to pet one of the terriers.

"That's a fine offer, indeed. I've been longing to leave home, but I'll need my father's approval. Fortunately, there are other sons on whom he can rely. Where would I lodge? Would I have a roof of my own?" Chrétien's impassive demeanor concealed an inner flight of fancy, which was leaping and bounding ahead, out of control.

"We've got a vacant cottage that may need some minor repairs, but you're just the sort to do the job. Should you decide to marry, there'll be room for your family as well. I'm also willing to provide you with the added luxury of a scullery maid and a cook."

"Thank you, milord!" said Chrétien, with a deep bow.

◆

Chrétien was in high spirits and whistling a tune when he returned to the village. He stopped at the inn for a cup of ale in order to reflect on his future. For once, Sylvie's overbearing attentions were unable to dampen his mood. He even let her sit by him for a moment until Guillemette ordered her to go about her tasks.

"You look like a cat who's swallowed a mouse," said the innkeeper's wife.

"I have a lot on my mind," he replied. "Knowing how you love idle prattle, I'm sure you'll be one of the first to know of my plans, but for now mum's the word."

"It must be love," said Guillemette, with a toothless, dimpled grin. "Poor Sylvie! She's been pining for you for so long, you know. By the by, have you heard that Yves Roussin, that fellow you were asking about, has been found dead? I'm surprised it took this long for someone to dispatch him to the underworld."

"Good God, woman! How do you come about such information! The gossip mill is alive and churning, I see!" He took a long swig of ale.

"So you knew . . ."

"Enough! You won't get any information from me. Bring me a pint and a bowl of stew, and leave me in peace!"

The innkeeper waddled back to the kitchen reluctantly, loath to abandon her inquiries. Her foul-humored husband eyed her suspiciously.

Chrétien mused over his feelings for Catherine. He longed for her to the point of distraction, but even his newly elevated station in life was too far removed from that of lady-in-waiting to the Grand Dauphine Victoire, a princess who might someday become the queen of France. They had seen each other several times since their fateful encounter in the woods. Their lovemaking was fraught with the fear of being caught, deliciously dangerous, but in late October there was a chill in the air and shelters were few and far between. He knew he had to ask her to marry him, however slight his chances. It was the only honorable thing to do, but for the first time in his life he feared rejection and ridicule. And even were she to wish to be his wife, and live in a humble cottage on d'Effiat's estate, how would her family react? His earlier mood of elation suddenly turned sour. He dropped a coin on the table and was preparing to leave, when Guillemette reappeared with a bowl of piping hot ragout.

"What, child? No more appetite?"

"None whatsoever," he replied, crestfallen, and made his way to the door under the innkeeper's watchful scrutiny.

Halfway home, Chrétien made an abrupt about-face and took the shortcut to the palace. It was nearly suppertime, and most of the courtiers would be preparing to leave their chambers. Catherine would no doubt have a bit of time on her hands, as her mistress was a woman of little vanity. A few minor adjustments to her gown, and perhaps a change of wig, would be all that was required for her appearance. She left it up to others to garner attention, and was quite content to disappear into the background.

With a sense of dread, wondering if this meeting was fated to be their last, Chrétien cast a pebble at Catherine's window-pane. Her slender silhouette appeared immediately against the candlelit room. She looked over her shoulder, and having made sure she was alone, she opened the window to peer into the darkness.

"Chrétien, is that you?"

"Yes, my love, I've come to steal a bit of your time, for I can't stay away."

"Meet me under the north-wing arcades. I'll be there as soon as everyone is seated at dinner. I'll tell my mistress that I'm unwell and need some rest."

Chrétien waited for what seemed like an eternity, pacing back and forth. The gallery was nearly deserted, and the moonlight illuminated the symmetry of the columns that stood guard like silent, lonely sentinels. Every now and then, the hurried clicking of a servant's heels broke the silence. Finally the maiden appeared, and her eager kiss dispelled his misgivings.

"Sit by me a while, lass," he said, cloaking her in his arms. "I have news that cannot bear waiting."

Catherine settled snuggly into the crook of his arm, and he told her of his impending independence.

"I've not yet asked my father's permission, but it would seem unlikely for him to oppose my good fortune." He caressed the down on the back of her neck and could feel her tremble inside.

"It would also most certainly enhance your family's reputation and their financial standing as well."

"Robin has offered me an income, a modest abode, as well as two domestic servants. I could live on the d'Effiat estate."

Catherine looked down and shuffled her feet.

"What is it, love? Are you not happy for me?"

"That I am, however, our meetings will be less frequent, and I fear you'll forget me."

The young man held her closer and felt her shudder beneath her cloak. "That's what I've come to discuss. Summoning all his courage, he got down on one knee and said, "Will you marry me? I can't offer you the life you deserve, but I swear that I will love and honor you as long as there is breath in my body."

Catherine reached out to stroke a windblown curl from his brow and kissed his forehead. There was a touch of sadness in her soft voice as she answered, "I could wish for nothing more in life, but I fear that my widowed mother will object. She would see it as a stain on our family's already tainted reputation. I fear she'll send me to the convent should she get wind of this. But for her, I would gladly throw caution to the wind."

Now that Chrétien had finally pronounced himself, he was not going to back down without a fight.

"What do you owe your family? They're penniless, their estate is in ruins, and they have left you no dowry, yet they have pretensions well above their means. My father's lifestyle may be humble, but he's provided all of his children with life skills, a loving home, and a moderate education. I could do the same for our children, if not better." He turned her to face him, as if to give more weight to his words.

"In aristocratic families, children are a great commodity if they marry well, but a liability and a burden when they don't. When I was fourteen, my mother despaired of my future. Not only because we were destitute, but also because certain rumors had circulated that I was of illegitimate birth and of mixed race. Having few suitors, and none my mother was willing to consider worthy of my lineage, I was on the verge of being cloistered, had it not been for the kindness of the grande dauphine, who took pity on me." She looked at Chrétien, willing him to understand.

Chrétien released her from his embrace and stood up with dignity. It took all the willpower he could muster to tear himself away from Catherine, who looked up at him woefully, eyes brimming with tears.

"I love you more than words can say, but we can no longer go on this way, meeting in secret, hiding our love. If you won't have me, I must take my leave. By your own admission, my station in life is unworthy of you. What if you were to become with child? It grieves me to part, but it's the only honorable thing to do. Should you change your mind, I'll face any obstacle to have you. And Robin d'Effiat is a powerful protector if only he can be persuaded to side with me."

"But I love you, Chrétien!" She held out her arms to him, but he turned and left her to her sorrow.

"Then you, my love, must have the courage of your conviction," he said, with one last parting glance.

THE HUNTER'S MOON

*R*obin stood staring out at the full moon. A thin streak of clouds traveled slowly across the night sky, beneath the pale orb. The shimmering light reflecting off the delicate veil of mist created the illusion of a translucent globe, indolently rolling on an ocean wave. It illuminated patches of milkweed pods that shone like tiny stars in the nearby forest.

In the distance, a clatter of hooves, faint at first, then thunderous on the cobblestone courtyard, announced the arrival of Mathilde and Julie. He greeted them in person, lantern in hand, having dismissed his servants early that evening. The girls wore dark hooded woolen capes that billowed in the autumn wind. Robin swallowed hard at the mystical vision, vaguely grasping the ancient, occult nature of feminine power.

"In the not too distant past, the two of you would have been burned at the stake," he said, but without the slightest trace of his customary sarcasm. With a sense of awe, he led them up the winding stairs and into his chambers.

Julie broke the silence, and the spell he was under.

"Stand by the curtain and don't approach until you are bid

to do so." Untying her cloak, she announced, "Let's start with a lesson in lovemaking."

"I hardly need schooling in such matters," replied Robin with a proud edge in his voice.

"That's not what I have heard. Rumor has it that you're a bit quick on the draw."

"If Mathilde has any complaints, she's never . . ."

"Leave her out of this. She can hardly be expected to know what she's been missing."

Julie began to undress Mathilde with deliberate slowness. She left on her gauzy petticoat and partially undid the laces of her bodice. Mathilde's skin shone like a pearl in the moonlight.

"Lesson one," said Julie, "begin by standing back and taking in the full measure of your lover's beauty from a distance, before rushing in like the fool you are."

Julie then proceeded to undress herself, again partially, and bid Mathilde to lie with her on the bed. Robin made to join them, but he was once again told to wait.

"Lesson two: always leave something to the imagination . . . a mystery for the mind to ponder after your lover has left. You'll be all the more eager to see her again and find greater pleasure in your lovemaking."

With that, Julie unlaced a bit more of Mathilde's bodice and uncovered her breasts. Mathilde's breath had quickened sharply, but Julie avoided touching them and gently began to stroke her arms and lower stomach, then reached under her skirt to lightly caress her inner thighs.

"Lesson three: bide your time before touching your lover's most sensitive parts, until she can wait no more. Begin with a featherlike stroke, and take your cues from her breathing to pace the quickening or slowing rhythm of your movements. Stop, then move and breathe in unison when you've almost reached your peak, wait for her to come, and let your two bodies climax together."

By the time Julie had finished demonstrating, Mathilde was clutching the bedposts and arching her back with pleasure. Robin could stand by no longer. He had never before felt such wild desire.

"Enough with the lessons," he said, removing his pants and climbing onto the bed. But in a flash, he found a rapier pointed at his cock.

"You see," said Julie, "lesson four: remain clearheaded at all times, never falling victim to your own blind passion or you'll become easy prey to your enemy. Many a man has been slain in the arms of his lover."

Robin's erection wilted instantly. He watched helplessly as Julie put on the garments she had shed, and made to leave unceremoniously.

"I've kept my share of the bargain, and I must be off. I'll be leaving for Paris in two days. But mark my words, I'll see you again, my love," she said, with a sidelong glance at Mathilde.

"No, you have not!" said Robin, regaining some of his lost composure, but being unarmed, he didn't dare lay a hand on Julie to detain her. "I haven't lain with either one of you."

"A *ménage à trois* means many things to many different people. You had the good fortune to play the voyeur in our little triangle. How many people would stop at nothing to have been in your shoes? There's many a peephole on the palace grounds."

"But…"

"But… you were also offered instruction as an additional benefit. My four lessons, should you decide to heed them, will stand you in good stead with the ladies. Thanks to me, you may someday become master in the art of love and the mysteries of intimacy, rather than the mediocre toy boy that you are now. Mathilde, however, will stay with you now, to reap the immediate benefits of your newly acquired knowledge. Adieu!"

With that, Julie threw on her cape, fastened her sword to

her side, and as she made her way toward the door, her sensual sway suddenly changed into a determined, almost military stride. Robin followed her with his gaze as she left the room, and he felt as though he were witnessing a mystifying instance of transfiguration.

Truly, she is a witch, he thought.

He turned toward the bed to see sadness in Mathilde's eyes and a feeling of immense tenderness came over him.

"Do you miss her already?" he whispered, removing a lock of hair from her damp forehead.

"No, it's not for her I cry but out of yearning for you, for the boy you once were, for the days in which we were so close. What's happened to you, Robin? My feelings for you are still the same."

"Hush," he said, pushing her down slowly onto the bed. He realized that for the first time since they had become lovers, they had the luxury of spending the night together. He cradled her in his arms and felt her skin, dewy with perspiration through her clothing. Taking his time, he fondled her beneath her skirts. Her skin was as soft and fresh as that of an infant, and she was wet with desire. He wanted to explore the smoothness of her body slowly, but she was ready for him, and as he came inside her, she exploded with a shudder. He could feel her body tremble from within, as a series of convulsions shook her inner core.

They made love twice more before they were sated that night. They drifted away toward dawn, but Mathilde awoke with a start. "I must be off before daylight, so as not to be seen," she said.

"Stay a while longer, my love," he said. When she tried to resist, he added in as casual a way as he could, "Will you be my wife?"

Mathilde was startled. "What about your betrothed?"

"I sent word yesterday that I want to break off the engagement. It was contracted by my guardian and without my consent, but now that he has been stripped of that role, it's been rendered null and void. So again, will you marry me?"

Mathilde looked him squarely in the eyes. "Nothing would please me more, Robin, though I know that even if you love me in this moment, you'll make me suffer some day."

"Fidelity is vastly overrated," said Robin with a grin. "I defy you to name one man at court who's a faithful husband."

"I've seen the long-suffering wives, but many find their consolation elsewhere. May I be allowed one condition?"

Robin looked at her with considerable surprise. He hadn't expected that she would waver or name her terms.

"You realize, of course, that marriage to me would be a great social advantage. But go ahead, name your condition."

"That I should be allowed the company of Julie d'Aubigny from time to time," she said with a grin.

"Why you brazen little vixen! Your provision only makes me want you all the more. What a couple we will make!" She wrestled herself loose from his embrace, pulled on her clothes, and blew him a kiss, as he watched her walk out the door. Then he fell back on his pillow and into a deep, dreamless slumber.

◆

Madame paced the floor, smoothing out the wrinkled message in Lully's handwriting that Julie had managed to salvage from the scraps of paper scattered around his bureau. This was more than she had hoped for, and she couldn't help but marvel at how foolish or foolhardy he was to leave his scribbling lying about. Of course, taken out of context, the message could be interpreted in several different ways. But Lully had been warned by the brotherhood, and he was now presumably under close surveillance.

A brief rap on the door announced Lully's arrival.

"Come in!" she said. She failed to rise from her armchair when he entered. It was obvious that he was wary of this summons, the first of its kind. He bowed before her in an overtly obsequious manner that could have been interpreted as sarcastic. She ignored the veiled insult.

"Monsieur Lully, it has come to my attention that your reputation has been sullied among my husband's *intimate* friends." She looked at him steadily to make sure that he understood her meaning. "Something that might make or break your career has recently fallen into my hands."

At that she handed him the note. He paled when he read it but looked up defiantly. He then read it out loud: "'Your Majesty, I shall meet you in your private quarters as per your request and at your earliest convenience with the information. D'Effiat and Lorraine need not know of our encounter.' This note is neither dated, nor sealed, and it's too vague to be incriminating," he added, but his countenance had altered, and he had begun to sweat.

"That would be so, under ordinary circumstances, but accusations are flying, and you're the prime suspect. I have no interest in you personally, Monsieur Lully, and would gladly spare you pain in exchange for some information. Word has it that your situation at court is tenuous at best. Should your friends' suspicions of betrayal be confirmed, you and I both know of what they're capable."

"I had already assumed that you'd brought me here for a purpose. May I ask what it is exactly?" Lully's eyes were puffy, presumably from a restless night.

"I'll agree to destroy my 'evidence' against you before your very eyes. In return you must help me destroy my enemies. Maybe in the future, you'll conceal your writings with greater care." Madame glanced warily at her own writing desk. It was securely locked.

"What can you possibly want from me? D'Effiat has left for Paris amid rumors of child molestation, and the king has just announced the chevalier's temporary banishment from court. What else could satisfy your desire for revenge?"

"Montespan needs to be brought down as well. Her involvement in the Affair of the Poisons almost cost her her head, but her sway over the king is still strong, despite Maintenon's objections. She is, after all, the mother of his legitimized children, whom he plans to marry off advantageously. I know that she and my opponents have consorted and conspired in the past, and I have reason to believe that she was made an honorary member of your little band of brothers."

"In that case, I'm not really sure in what way I can be of service, Madame."

The duchess stood to her full height; she was twice the girth of the slender Italian.

"I have heard some testimony tying her to the untimely and suspicious death of Henriette, my predecessor. I know that you can provide at least some of the missing pieces." She dangled the crumpled paper in front of him.

Lully seemed to be measuring her up and deciding whether to call her bluff, but she knew she had him by the balls.

"Madame, the court physician decreed that your husband's first wife died of a perforated ulcer," the musician said feebly.

"We both know the obvious, which is that autopsies cannot satisfactorily prove or disprove the presence of poison. I am quite aware of the official results, but that notwithstanding, Henriette had many enemies at court, and she had openly declared to her intimates that she was being poisoned already some time before her death. Since she had successfully requested the Chevalier de Lorraine's temporary banishment to Rome a year earlier, she had good reason to suspect someone in his inner circle."

"Everyone at court knows that," said the composer dismissively.

"Her symptoms were consistent with slow arsenic poisoning, such as swelling of the stomach, hair loss, and weight loss. The marquis's servant was seen to be adding something to her chicory water that very afternoon."

"But in what way does that information point to Montespan?"

"That's the missing information I am relying on you to supply, my friend."

"What I can tell you will not be as conclusive as you would like," said Lully in a low whisper. "Henriette's death came as a surprise to the brotherhood, though certainly a welcome one. Montespan, who had been dabbling in aphrodisiacs and charms, was indeed asked to have her page or on occasion her chambermaid administer small doses of arsenic to the woman she saw as her rival for the king's affection, not to kill her outright, but to lessen her desirability. In addition, she had stolen a lock of Henriette's hair, which she kept in her locket, as a charm to steal her powers over Louis."

"Don't tell me that Montespan, who had every reason to be jealous of Henriette, didn't finish her off! She once threatened to kill the king himself, and we know that she may have played an indirect role in eliminating her younger rival Marie Angélique de Fontanges, by causing her to abort."

"All I can add is that the night of Henriette's death, the brotherhood became justifiably fearful that the finger would be pointed at them. I believe that at that point, d'Effiat's factotum Roussin was sent to silence the page and to get rid of the locket."

"So indeed, murder was involved. The suspicions aroused were quickly suppressed, no doubt thanks to my husband's influence on the king. The poor page boy probably had no idea what he was being asked to do, nor any say in the matter, and being a commoner, was soon forgotten."

"As to who might have administered a final, lethal dose of arsenic, it's hard to tell," added Lully evasively, as he was eager to leave. Beads of sweat had started to gather on his brow. "However, I can tell you without a doubt, that the one person Roussin feared more than anyone, even more than the Chevalier de Lorraine, was Montespan's chambermaid Claude des Œillets."

"How so?" asked the duchess, reaching for her fan. The fire had just been stoked, and the room was sweltering. "I saw her at court recently. She looks like a middle-aged dowager, plain and unassuming, but at Versailles I know that appearances can be deceiving. It was clear that there was no love lost between her and her former mistress, as they were forced to sit together during the Turkish festivities. In fact, now that I think of it, it was downright shocking to see a person of her class seated beside high-ranking members of court. I believe her mother was a famous actress at one time."

"Until the Affair of the Poisons erupted, Claude was the principal contact person between Catherine La Voisin, the sorceress who was burned at the stake, and Montespan. In the process, the chambermaid acquired wealth well beyond her lowly station and gave birth to at least one of Louis's royal bastards. Although she harbored resentment toward the king for refusing to legitimize her child, he had his architect build her a splendid residence on the outskirts of town."

"Even if at the time she may have been in a position to blackmail her mistress, why was Roussin so terrified of her? He implicated Lorraine and d'Effiat under duress of torture but never mentioned the involvement of Montespan or des Œillets."

"You have no idea, do you, what those she-devils were capable of?" Lully looked surprised.

"I know that Montespan used aphrodisiacs to lure the king away from Henriette of England, and later Louise de La Vallière. I also know that when the king replaced her with Marie-Angélique Scorailles de Fontanges, she threatened both their lives."

"The aphrodisiacs were only the tip of the iceberg. The two women also attended black masses conducted in private by a priest. In one such instance two pigeon hearts were placed in the communion cup, symbolizing those of Athénaïs and Louis. A spell was cast to invoke the death of La Vallière, and though she didn't die, she left the court to become a Carmelite nun."

"That's as near to death as it gets," said the duchess grimly. "So Montespan got her wish and became the king's favorite. But spells and incantations wouldn't be sufficient to shake a man like Roussin, would they?" Madame reminded herself not to believe hearsay, tempting as it was.

"Although this rumor has never been substantiated and can probably be simply a matter of superstitious confabulation, it is said that for the tidy sum of fifty pistoles and a donation of two thousand pounds to the church of Villebouzin, Claude des Œillets, passing herself off as her mistress, may have had the Abbé Guibourg perform a mass on her womb. She was stark naked, but her face was shielded by a large headdress that had been folded down over her breasts. An infant's throat was savagely slit over her lower body. Although Guibourg confessed to this horror, the identity of the woman was never certified. This time, however, the motive of the conjuration was not the *love* but the *death* of Louis of France."

"How dreadful! Is it possible that such atrocities could have taken place under our very noses? I can barely fathom it! The motivation is questionable as well. Why would Montespan want Louis dead? She may have threatened him in the heat of the moment, but he was her lifeline at court. And if it was des Œillets, how could *she* have afforded two thousand pounds?"

Lully shrugged. "I have no idea, Madame. For a while, Claude was frequently seen in the company of a mysterious Englishman, whom many assumed to be her lover. Perhaps he was a man of means. However, the story is indeed preposterous, and I give it little credence, as did the king himself at the time. But what I am trying to say is that Roussin, superstitious fool that he was, would have been terrified of a woman he believed to be in league with the devil and who seemed to have an ill-begotten fortune at her disposal." He looked at the door, waiting to be dismissed.

"I am not sure whether to trust you, but very well, you've earned your stay of execution," said the duchess, as she held the paper to the candle flame and then threw it into the hearth. "God save you, if you've been lying to me! The final piece of the puzzle is still missing, but I'm close to solving the mystery. Unfortunately, Montespan will probably come out of yet another scandal unscathed, as she's been pardoned for worse in the past."

As Lully slunk out the doorway, Madame returned to her writing desk. She had the vague feeling that the key to the mystery was within her reach but that someone was withholding information. Could it have been the composer? Or someone closer? Her own husband perhaps? They barely spoke to each other these days.

◆

Mathilde was heading back to Madame's apartment when Catherine rushed up to her from behind.

"You nearly gave me a heart attack!" she said to her friend. "You look ill. What's wrong?"

"I need your advice, Mathilde!" There was a soft tremor in Catherine's voice.

"I thought you were the sensible one! I never imagined that

I would have to counsel *you*! In fact, I was looking for you as well. But you go first."

"I don't know what to do! I know you'll be angry with me, but you've been so preoccupied yourself lately that I didn't dare bring up my own problems."

"This wouldn't have something to do with Chrétien, would it? You've been distracted of late."

"I tried to tell you, but my cousin seems to have your ear these days. I thought you couldn't abide her!"

"You know she's leaving to make her way in Paris at the Palais-Royal opera. My mistress has offered to promote her career as a singer," said Mathilde, with a tinge of regret. "So what is it?"

"You've trusted me with your secrets, and now I beg of you not to judge mine, because there's nothing you can say that I haven't told myself a thousand times over."

"So you're in love . . ."

"Head over heels, and what's worse, is that we've been meeting in private almost every day until last week. We can't keep our hands off each other, and I'm afraid that we'll soon be discovered and shamed in public."

"No, I won't judge you," said Mathilde, reaching out to hold her friend. "But you know that your mother will send you to the Ursuline convent if word reaches her that you're having an affair with a commoner."

"Chrétien has asked me to marry him. Robin has offered him the position of head groundskeeper on the marquis's estate, and even a modest house for his future family. Chrétien is fully aware that his offer would require me to accept living in humble conditions, and I believe he expects me to refuse. Since his proposal last week, he's refused to see me, and I'm so miserable I can't stomach the slightest bit of food."

"So you've not yet answered him. I must say that I'm impressed by his willpower and sense of honor. But you, dear, aren't accustomed in the least to manual work or to running a household. Your skills are limited to needlework and tending to your mistress's wardrobe, hair, and rouge. Ladies of your social station don't raise their own children. Imagine those noisy brats wreaking havoc in your home and you playing the servant to your husband and master!"

"I could imagine nothing more joyful than being surrounded by my own children. And the pleasure of knowing Chrétien would be mine for life."

"My God, the publication of Madame de Sévigné's correspondence with her daughter seems to have made motherhood unjustifiably fashionable at court! But don't forget that that very same daughter, the Countess de Grignan, the apple of her mother's eye, shipped her own infant girl Marie-Blanche to the convent at the age of one, and that the girl's been there ever since."

"The Countess de Grignan was rumored to prefer her husband to her child, but I know I would love them equally," said Catherine glowingly.

"I think you have a very idealistic view of marriage. As for me, though I love Robin, I see it from a more realistic perspective. Our passion won't last, and there'll be other lovers for both of us. We'll have our share of disagreements and hurt, but I do believe that, since we began as friends and lovers, we can both benefit from the arrangement."

"Mathilde, you speak as if you weren't aware that Robin is engaged to another."

"He sent word to Madeleine yesterday that he intends to break off the engagement, owing to the fact that his uncle no longer holds legal guardianship over him. He claims that he entered into the agreement against his will."

"Do you have any idea how she reacted to the news? She seemed quite keen on the marriage, and I doubt she will go down without a fight. Breach of contract is a serious thing."

"In exchange for key information from Robin, my mistress has supplied him with some damaging information about his fiancée's dodgy past, which would make the most intrepid man hesitate to marry her. She won't want the matter to air at court, knowing that Robin could now claim her to be unfit for marriage and mentally unstable."

The two girls interrupted their conversation as they reached the door. A guard in royal livery moved forward to open it for them. Mathilde breathed in the crisp, clean autumn air and the sharp scent of decaying leaves. They sat down on their favorite bench and huddled together.

"Any idea what she did?"

"No, but I will eventually find out. Robin has asked me to be his wife."

Catherine embraced her friend with true emotion, then moved back and said, "I don't know whether to be happy for you or sad. Tying your destiny to that of the future Marquis d'Effiat is risky business, although you won't be lacking for money. I fear you're more in love with him than he with you."

"Love has very little to do with our arrangement. I would be a fool to reject a man for whom I have a great deal of affection. He's rich, handsome, and although we lust for each other now, our mutual friendship will outlive the passion. How many women in our social class can say the same? Marriage is usually nothing more than a business arrangement."

"A powerful and handsome man is wont to have his fair share of mistresses."

"Perhaps, but I know that I'll have a means of consolation," replied Mathilde with the hint of a smile, then looked at Catherine's expression, and added "You don't seem happy for me, Catherine. Could you be envious?"

"It's not that at all, Mathilde. It's just that I, too, am in love. But my situation is the exact opposite of yours. I know that Chrétien would never betray me, but he has little to offer outside of love and constancy. Accepting his proposal would put me at odds with my mother and break her heart. Rejecting it would break mine. Am I to sacrifice my one chance at happiness for our illusory family honor?"

"Have you considered that my marriage to Robin would allow me to help in some ways? We wouldn't be able to consort in public, but in private we could maintain our friendship. I think Robin is sincere in his regard for Chrétien. Were they not separated by class, I'm sure he would consider him a friend and an able counselor."

"So what would you advise me to do?"

"Follow your heart, as I have mine. You'll have plenty of time to be reasonable in your old age."

◆

Chrétien had been waiting at the Auberge du Cerf Blanc for his father's arrival. His ale mug was still full, as he stared absentmindedly into the foam. He had asked him to meet him there for a conversation far away from the unbearable din of his siblings and his mother's watchful eye. Goliath was at his feet, happily gnawing on a bone. When Jean Desforges appeared, Guillemette ushered him over to the table with effusiveness. He was still handsome at forty-five and held the respect of the community for his position and integrity. He was slightly shorter and bulkier than his son, but his frame was upright and proud. Chrétien noted that his father's blond hair was turning lighter with age so that it appeared to be a halo above his ruddy forehead. The resemblance between the two men was striking and the innkeeper remarked on it flirtatiously, like the old coquette and businesswoman she was.

Having ordered the mutton pie, Jean sat down wearily and took a gulp of Chrétien's beer.

"It looks like you've lost your appetite as well as your thirst, son. What's the reason for this private meeting?"

"I've been offered the position of head intendant of the grounds at the d'Effiat's estate. It will pay well, and lodging will be provided. I've come to ask for your permission to accept."

"I've heard that the marquis has left for Paris, amid rumors of sexual misconduct. Under ordinary circumstances, the offer would be a great honor, but why would you want to work for a scoundrel?"

"It's his nephew Robin who's taken over the reins of the estate, and he holds me in some regard. One might even say we're friends."

"Beware of the friendship of the powerful! There's always self-interest involved."

"Perhaps, but I'm not such a fool as to consider myself anything other than his servant. Nonetheless, you yourself work at the palace of Versailles, where scandal's a way of life. The moral climate's no reason to decline an advantageous offer."

"I can't disagree with you there, son. As the eldest, it'll be your responsibility to ensure the family's good fortune after I die. I believe I can entrust that to you?"

"You can indeed, Father."

"Well, then, there's one other condition. I've had a mind to bring up this matter for some time now. You'll need a wife to look after your home and well-being once you've left the family abode. They say a man may build a house but a woman creates a home. More than one lass would be pleased to attend to those duties, especially in light of your sudden stroke of luck. Have you considered a suitable partner?"

Chrétien could not bring himself to admit that he had already asked Catherine to marry him without his father's consent. That would only serve to enrage him.

"I do have someone I'm fond of, but I'm afraid that being of noble birth, she'll no doubt refuse. Nonetheless, I beg your permission to ask, just in case fortune should smile on me a second time."

"No noblewoman could be of any assistance in the life of a working man. Her fancy airs and lack of basic skills would be more of a hindrance than an advantage to you. She would spend her days wasting your money on new gowns and rouge."

"Father, this girl is different. She's modest, discreet, and most of all, devoted to me, as I am to her. Her name is Catherine de Sauvignon, and she's lady-in-waiting to the grande dauphine."

"Well, you certainly have high aspirations! How can you expect her to lower her standards and thwart her family's expectations? She may end up harboring resentment toward you for the loss of standing, and you may eventually grow tired of her lording that over you. As the saying goes: the man who marries above his station finds a master! Would your family feel welcome in her home? I wonder."

"Again, Father, I swear to you that she is as kind as she is beautiful."

"I'm going to surprise you by giving my consent. But be prepared to be rejected by your lady love. It's good to aim high but not to shoot at the moon, my boy. It'll only lead to disappointment. Be content with what God has granted to you. I'll give you one week to win the maid's hand, after that I'll be the one to choose a wife for you from your own class. Take it or leave it."

With that his father stood up, tossed a few coins on the table, and made his exit. Guillemette prattled on while walking him to the door, but he didn't turn around. Chrétien was startled by his father's wary approval, but he knew that is was based on his lack of faith in such an improbable union. His father was betting against him in the hope of gaining the advantage. Chrétien cringed to think what type of wife his father might choose for him. At that thought, Sylvie appeared from the kitchen. It was his signal to go. He stretched to his full height, made for the door, and braced himself against the chill of the evening. On his way down the path to the main square, he was startled by two hands that caught him from behind, to form a blindfold around his eyes. He was irked by Sylvie's persistence, having made his lack of interest clear enough, and was about to shrug her off, when he recognized the light touch and the pressure of Catherine's slender body against his back. Turning around swiftly, he slid his arm around her waist, drawing her close. She smiled up at him. It was all the answer he needed, as he bent down to kiss her lips.

◆

After having taken leave of Catherine, Mathilde reckoned it necessary to inform her mistress of recent events. She knew Madame was unhappy with her for having lost the locket and for her recent distractedness, but she hoped that her present circumstances and good fortune would explain her behavior. As she was walking down one of the lesser traveled hallways where the single ladies-in-waiting resided, she suddenly sensed that she was being observed. This impression of being followed had become all too familiar of late, and gave rise to a heightened sense of awareness. She felt a tingling sensation as the hair rose on the back of her neck and heard a light footstep that stopped when she did, but not quite quickly enough. Suddenly a ghostly face appeared out of a poorly lit passageway. Fear paralyzed Mathilde momentarily, just long enough for Madeleine to get the better of her. Yanking her by the hair, she pulled her to the ground, causing her to briefly lose consciousness. When she regained it, Madeleine was sitting on her chest, choking the breath out of her. Though Mathilde was the stronger of the two, her arms flailed helplessly under the attack. Her rival's fury had given her an almost superhuman strength.

"You dirty little bitch! Didn't you suspect that I would have you followed? You and your little friend Julie? You thought you could outmaneuver me, but I won't go down quietly! You'll be going down with me!" She looked every bit as mad as Madame claimed her to be.

Mathilde started to black out for a second time, when Madeleine suddenly loosened her grip and appeared to levitate into the air, hovering above her. It all seemed to be a hallucination, but then Wendt's face came into view. He was holding the slight frame of Madeleine de Noailles in the air as she kicked and screamed. This attracted the attention of the palace guards and several courtiers, who came running to gleefully witness the catfight. Wendt handed Madeleine over to the guards and carried Mathilde back to Madame's quarters.

◆

Her mistress was all aflutter, tending to her lady-in-waiting. Mathilde's throat was bruised, and she spoke in a hoarse voice.

"Don't concern yourself, Madame. My pride is more wounded than anything. I can't believe that weakling got the better of me!"

"Sit here a while and have a glass of Glühwein. I should call the doctor, but I am afraid he'll do more harm than good. A bleeding is not what's needed right now."

Wendt explained briefly and bluntly what had happened but seemed eager to take his leave.

Once he had left, Madame asked, "Tell me why that madwoman attacked you! Rumor has it that Robin has broken off his engagement with her. This little episode and her arrest will certainly free him from any breach-of-contract charges. But why you? Has Robin finally proposed to you?"

"That he has, Madame. I was on my way to tell you of my plan to accept his marriage proposal."

"The offer is indeed an advantageous one, and one that many a girl might dream of, my dear. But have you considered what it means to become a member of such an infamous family of rogues? Your own reputation may be dragged through the mud in the process."

"I've taken those matters into due consideration, but the benefits outweigh the disadvantages. My family is noble, but my dowry is small. I could never hope to aspire to such a match, were it not for the genuine affection between Robin and me. We grew up together, and I know his flaws and weaknesses. But I'm the only one who can love him despite that knowledge."

"Your path will be a difficult one, Mathilde. A good marriage requires more than four bare legs in bed!"

"Perhaps, but we shall learn to compromise. I'd rather have a brief period of passion than a long life of boredom. My parents were at one time considering marrying me off to an elderly widowed country squire, however even *he* lost interest when he found out that I'd be more of a financial burden to him than an asset."

"You know that you have my blessing, girl. Whatever you decide, I'll lend you my support. I'll never forget my own distress when I was forced to leave my home in Heidelberg to marry the king's brother. Marital relations have always been an irksome duty to me. Fortunately for me, my husband felt the same way and left me alone most of the time."

"I'm afraid that Catherine's future will be even more diffi-cult than mine. She's bound and determined to marry beneath her station, and her mother will no doubt disown her once she learns of the mismatch. As Robin's wife, I'll make it my duty to protect her from being forced into a convent, and it would please me if you and the grande dauphine would consent to do the same."

Madame simply shook her head. "What is it with you young folk? Insubordination seems to be the rule of the day. I shouldn't agree to any of this, but I remind myself of my own unhappiness in matters of the heart. I'm assuming it's the young groundskeeper she's after. . . ." Her voice trailed off, as she was reminded of her own forbidden attachment for Wendt. "It's fortunate that Hermann was there to rescue you from harm. I often wonder what I would do without him."

"I owe him a great debt, Madame, but it does seem a bit odd that he's always on hand when needed. I've had the feeling of late that I am being watched. And the more I think of it, the odder it seems that the locket went missing shortly after I went to his quarters."

"Silly girl! Noailles herself told you that she's been having you followed. How dare you imply anything other than honorable conduct from Herr Wendt! I trust him more than anyone else, including my husband! I won't hear of it!"

"Very well, Madame. It's my own fault that the pendant went missing. Had I not been so eager to see Robin, I might have been more careful. But I swear to you that I did a thorough search, and it all seems to lead to your courier."

"Nonsense! Unfortunately, thanks to your carelessness, we've lost a key piece of the puzzle. It would appear beyond doubt that the locket you found in the woods belonged to Montespan. I was able to wrangle some information from Lully, who explained her connection to d'Effiat and Lorraine. The lock of hair belonged to my husband's first wife. It was being used as a talisman to weaken her hold over Louis. That Montespan is a superstitious shrew, as has been proven in the past, and possibly even one of monstrous proportions. But our investigation is at a standstill for lack of further evidence. We may never know who administered the fatal dose of arsenic to Henriette of England."

"In any event, the chevalier has been exiled once again over the recent scandal and d'Effiat has fled to Paris, perhaps even permanently. You'll have some peace, at least for a while."

"True, but thanks to my husband, they've gotten off lightly yet again. They deserve the gallows for their crimes against nature!" Madame's face looked positively apoplectic as she considered the injustice of it all. She sat down abruptly to steady her countenance. "Well, Mathilde, I hope you know what you're getting into. I'll miss your daily presence more than your services, which have been somewhat sporadic of late. Off with you, now. I need some time to think." But it was with great regret that she saw her leave. An overpowering sense of loneliness weighed down on her soul.

Once Mathilde was gone, Liselotte realized that the girl had touched a raw nerve. There was some truth in what she had said, although the duchess was loathe to admit it. While she knew it would be best to put the matter to rest, her obstinacy would not let her do so. She needed to satisfy her curiosity and attempt to follow the locket one last time. With a trembling hand she opened the door to her private chambers and made her way down to the servants' quarters. She was convinced that Wendt was protecting her from dangerous waters and that he knew much more than he was willing to let on. It was rare for her to visit the lower lodgings, and her presence there would normally attract attention. However, she knew that the king's latest *divertissement* was in full swing, and had she summoned Wendt to her chambers, she would lose the advantage of surprise.

When she got there, she found the room to be empty. It was fastidiously organized, with very few possessions, apart from a miniature of Wendt's wife on the writing table, an inkwell, and a pen box. She knew better than to nose around, but she couldn't help opening the box. The man was such a mystery to her. The coffer contained the usual writing implements, quills, a sharpener, sealing wax, and cachets. Much to her surprise, she noticed that among the seals was one bearing the insignia of the House of Hanover. As she was trying to digest this revelation, she was startled by a figure in the mirror above the desk and dropped the object in her hand. Wendt was standing right behind her, so close that she felt suddenly threatened by his presence, but at the same time she blushed with embarrassment at being caught in the act of prying into his personal life.

"Perhaps this is what you were looking for, Madame," he said, pulling Montespan's pendant from his vest pocket. He handed it to her for inspection and when she opened it, she saw that it still contained the lock of hair that allowed it to be identified as belonging to the king's former mistress.

The duchess was speechless and confused. Was the trust she had placed in her courier just as much of an illusion as everything else at court? Was her reality but a reflection that hid a sinister truth just below the surface?

"If you will humor me, Madame, I'll tell you the complete story of your husband's first wife. Your aunt Sophie has summoned me back to Hanover immediately, because your investigation has opened up some cracks that we assumed to have been covered up for many years. Once you have heard the report, I shall rest my fate in your hands. You'll have the ultimate say and determine my guilt or innocence in the matter, as is only right. Please have a seat."

"So it was *you* who opened my last letter from Hanover and later resealed it!" said the duchess, finally able to regain her composure and her wits.

"Yes, it was. I'd notified your aunt of the powerful enemies whose anger you'd aroused, and she was concerned for your safety. It has been my privilege and my mission to serve and protect you since the day you arrived at court."

"But you arrived here many years earlier, shortly after Henriette was wed to Philippe d'Orléans."

"I've lived at court intermittently for the past twenty years. And I was sent here by none other than your aunt Sophie's husband, Ernst August of Brunswick-Lüneburg. Henriette was very close to her brother Charles the Second, and there was due concern over her influence on him regarding matters of faith. She and her mother, Henriette-Marie of France, were Stuarts and Roman Catholic fanatics. When Charles the First of England was executed in 1649, his wife and young daughter sought exile at the court of France."

"I had heard that the mother's ambition was to contract a union between her daughter and the present king, but when that plan failed, she settled on his brother, Philippe."

"Most of all, the mother wanted to turn England away from Protestant rule. When she saw that Louis was smitten with Henriette, she used her daughter to push France and England into a pact. And her plan nearly succeeded at the time of the not-so-secret Treaty of Dover."

"But Henriette's untimely death put a convenient end to that."

"Yes, but you might say that she was given a slight *push* in that direction. As you suspected, Lorraine and d'Effiat conspired with Montespan to administer slow arsenic poisoning, in the hope of weakening her sway over the king. He was very much enamored with the spritely Minette, as he called her. Henriette suspected the two men of poisoning her and had voiced her concerns to Louis. All it took was for someone to administer a final, lethal dose, and the blame would rest on the chevalier and the marquis."

"So no suspicions ever fell on *you*," said the duchess, completing his story.

"I was sent here as a spy, and my mandate was to inspect the official correspondence between the court of France and

England. Being a courier for the House of Orléans made that job quite easy. When you came to court, your protection became my second assignment. I've ever been your loyal servant."

"But you didn't hesitate to kill when ordered to."

"I did not. Or rather I did not hesitate to employ the services of Mademoiselle Claude des Œillets to that effect. She had easy access to the poisons and aphrodisiacs that she procured for her mistress. It was so simple really. She poured a fatal dose of arsenic into Henriette's chicory water, which she then handed to her mistress. Montespan was in the habit of administering tiny doses, so when she handed the cup to her page to give to Henriette, she unwittingly eliminated her rival. Claude des Œillets was handsomely rewarded by the Protestant faction, but Montespan never trusted her again."

"Murder by proxy!" said the duchess. "The chain of command is like a series of mirrored images, and virtually untraceable, disappearing into the distance like a hallucination!" There was a deep sadness in her eyes as she looked at her long-time ally. "So even you, in the end, cannot be trusted!"

"If England had returned to papism, an ensuing bloodbath would have been unavoidable. I spared many a life with my single act. Furthermore, your aunt Sophie is also a Stuart, albeit of the Protestant line, and a remote contender for the throne of England, since her mother, Elizabeth, was Charles the First's sister and she is the late Henriette's first cousin."

"Surely, she would never have ordered her own cousin's murder!" said Madame with a shudder, again feeling the ground shift beneath her feet.

"No, she did not. But she is to some degree complicit as she took no action to prevent it. The order came from higher up, but I'm not at liberty to reveal that person's identity to you. I've said enough, however, for you to understand why I am being sent back to Germany. Of course, you could have me arrested for high treason, but in the process you would have to implicate your own family. I have no regrets for what I did. I consider myself to be a soldier in service to my country."

There was no arrogance in Wendt's voice as he spoke, just quiet confidence. How well he knew her, her loyalty to her family, her religion, and her native land, she thought. She wondered if he had ever guessed her feelings for him, too.

She stood up wearily and went to face the window. Her lips formed a thin line and her heavily jowled chin was set with determination as she watched a few drunken stragglers stumble amid gusts of laughter. She turned back to face him, feeling betrayed by his departure. Her isolation at court would now be almost complete. Her meddling had led to this, and she had no one to blame but herself. And what had she gained? The loose ends would be swept under the table and the lost boys would never be totally avenged. The chevalier's exile, which would be brief, was nothing but an empty gesture, the duke would see to that. The king cared little for the village children, but he did love his son Louis de Bourbon. Lorraine's punishment was the result of that instance of abuse, nothing more. His ally d'Effiat had gotten off scot-free. No one cared about Roussin's murder, and most of his secrets had died with him. Meanwhile, Claude des Œillets was living comfortably in a country manor.

"I shall no doubt have to account for my absence at the festivities tonight. Life is but a masquerade at Versailles. Godspeed, Hermann!" she said, her voice quavering with emotion. Using his first name was so intimate a gesture that she immediately regretted it.

Wendt bent down to gently kiss her lips, turned on his heels, and silently left the room. And in that moment she understood what it meant to feel unconditional love. She understood her husband's tenderness for Philippe de Lorraine, she fathomed Louis's ability to forgive Montespan, accepted

Mathilde's blindness toward Robin and Catherine's willingness to fall from grace. The inscription on the locket came to mind. *Qui m'aime, me suive* was no longer ambiguous. To love meant to follow. It was not experienced in the grand passions and lustful encounters, but in moments of sacrifice, service, and kindness. But most of all, in forgiveness. Her heart was as full of love as it had ever been.

"Godspeed!" she whispered again, unsure whether she was uttering a blasphemy.

NOTE TO THE READER

I must thank you from the bottom of my heart for choosing to read Hall of Mirrors. I sincerely hope you've enjoyed it and I hope, good or bad you will let me know what you think by leaving a review on Amazon or Goodreads.

It makes my day to read the thoughts of those who have read my works. Please feel free to follow me on Facebook I love connecting with my readers!

ACKNOWLEDGMENTS

I would like to thank Lafayette College for having funded some of the extensive research that went into this book, including trips to the Bibliothèque de l'Arsenal in Paris and to the University of Heidelberg. Most importantly, however, the college afforded me the luxury of an invaluable research assistant, Leo Mackenzie, who helped provide information on daily life during the late seventeenth century at the French court of Versailles. He also proved to be instrumental in establishing a chronological timeline of the historical characters and events that provide the framework of the novel.

Furthermore, I want to express my deep gratitude to friend and author Laurie Loewenstein, whose continual encouragement and faith in my ability as a writer helped me to bring this project to completion.

Made in United States
Orlando, FL
15 January 2022

13489616R00168